This book is dedicated to the memory of Tracy Eichelberger whose smile could clear out the darkness. Tracy was an inspiration throughout my life. She will always and forever be remembered.

Tracy, I hope I captured your essence in these pages.

Thank you for whispering in my ear while I was writing this novel.

When I'm in writing mode my shenanigans can be rather dramatic, yet somehow my family always manages to remain supportive and inspirational.

More Than One Way to Breathe is also dedicated to them.
Thank you, Joseph, Noah, Jacob, and Ian: together you form the light of my world.

To Michaela Fetterolf, who allowed me to tap into her memories of Tracy so I could portray her in a magical way—I hope I did your love for Tracy justice. Thank you for guiding me.

Also, a special thanks to Michelle Liddick, Robin Spicher, and Alexia for taking the time to reminisce and send me their favorite memories of Tracy, so that I would be able to understand her essence from all angles.

To Eddie Eichelberger, thank you for sharing Tracy with the world!

Thank you to Skai de Leon, who offered an informative teen voice to the words in this novel. Your advice added authenticity.

A special note of gratitude goes out to my editor at Cable Creek: Laura. Thank you for pushing me to write the best book my fingers and brain could possibly create. I'll be grateful for the rest of my days for your thoughtful insight and pressure to get the words on the page.

Thank You!

- Chapter One -

"You're a pain in my ass. Do you know that?"

"Mom, what the hell?"

"Don't talk to me like that." She pointed at me. Her bright red nails seemed like they could have slashed my face. "You are so ungrateful."

"What are you talking about?"

"You know exactly what I'm talking about." She pointed at me. "Your incessant laughter and giggling kept me up all night."

"How?" I scooped another spoonful of ice cream into my mouth. This was something I was used to. It happened every time Sophie slept over. We were always too loud for my mother. "We were in the basement. There's no way you could have heard us."

"You know what? Get out of my house. I'm sick of you."

"Mom, stop." I rolled my eyes.

"No, get out."

"What do you mean?"

"I meant what I said. I don't want you here anymore," she said with a wave of her hand.

I stood up and stared at her for what felt like an eternity. This was not the first time she had said this to me, but it was the first time she wasn't backing down. Her cold eyes stared into me. I shivered.

She opened her mouth and slowly whispered, "I said - get - out - of - my - house, you - disrespectful - waste - of - space."

I grabbed my phone and turned just as she bum-rushed me and grabbed the phone from my hand.

"I pay the bill." She held the phone up in my face. "This is mine."

"Mom, you can't be serious."

"You show no respect. None. You think you can just live here and treat me like this?" She waved her hand at me, swooshing me away. "Get out."

My heart started racing. I couldn't believe she was serious.

"Just because Sophie and I were loud?" I screamed back at her, tears falling from my eyes.

"Because you weren't just loud. You were disrespectful."

"I'm calling Dad!" I tried to grab my phone out of her hand.

"No. He's not going to rush home and save you. When will you learn that?" she said as she recoiled.

"What about grandma?" My legs felt like they were going to buckle from under me. What was I going to do? We lived in the woods, on a mountain, in the middle of nowhere, and it was snowing. I wasn't sixteen yet, so I couldn't drive anywhere. Not that she would have let me take the car anyway.

"I said you can't have your phone."

"Mom."

"GET - OUT - OF - THIS - HOUSE!"

I turned toward the front door, stunned with my eyes wide and my mouth open. My face was hot and tears were forming in the corners of my eyes. I didn't want to appear weak, so I closed my mouth and bit my tongue to stop crying. I still didn't think she'd actually make me leave, so I walked slowly and carefully. Every step grew heavier and heavier until I got to the door and turned to face her. I looked at her and waited for her to change her mind.

She didn't.

We stared at each other for what seemed like an eternity. I sat on the floor to put on the shoes I had haphazardly kicked off the day before. I stood up again, still staring at her. Holding my breath, I stood back up and slowly reached out to the coat rack and grabbed my jacket. "Can I pack some things before I go?" I asked, hoping this would stop our game of chicken.

"No, just go," she said. Then she turned her back to me and walked into the kitchen. After that, she grabbed her mug, leaned against the kitchen island, took a drink, and picked up her phone.

I stood watching her as she called a friend. She acted like I was invisible. There she was chatting with a friend, laughing, as if she hadn't just kicked her daughter out of the house. I decided to open the door, thinking this would make the game stop.

She didn't say a word.

I realized she meant what she had said just as a big gust of cold wind rushed inside the house, blowing my hair away from my face. I turned around one more time. My face warmed as it faced our fireplace, with its bright red and orange glow. I stepped backward, away from the door, closing it. I would need my gloves, hat, and scarf.

I took a step toward the closet.

My mother slammed her phone down and yelled, "I told you to get out." She gestured to the door, her stiletto-shaped nails pointing the way out.

"Mom, it's snowing, I'll get sick." I couldn't believe she was serious.

"Get - Out," she said, enunciating each word slowly, loudly, and clearly.

I turned and opened the front door again. The cold made my face sting. I was still biting my tongue, sure that my tears would freeze to my face.

Without winter clothes, my phone, or any plan at all, I left my home.

I walked down our long, dirt driveway with my hands in my pockets, knowing that I had to stay warm as long as I could. I made my decision. I would go to Sophie's house. I could have gone to my neighbor's house, which was closer, but I needed more than they could give me. And besides, they probably would have walked me back home again, where my mother would have feigned love for me. Then they would have left, and she would have kicked me out again.

No. I needed that special hot chocolate with one lone marshmallow and caramel syrup artfully poured over it. I needed the warmth Sophie and her parents would give me. Emotional warmth. I needed to hear I was loved. Lisa, Sophie's mom, would make me feel wanted. Sophie would make me laugh. It would be okay. I just needed to get there first.

I held my arms tight against my body and walked with my head held low against the snow as it whipped me in my face. My entire body was tight, rigid. Why didn't my mom love me? Why did two teen girls giggling cause her to decide she didn't want me in the house anymore? I didn't understand any of it. I tried my hardest to keep her happy. I did everything she always asked of me, but it was never enough. I wasn't good enough to be her daughter. Why was I so unlovable?

Despite my best attempt, I started crying again.

I tried to stop, but I couldn't. Crying was making my face freeze. I knew the only way to stay warm was to keep my face dry, but I couldn't do it just yet. I tried to walk as fast as possible. It was growing dark, but I was still able to see around me. The trees appeared to grow taller and taller over my head. Their shadows menacingly taunted me. I could feel eyes in the woods. I could feel hunger. I stopped crying and began to run.

That's when I heard something run beside me. I had no idea what it was. But for some reason, I stopped running to see if it stopped too. It did. To my side, I saw two glowing eyes. Something inside of me knew it meant no harm, but still, I remained frozen.

I heard a sound behind it, like another creature lurking. The glowing eyes came toward me. I saw it was a coyote. It stepped out onto the snowy dirt road from behind the treeline. I shivered. It walked toward me and nudged my legs as if telling me to go. Then turned, ran into the trees, and disappeared. I heard howling, then growling. The sounds moved further away, one animal chasing the other.

I had no idea what had just happened, but I needed to get to Sophie's house as quickly as possible if I wanted to survive. Sophie lived in town; I lived on the mountain. I knew that if I could make it to the streetlights at the edge of town, I would survive. If I could just make it there, I could collapse under a light and someone would notice me.

By the time I reached the lights, I was out of breath from running. I felt like there was a heavy stone on my chest, making it impossible to take big breaths. My fingers and toes were completely numb. The rest of my body felt like it was burning—not from heat, but scorching from the severe cold. My hair was frozen. My face stung. I was exhausted. But there was light. I was going to be okay.

I felt like collapsing, but I was able to gather what little energy I had left to walk the five blocks to Sophie's house. Once I saw her rowhome in the distance I started crying again. I could not hold it in any longer. It hit me all at once, sheer terror leaving my body, sadness from what had become of my relationship with my mother, and happiness over the fact that I knew I would survive the night. I would be okay.

Sophie's outdoor light was on; it welcomed me. I sighed in relief to have made it as I walked up their section of sidewalk. I stepped up to her covered porch, shaking. This was the first time that snow and wind weren't slashing at my face. I reached my hand out and tried hard to uncurl my clenched fingers to ring the doorbell. It was harder than I thought it would be. But I was able to ring it once before balling my fingers up again and shoving them in my wet pockets.

The door opened and a warm welcoming glow spilled out from the doorway. Lisa, Sophie's mom, stood in front of me, looking at me in horror.

"Mia!" She grabbed my arm and pulled me into the house. "What are you doing?"

The heat from the warm home felt like fire on my face. It was a shock I was not prepared for. I sobbed loudly, finally allowing tears to roll down my cheeks freely. Lisa took my wet coat off me and threw it on the foyer floor, then started rubbing my arms trying to warm me up.

She yelled up the stairs, "Robert, get two blankets from the closet, bring me one, and put the other in the dryer to warm up. Quickly!"

I saw Robert, Sophie's dad, peek down the steps to see what was going on. He turned quickly after seeing the state of me. I heard the hallway closet door open and close. He ran down the steps, then quickly wrapped me in a quilt. Then he ran to their basement to throw the other in the dryer.

"Mia, I'm going to get you some of Sophie's clothes to put on."

"Thank you. I… I…"

"No, we'll talk after you warm up. Not before. Okay?"

I nodded.

She ran to Sophie's room. I could hear Sophie asking what was going on.

"Don't worry about it, honey. Finish your breathing treatment."

Sophie had no idea I was there. Her breathing nebulizer was always so loud, she probably didn't hear me come in, or any of the confusion. That was okay. She needed her breathing treatment more than she needed to know I was there.

Lisa ran back down the steps with new clothes in hand. "Sophie is in her room getting a breathing treatment, so you can go in my bedroom to get changed. I'll go make some of that hot chocolate you love so much, okay?" she said as she handed me clothes.

I sobbed again. No, it was a guttural wail. I couldn't stop. "Thank you," I choked.

I walked up the steps and peeked into Sophie's room. Her back was toward the door as she sat at her window watching the snowfall. I could see the cord from her nebulizer fall behind her back, leading to an air compressor. Her shoulders rose and fell with each breath. Instead of interrupting her, I turned and walked to her parents' room to get changed.

- Chapter Two -

My teeth were still chattering, despite the warm blanket wrapped around me. The hot cocoa was welcome, comforting even, but it didn't make me feel better. Lisa sat beside me, her eyebrows furrowed, the wrinkles on her forehead pronounced with worry.

"Mia, why were you walking in the snowstorm?"

"My mom told me to leave."

"What? Why? Ok wait, before that, why didn't you have gloves or a hat?"

"She wouldn't let me take anything."

"You should have called."

"She took my phone," I said, wrapping my fingers around the mug.

Lisa took a deep breath. "What happened?"

"I don't know." My face felt heavy. My fingers throbbed back to life. I started crying. "I was just eating ice cream, and she started screaming at me."

"About what?"

"About when Sophie spent the night."

"What about it? Did you guys do something you shouldn't have?" She sat up straight and rigid.

"Yes."

"What did you do?" She took another deep breath. "It's okay to tell me; my love is unconditional." She shook her head. "I won't kick you out."

"We were loud and laughing too much."

"That's it?"

"Yes." I nodded my head, worried that she would be angry too.

"Are you sure?"

"I may have talked back when she started yelling."

"Okay. It's going to be okay," she said, placing her hand on top of mine. "I promise."

"Am . . . am I homeless now?" I asked.

"Robert and I would never let that happen. Why don't you go talk to Sophie," she said, pointing up the stairs. "She'll be excited to see you. She has another ten minutes of treatment left. You can help her. Okay?"

"Okay." I picked up my mug, keeping the blanket wrapped around me, and walked back up the steps. I could hear Sophie's nebulizer buzz louder and louder with every step.

Before entering her room I stood and watched her as she took deep breaths of her medicine into her lungs. The nebulizer's sound kept her from hearing me when I stood in back of her. I could see the vapor of medicine rising above her head. No one was stronger than her. She may have been sick, but that didn't matter. She was strong.

I knocked. "Sophie?"

She turned toward me, took one more long breath of medicine, then put her mouthpiece down. "Mia! What are you doing here? There's a blizzard!" She got up, put her mouthpiece on the nightstand, and ran to me. She was shaking, that's what her medicine did to her.

"Why are you here?" she asked again, then started coughing.

I waited for her to stop before answering. "My mom kicked me out."

"WHAT?" I could hear the crackling in her lungs, her phlegm was breaking up. The bubbling sound scared me and grossed me out, but I knew that meant it was working. Coughing was normal for her.

"Sophie, do you want to do percussion?" I asked, hoping she'd say yes. She normally had a vest she would wear that would vibrate to break up the phlegm further, but I always liked doing it for her.

"Sure," she said.

"Okay, Soph, sit back down and finish your breathing treatment."

"Mia, not yet, I want to hear what happened first."

"As your mom always says, 'Cystic Fibrosis waits for no one.' Lie down."

She started coughing again, but was able to get out, "Fine!" She was taking the deepest breaths she could, staring at me the entire time. Once finished she got up from her spot near the window, walked to her bed, and flopped down on her stomach.

I knelt down next to her, cupped my hands, and began hitting her back with cupped hands and a rhythmic thud.

Sophie's mom came in and sat down next to me, "Mia, are you sure nothing more happened? I'm really trying to figure this out."

"Yes. I promise." I replied over Sophie's watery cough.

"Okay," she said, then sighed and stood up. "Ten minutes of percussion, okay?"

"Okay. I got this," I replied.

When Lisa left, I continued doing percussions.

"What's happening?" Sophie said, her voice warping up and down with each hit.

"Mom kicked me out. So, I walked all the way here."

Sophie tried to sit up, but had a coughing fit and gave up.

"Stop. I'll tell you everything. Calm down."

"Fine."

"She came into the kitchen and yelled at me for how loud we were on Friday night," I explained.

"But we weren't that loud."

"I know. Then I guess I snapped back. Because, you know, who wouldn't?"

"Right."

"And she told me to get out."

"Are you sure that's what she meant? For you to leave?"

"Oh, I'm certain. She wouldn't even let me go to the closet to get a hat and scarf."

"Did you really walk all the way here?"

"Yes."

"All the way off the mountain?"

"Yes."

Sophie turned around and sat up, taking my hands in hers. I knew she was trying to keep herself from coughing. Her face was turning red. "You shouldn't be hitting my back, your hands must hurt."

"Sophie, of course, I'm doing your percussion. It keeps you alive. And, of course, my hands hurt, but it doesn't matter. Lie back down."

She looked me straight in the eyes and whispered, "I love you, too." Then she winked.

We started hearing talking coming from downstairs. It got louder and louder. There wasn't a fight—only one person was talking, and that was Sophie's mother. We both got up and slowly crept to the middle landing of the stairs. Sophie's face was still red from holding a cough in. I pointed to her bedroom to tell her to cough there. She got up and made it to her room before the coughing started. Her mom, holding her phone, stopped talking and looked upstairs, but she didn't notice me sitting there; her eyes were only on Sophie's room.

"Look Kim, this is insane. You kicked her out of the house during a blizzard. No phone. No gloves. No scarf. No hat." She stopped talking for a moment, listening to the voice on the other side of the call. I could see her whole body start to shake and her face turn red. "No. You live on a mountain by yourselves. This is not the same as her sledding with friends. It's completely different. It's freezing out and there's barely any visibility." She started pacing. "Kim! Get real! She is lucky she made it here at all." She stopped talking for a bit, then said, "No Kim, she's lucky she's alive."

She stopped yelling just as Sophie came back to the steps and sat next to me. Sophie and I simultaneously reached out for each other's hands.

"Where is Dennis? Is he home? Did he allow this?"… "Right, I had an idea he was out of town." … "No, I'm sorry. I believe Mia." … "No, I do." … "Why would she choose to walk down the mountain, all the way to town, without her hat or gloves." … "Kim, she didn't even have a phone, that's how I know you are lying. What TEEN would leave a phone behind?" … "Oh, stop crying, you did this to her." … "Look, I'm going to be brutally honest with you, this is child abuse." … "It is." … "Okay, I'll tell you what, I'll call Child Protective Services and ask them. How's that?" … "No, I don't think you should come and get her. Leave her here for now." … "Fine, you can drop off clothes. But if you come into my house and start anything, I'm calling the police. Do you hear me?" … "DO YOU HEAR ME?" … "I can't promise she'll want to see you." … "Fine." Lisa threw the phone against the wall. Sophie and I jumped. I'd never seen her that mad before.

Robert walked up behind her and massaged her shoulders. She flinched away, "Please, not now." She stomped over to retrieve the phone, then turned back toward her husband and beckoned him to her. "No child should have to deal with this," she said through her tears. "That woman is a psychopath."

"I know. We'll do whatever we need to do to keep her safe."

A wave of guilt came over me. They had enough to go through with Sophie, they didn't need my issues as well. I got up and walked to Sophie's room. She followed after me.

I turned to her, "Soph, I'm going to go home."

"What? No. Stay here for one night, please?" She closed the door behind her.

"I can't. I need to face this."

"But we'll have a snow day tomorrow. We can go sledding or something."

"I can't."

"No, you can. Just one day. You need a break from her." She looked at me like she was trying to push her will into my soul, her lips were pursed together and her eyes were squinted tight. She wasn't going to budge on this. She repeated herself, "You need this break."

"You're right," I said with a sigh.

"We'll have fun. I promise." She walked up to me and hugged me. "I know this is hard, but just stay here tonight. Just one night. Okay?"

"I feel like all of this is too much for you guys."

"It's not, we love you. Honestly, I'm not sure my mom would even let you leave. So, just get used to it."

There was a knock on Sophie's door. "Come in," Sophie said.

Lisa opened the door and said, "Hey, girls. You finished the treatment?"

"Yes. Mom, we heard you on the phone. What's happening?"

Lisa sat down and clasped her hands together. "Mia, your mom is coming to bring you some clothes," she said, then looked at me. "I need you to know that she said you ran away."

"But… but, I didn't. I wanted to stay home."

"I know, trust me I know. No teen would leave their phone behind. I believe you."

"Thank you."

"You don't have to go with her," she said, reaching out to hug me. "You are welcome here."

After a while, the doorbell rang once, then twice, then two more times after. It was obviously my mother. I knew she would whirl into the house like a tornado. At home, she was always either aloof or screaming at me. There was no in-between. In public, she showed love and concern for me, to a dramatic level, like she was performing. Of course she'd say I ran away from home. She couldn't get sympathy with the truth. Crying and begging are more her style, but only in public.

"Stay here," Lisa said. She got up and walked out of the room. I could tell she was worried by the way she rubbed her forehead.

"It's going to be okay," Sophie assured me. But it didn't matter. I was shaking. "Do you want to go listen on the steps again?"

"No. She's just going to lie."

"Okay. You know what? I have an idea." She jumped off the bed, reached out to the top of her dresser, and grabbed a stone from her collection. "Here, hold this, it will help." She put the stone in the palm of my hand, I closed my fingers around it, and she wrapped her hands around mine. The stone, and her hand, rested perfectly on mine. She tilted her head ever so slightly toward the ceiling and took a deep breath. These were the moments when she became magical, otherworldly. Her deep breath showed no signs of wheezing and was done with a grace that only she possessed. As she exhaled I felt a sense of peace come over me. The air seemed lighter. I felt freer somehow. She lowered her head, opened her eyes, looked at me, and said, "You're going to be okay." Then she took her hand off mine and smiled.

I ran my thumb over the stone. It was light gray and perfectly smooth. She must have found it in the river. She liked to go stand in the river to find peace. Whenever all the doctors' appointments, breathing treatments, and IVs wore her down she would ask her mother to take her to the river so she could find peace in the water. She said it gave her the energy she needed to keep living. Like she could feel God in the current, washing her problems away.

"Hold onto the stone. Don't put it down until after your mom leaves. Okay?" she asked.

I simply nodded. I don't know how she did it, but she was able to calm my nerves. And the stone in my hand kept that feeling going. She would often find meaning in the smallest of objects. Sometimes it was a burnt match or even just a thimble. But her special objects usually had something to do with nature. Oddly shaped sticks and pebbles were her favorite. Her room was full of small objects others would ignore. She would see their beauty and attach meaning to each.

"Let's go listen now," she said, sitting up.

I simply nodded at her suggestion. We got up and went to the top of the landing and sat. I held the stone, rubbing my thumb over it.

"I just don't know what she was thinking," my mother said. I could hear her crying in fake hysterics. "Why would she leave like that, and in the middle of a snowstorm?"

"Kim, you kicked her out." Lisa pointed out. "I'm not stupid."

My mother gasped. "What? I would never. She could have gotten killed out there by herself."

"Stop. Don't lie. I know you well enough to know you are–"

My mother started talking over her, "I just can't understand; she left her phone. She didn't even have proper winter clothes. Did she even put on boots?"

"No, no, she had no–"

My mother interrupted again. "She could have died out there." I heard her footsteps, she was pacing, something she always did to let people believe she was panicking.

"Yes, she absolutely could have died, as I said to you on the phone. She was wet and frozen to the bone when she got here," Lisa said.

"Oh, God!" My mother was wailing now.

"I took care of her, she's fine. But she's going to stay here with us for a bit." Sophie's mom was trying to sound calm and soothing, probably just to get my mother out of the house as quickly as possible.

"Oh no, no, no, no. I have to take my baby home." My mom started yelling through the house, "Mia. Mia! Mommy's here. Mia, dear!"

Sophia lightly tapped my leg as a way to tell me not to get up or make a sound.

"I'll go see if she wants to see you," Lisa said. She rounded the corner to go up the steps and saw us, but didn't let Kim know. She used her right hand to shush us up to Sophie's room in a secretive way. Following her lead, we got up and tiptoed to Sophie's room.

When Lisa came into the room, she quietly shut the door. "Look, Mia, if you want to see her, you can. It's up to you. But I don't want you to go home tonight."

I realized there would be nothing my mom could do to me with Lisa standing there, so I nodded my head. "I think I have to go down. Can you come with me?" I said looking at Sophie.

"Of course," she replied.

I took a deep breath and squeezed the river stone. "Ok, let's do this."

Sophie and I walked out of her room and down the steps together, holding hands. As soon as we reached the bottom, my mother screamed and ran to me, grabbing me into her arms and holding me—all while crying very large, very fake tears.

"My baby! I was so worried." She backed up and took my face in her hands. "Are you okay?"

"Sure, Mom."

"Never, ever run off like that, you've scared me so bad." She squeezed me tighter.

"Mom, you—"

She cut me off. "Let's not rehash this. Just come home with me."

"I think I want to spend the night here, Mom."

"Oh no. No, no, no. I've failed you as a mother. I'm the worst mother in the wwwwoooorrrlllllddd." She could cry on demand anytime she needed to. That's one of the ways she controlled people.

"Mom, stop."

"Just come home, baby."

"Kim, she said she wanted to stay here." Lisa approached her. "You said you brought her some clothes and her cell phone? Where are they?"

"NNNNooooo!"

Part of me started to falter, to tell her I'd come home. But I took a deep breath and centered myself and said, "Mom, I'm going to stay here."

"Kim, is her stuff in your car?" Lisa asked a second time in a louder voice. At that point, Sophie's dad, came back into the room with his eyebrows furled and a frown on his face.

"She's coming home with me. Her stuff can stay in my car," she said, still holding on to me.

Robert's voice boomed from across the house. "I'm sorry," he said, then stopped himself and spoke again, "No, no I'm not sorry." He held out his hand to create a barrier. "Mia showed up at our doorstep after walking from your house, on the mountain, all the way into town, in the dark, in the snowfall, with no phone or proper clothing." He took a breath, then said in a voice that was probably meant to be more calming than menacing, "Kim. She's staying with us." He walked toward us. His face was bright red. He turned back around toward my mother. "Now, if you don't want us calling social services, you will walk out to your car with me and give me her stuff, and then you will leave."

My mother's face went blank. I could feel the anger boil inside of her. She never liked to be called out in such ways, and I was sure I would pay for it later.

She released me and took a step back, wiping the tears from her cheeks as she stared me in the eyes. Without breaking the stare she said, "Yes, let's get her stuff." She turned away from me slowly, eyes still focused on mine. Then she looked me up and down. "Well, I'm happy you didn't die." Her voice was suddenly cold. She turned on her heel and headed toward the door. Just like that, all of her fake emotion was gone, yet the air in the room became heavy. Actually, no. It became hot. That's how she was, she could change the entire atmosphere of a room with no effort. She projected emotions, fake or real, and made sure everyone could feel them, without even saying a word. This is what made her so scary.

Robert took her by the arm and led her to the door. She didn't look back at me once.

Once she was outside and Robert closed the door behind her, we all let out a breath of relief. "Are you okay?" Lisa sped next to me and grabbed me in a tight hug. Sophie stood beside us, rubbing her hand up and down my back. I started crying. We stood there for what seemed like an eternity. "Listen to me, Mia. We love you."

"I love you, too," I said through sniffles. Sophie's rock was still in my hand. I was squeezing it so hard that my hand was cramping, but I wasn't ready to let it go. I felt like the rock was allowing me to stay in one piece. To not shatter. To stay alive.

The front door blew open with a whoosh, letting in the evening air. The coldness was cleansing and let what was left of my mother's heavy energy out of the house. Suddenly, we all felt at peace. When Lisa let go of me to close the door, Sophie took over hugging me. It's strange how the cold can feel like it's going to kill you, then a few hours later, cleanse you.

"Well, glad that's over," Sophie said with a giggle. Before I knew it, I was giggling with her. I couldn't help it. I was scared, but the giggling helped to cure me of my deepest pain. It always did. Sophie called it "laughing medicine." She always made a point of laughing as much as she could. She used to say that life was too precious to not laugh as much as possible, that there was more than one way to breathe, and laughing was one.

"Sophie, your laugh is entirely too loud," I said back to her with a fake authoritarian voice. Those were the famous words Sophie heard every day when she would start laughing in the middle of class. She couldn't help it, it's how she burned off the steam she had building inside of her all the time.

Then I busted out in a full roar of laughter. I couldn't control it. We both collapsed on the floor with her parents standing over us, not looking at all amused.

Sophie's parents shook their heads and turned and walked upstairs. Faces dreadfully serious, bodies held rigid. They look exhausted.

"Hey, Mia," Sophie said in a breathy tone, holding back a cough.

"Yeah?"

"Did the stone help?"

"I think it did."

She took my hand in hers and pulled my fingers away from the rock. It had changed from light gray to black. "Well, look at that, it took all your negativity and gave you the laughs. Just what I was hoping it would do."

"What?"

"Oh, Mia, one day you'll learn."

"What are you talking about?"

"I just see more because I won't live as long as you. Sometimes, when you are close, you see things others can't."

"Close to what?"

"Mia, I'm not going to be here forever."

"Sophie, no. You're never leaving me."

"No, you're right. I will never, ever leave you."

"Okay, Sophie, you are freaking me out. What's going on?" We still lay on our backs next to each other, breathing heavily from the laughing fit. We turned our faces toward each other, our noses almost touching.

She looked away, coughed a bit, then looked back at me, "Mia, I'm never leaving you, but I'm never going to get better. You understand that, right?"

"Mia. Did you get bad news?"

"No, I just know. But, it's okay. I'm okay," she said with a small smile. "You know?"

"I know. But we are all just spirits anyway," she said waving her right hand in the air as if it was not a big deal. "This is just one part of our journey."

- Chapter Three -

I couldn't sleep that night. My mind just kept replaying Sophie's words over and over again. As I lay next to her and listened to her breathing, I could hear the wheezing from deep within her lungs. I also heard a faint gurgling sound, and every once in a while she would let out a small cough without waking up. I couldn't imagine life without her. She was my person. She was the only one who understood what I was going through. She loved me.

The darkness broke before it broke me. Someone had turned on a light downstairs. I got up to use the bathroom, then quietly crept down the steps to find Lisa sitting, drinking a cup of tea. I walked slowly toward the table and sat next to her.

"Lisa, are you okay?"

She smiled at me faintly and said, "Yes, dear. Why aren't you sleeping?"

"I can't."

"Me neither. But you know what helps me when I can't sleep?"

"What's that?"

"Camomile tea. Let me make you some." She got up, pausing a moment to touch my shoulder on her way to the kitchen. I couldn't shake the heavy feeling of unhappiness that filled the room. She came back and put a hot mug in front of me. I wrapped my fingers around it to feel the warmth. "Mia, I'm thinking we need to call Social Services."

I looked at her, holding my breath. I started to tremble. "No, no. It's not that bad. She just has her moments. It will be okay." I bit my tongue in the hopes my tears would not start.

"I'm concerned it IS that bad?"

"No. It's okay."

"I don't think it is, but I need to talk to your dad. Does he have any idea of what happened?"

I looked down at my mug. "No, she wouldn't let me call him."

"Okay. Well, Robert and I are going to get you a cheap cell phone to keep on yourself. Can you do that? Keep it on you at all times?"

I nodded.

She ran her finger round and round over the tip of her mug. "It wasn't safe for you to walk through the blizzard off of the mountain like that." She picked up her mug and held it close to her lips, blowing on it. The mug was shaking. "I keep thinking about what could have happened."

The tears were running freely down my cheeks. I nodded.

"I think it's best if you stay with us until your father gets home from his business trip. Is that okay?"

"Yes." Knowing how much they cared made me cry even harder. I needed them.

Lisa sat with me while I cried. Afterward, we sat and drank our tea together. The tea made me drowsy; my eyes drooped.

"Why don't you go back up to bed. I doubt you'll have school tomorrow after all this snow. It might be a fun day."

"Okay, yeah. Thank you for the tea. And for helping me."

"I'll clean up you just get to bed."

We both stood and she gave me a hug. As she was holding me I imagined that she was my mother, loving and kind. "It's going to be okay," she said in a soft tone.

I didn't answer her I just turned and walked up the steps. When I got to Sophie's room she was fast asleep, but her lungs were making a horrible gurgling sound. She always had a wheeze, but the gurgling was new. I stayed awake, for a while, thinking about how Sophie had said she wouldn't be here forever.

- Chapter Four -

"Rise and shine, sleepyhead." Sophie was kneeling over me with her hand on my back.

I pushed my body up to a sitting position and stretched. She walked to her curtains and opened them. A blinding light filled the room.

"Mia, come here! Isn't it all just so beautiful?"

I got up and ran over to the window. It had stopped snowing, but it was piled up deeply. A cardinal perched in the middle of her backyard, inexplicably standing on a snowdrift, watching us. Everything was quiet. So quiet that all the worries about my mom disappeared. I looked up at the sky, past the glistening icicle hanging from the edge of the roof. The sky was a clear light blue, a sharp contrast to the anger the skies showed me the day before. I looked down at my hands. The night before they felt frozen stiff. Now I was able to move them without thought.

Sophie interrupted my thoughts. "School is canceled. Wanna see if my parents will take us to the diner for breakfast?"

"Oooo, I'm in the mood for hot chocolate and french toast. Are they awake yet?"

"Yes, I think I can smell coffee brewing."

***

After Sophie's dad shoveled, Lisa lent me a pair of boots, gloves, scarf, hat, and old jacket so we could all go outside.

We stepped into the cold winter wonderland. Today, the cold was more peaceful than the night before. Today, it was beautiful and refreshing and all I could think was that I was safe.

The diner was two blocks from the house, but we walked slowly so Sophie would not become winded. As we rounded the corner, we could see that a lot of our classmates had the same idea. Emma saw us first and came running, then slipped haphazardly on a patch of ice in a way only Emma could do. Lily busted out laughing. They were best friends, but that didn't stop Lily from laughing at Emma's clumsiness.

She promptly walked over to Emma and put her hand out. "Come on, klutz. Get up." After Emma was up, Lily, with her hands on her hips, said, "Do you need me to hold your hand so you don't fall again?"

"Shut up, Lily!" Emma said with a huff. Then she rolled her eyes and said, "Yes. I do need help." Emma held out her hand and they both walked over to greet us, hand in hand.

"Soph, wanna get a table with us?"

"No, maybe later. We're here with my parents."

"Mia?" Emma asked.

"I'll eat with them; we have a lot to talk about."

"Suit yourselves. Oh hey, I got a text from the guys," Lily said, giving me a small wink. "They're on their way." She smiled. "Max is coming too."

"I don't know why you guys think I like him."

"Because you do," Emma said with a loud snort.

Lisa interrupted, "Come on girls, let's go get a table."

Sophie turned to her mom, "Okay," she said. To the gang, she said, "See you inside."

Sophie and I followed behind her parents. The diner was full of the town regulars, most looked exhausted from a morning of plowing and shoveling. Men in overalls and beat-up John Deere caps with women who looked like they were savoring their first cup of coffee in the morning. Small kids scrawled pictures of snowmen on their menus, while teens sat at the bar eyeing up the desert case. The smell of maple syrup, mixed with bacon and strong coffee, filled my nose. The smell was welcoming and made me feel at home, made me feel grounded.

Ruth, a small, older waitress who had probably worked there since she was a teen, thrust menus into our hands. "Seat yourselves. I don't have time to figure it out for you today." Sophie and I looked at each other and giggled. Ruth yelled into the kitchen, "Jack, are those waffles done yet? They've been waiting for a lifetime already."

Jack yelled over the flat grill, "Moving as fast as I can, Ruth. I'm the only one back here today." I looked around. The tables were full, but I couldn't see many workers. They must not have been able to make their way to the diner. Only Jack and Ruth were keeping the place moving.

"All right, ladies, go pick a table." Robert pointed to the dining room. "We'll follow."

I grabbed Sophie's arm and together we found a circular table in the corner. It was bigger than we needed, but there weren't many choices. We took off our coats and slung them over our chairs before sitting. Ruth was behind us with a pot of coffee. She began filling four mugs before we even told her we wanted any. Lisa and Robert walked over together, arm in arm. Lisa sat, then wrapped her long fingers around her mug, bringing it to her nose and inhaling deeply. Robert sat next to her before adding cream to his mug.

Sophie and I looked at each other. "I guess we're having coffee," she said to me.

"Guess so. Pass the cream and lots of sugar, please," I said to Robert.

"I think it's fine, you'll be outside most of the day anyway," he said, passing the sugar and cream.

"Do you know what you want yet?" Ruth asked sternly, tapping her pencil on her pad of paper. We were lucky we knew the menu well, she was not messing around.

After we had ordered and suffered through Ruth's eye rolls at the various types of eggs we wanted, we all got comfortable and started chatting.

"Girls, I brought something for you to look at," Lisa said. She dug around in her bucket-sized purse before pulling out a pamphlet and handing it to Sophie. "We thought you might want to try a summer camp this year. Richard and I think it would be good for both of you. And Mia, we need someone there who knows how to give Sophie breathing treatments." She paused. "So, well, we thought we would pay for the both of you to go."

"REALLY?" Sophia said with a squeal. She had always wanted to go to summer camp, but her parents had been too afraid to send her–until now, apparently. I know her well enough to know when she's struggling, and over the past year, I had learned how to help with her breathing treatments. We were ready for the adventure. I felt good that her parents would trust me with this, trust us with this.

"Do you think you'd be interested, Mia?"

My mom would never support me like this. She would never spend the money to send me to camp. She would always complain that I wasn't worth the cost, or that I would just embarrass her, or something. "I don't know what to say." I looked at them. Tears welled up in my eyes. "Are you serious?"

Lisa reached out and lightly touched my hand. "Yes, we are serious. We've been saving up for it, and we would feel so much better if you were there with Sophie. You could keep an eye on her for us. You know what to do if anything goes wrong."

"MOM! Nothing's going to happen"

Lisa looked at Sophie then turned back to me, "Mia, we love you, and we want you both to experience camp. It's important."

"I… I would love to. Thank you." I pulled my hand away to wipe a tear from my cheek.

"Look over the pamphlet and choose something. Nothing too hard, okay? They have a cute programming camp."

"Eeew! No. Mom! That's boring. I want to do something outside. And fun," Sophie said, grabbing the pamphlet. "I want to do the naturalist camp. Mia, look!" she said, pointing to the description.

Just as she said that, the bells on the door rang as it opened. Our entire gang came inside, including Max. Sophie poked me in my side and whispered, "Once they sit, you should go say hi."

Heat flooded my face. I was sure I was bright red. "No. Don't be silly."

"Just saying," she said, then looked at the pamphlet again.

We moved in closer together to look at the camp descriptions. I felt someone scoot in right behind me. I knew it was him. I could smell his cologne.

I turned around slowly and discovered I was right. There he was. "Hey, Max!"

His bright blue eyes looked down at me, then glanced at Sophie's parents. "So, um. That's a lot of snow. Isn't it?"

"Yeah." I felt stupid. I could tell I was blushing again. *I answered with just… yeah?*

"What are you two doing today?"

"Just hanging out, nothing special." Sophie replied. She totally played it cool.

"We were going to the school hill to sled. Wanna come?"

"Maybe," I answered back, realizing I had forgotten to answer in full sentences.

Sophie cleared her throat. "Max, do you want to sit with us?"

Yeah, um. Cool." He quickly sat down next to me. I felt a jolt of electricity flow through my body. My hair stood on end. Sophie put her hand on my knee, then gave me a smug smile.

Ruth walked back to our table, flipped over the coffee mug sitting in front of Max, and said, "So, I guess you want to add him to your order?" She filled his mug before anyone could answer.

"Yes, yes that's fine," Lisa responded.

"Right." Ruth slapped a menu in front of him, then muttered under her breath, "Like I have nothing else to do right now." She scurried away. We looked at each other and laughed nervously.

"Mia. I was wondering. Can I have your number? I realized I didn't have it, and… I'd like to text you sometime."

"Oh, really?" I stammered.

Sophie snapped, "Yes! You can! Here, hand me your phone." She grabbed his phone and put my name and number into it with no reluctance whatsoever, then handed it back to him.

"Cool," he muttered under his breath.

"Cool," I muttered under mine.

"Oh Lord! Mia, give your phone to Max so he can put his number in," Sophie said with a strangely loud eye roll.

"So, what are you guys talking about?" he asked, looking at the camp pamphlet.

"Sophie and I were thinking about doing a camp at Hemlock this summer."

"Oh cool. I work there every summer. I'm a hiking guide for the younger kids."

"We were looking at the Naturalist Camp," Sophie volunteered.

"Sophie! You can't." Lisa snapped her head toward Sophie.

"MOM!"

"Oh cool. They hike in that one too," he said, nodding, still staring at the pamphlet.

"Would you be our guide?" I asked.

"Probably not. But that's cool."

"Cool," I replied.

"OMG, seriously? Cool, cool, cool," Sophia said, laughing.

"Hey. Wanna come sledding with us? I'd like to spend time with you," he said, looking straight at me.

"Yeah. I'd like to, too. I just have to make sure Sophie has her breathing treatment first," I said.

"Okay. If it's a problem. It's no big deal. Maybe we could go to a movie next weekend or something."

"Or both!" Sophie blurted out. "Honestly, my breathing treatment won't take THAT long."

"Yeah, or both. Would you be okay with that?" he asked me.

I nodded and bit my tongue so I wouldn't start smiling.

Ruth delivered our food and asked if Max was ready to order. He said he would sit with his friends, so she could get his order there. As she turned away from us we heard her say, "Great, that doesn't make things confusing at all."

"I'll let you guys talk. I hope to see you later," he said, looking at me. Then, without giving me time to answer, he got up and went to sit with his friends.

I couldn't believe it. I had been dreaming of him for so long. And now suddenly, he was asking me for my number.

"So, are we going sledding?" Sophie asked.

"Are you feeling up to it?"

"Yeah, I'll be fine. I can just watch if it gets to be too much."

"We can leave whenever you want."

"That's something we wanted to talk to you about, Mia. I mean, besides the fact that you are interested in a Junior, that's a whole other matter," Lisa interrupted. "Sophie will probably be going into the hospital for a few days soon. She just needs to get some of that stuff out of her lungs."

"When?"

"Depending on how she does, it might be next week? I'm sure you've noticed her struggling a bit?"

"Mom, OMG, I'm fine."

"Well, I am concerned about you going sledding. You know what the cold does to your lungs."

"MOM! I have to be able to live."

"And to live, you must breathe. I'll tell you what? Mia, why don't you go sled while Sophie and I do some crafting. Then tonight the two of you can watch a movie and make smores in the microwave?"

"Can't I just go for a little bit? The school is right around the corner, and you'll be close. If I have problems breathing, I'll call."

"Lisa, I think it's fine for just an hour. Let her live a little," Robert spoke up. "She'll have a scarf across her mouth and nose. She's got to live."

Lisa sighed. "Okay. But just an hour. And make sure your phone is charged."

- Chapter Five -

Sophie and I took the trek to the old church near the school. We climbed the hill, pulling sleds behind us. Sophie was struggling to breathe, but that wasn't necessarily odd There was just something different about it this time.

"Soph, we don't have to go to the top. We can hang out here and cheer for everyone coming down."

She wiped her hair from her face. "No…" —she wheezed—"I'm fine." Struggling. "I can do this." Coughing. "I'm not ready to give up, yet."

We stayed quiet the rest of the way. I didn't want to talk because if I did, she would too. I wanted her to save her breath. Part of the way up, I stopped and acted like I was winded. I flopped down by the road to catch my breath in the snow. Sophie settled next to me. We rested in silence as I listened to her wheeze. She had been able to do this entire hill last year.

She took off a glove, reached into her pocket, and brought out her inhaler. She sucked on it a few times, heavily. I could hear bubbling in her chest.

"Do you want me to call your parents?"

"No, I need to do this. I'm fine; trust me." She said no more.

A red cardinal flew over us and landed across the road, standing in the snow, watching us. It stood there staring. Sophie propped herself up to look at it more closely. The three of us sat there, Sophie, me, and the bird. The cardinal stood watching Sophie as she coughed. Her breathing became calmer, and the wheezing went silent. The bubbling in her lungs stopped, then the bird flew away.

"Thank you," she whispered.

"You and your animal thing!"

She looked at me. "Okay. I'm ready. You ready?"

"Yep. Let's do this." I had no doubt she would be able to make it the rest of the way.

She struggled a little, but she had the energy and air she needed to be able to get up the hill.

"Hey! Head's up!" Madison yelled. I dodged my head quickly enough to miss a spiraling snowball. "Sorry, bad aim." She ran up to us and gave Sophie a hug, then took her hand. "They're here!"

Everyone crowded around Sophie. They made a big deal over her being there, and I was glad for that. It WAS a big deal that she was able to come out in the snowstorm. Sometimes they forget about me when she's around. That's just part of being her friend. Everyone loves her.

Olivia popped up beside me, "Hey, girl. My mom made us hot cocoa." She was holding a thermos in one hand and cups in the other. "You want some?" I could always count on her. She poured me a cup. "So, what's up? You spending the snowstorm at Sophie's?"

"Uh, yeah." I didn't want to tell her what had happened with my mom.

"Cool. We are just waiting for the guys to get here before we start sledding."

I spotted the guys driving up over the hill to the parking lot. Sophie looked at me and winked. She knew I was nervous about Max. Then she turned to finish her conversation.

Olivia was always a bit nosey. I was used to it, but I didn't want to be pumped for information about the latest gossip at the moment. I wanted to get myself ready to talk to Max. I was nervous as hell. Despite feeling frozen, my cheeks grew warm when I saw him get out of the truck. Then my palms started sweating, and I felt like I needed to take off my coat.

"So, is Sophie actually able to be here? This seems unsafe for her." Olivia started pressing me. "Do her parents know she's here?"

I still had my eye on Max, but whipped my eyes back to her. "Olivia, this was Sophie's decision. And yes, her parents okayed this. She's stronger than you realize."

"I don't know—seems stupid to me."

I looked from Olivia to Sophie and smiled. Sophie was spinning around, her arms outstretched, head facing upward. "Look at her," I said, "Really look at her."

"I mean—"

"Olivia. She's happy."

Olivia turned her head toward Sophie. She did not smile. *Who doesn't smile at the sight of Sophie's happy face?* "Okay, true," she finally said.

The guys were busy getting toboggans out of the bed of the truck. Steven yelled over to us girls. "You sure you're ready? Because I greased these up. You're going to go flying."

"You think we're scared? We aren't scared," Madison yelled back.

Another car drove over the hill and parked next to the guys. Out popped three seniors: Reagan, Brooke, and Izzy. "Let's do this, guys! We haven't had snow like this in two years!" Izzy yelled. She looked over at Sophie, Olivia, and me and asked, "Are we babysitting today?" Then pointed to us and said, "I hope you ninth graders are ready." She laughed to herself.

Just then, Marco and Larkin drove up. They parked next to Brooke's car and got out. Larkin leaned against the side of Marco's car while Marco pulled a blanket from the back and wrapped it around her. He produced a thermos and handed it to her, while she put on a pair of sunglasses.

Sophie started laughing in the only way she could—crackling giggles and all. "No, you don't need to babysit, we are tough." She ended the laughing fit with a bunch of coughs. As I walked over to her, I could just see Olivia out of the corner of my eye, shaking her head.

"Soph, are you okay?"

She was coughing heavily so she simply nodded to me, with her face turning red.

"Do you need your inhaler?"

She moved her head from side to side, signaling no while coughing.

"Okay, well, I'm giving you my scarf. We can filter the cold air with it." I took off my scarf and wrapped it around her neck and her mouth and nose. After a few minutes, she stopped coughing and gave me a hug. "Are you sure you're okay?"

"You're being silly. I'm fine." Her voice sounded muffled from under her scarf and mine. "I think I'll just watch though."

"Okay, I'll stay with you."

"Mia! That's stupid. Go, have fun," she said with a wave of her hand as if to dismiss me. "I'm having fun, you should too."

Olivia walked over. "Soph, want some hot chocolate?"

"Not yet," she said, then started spinning in the snow again. Doing what she knew was best for herself, feeling nature happen around her. As she raised her arms, the snow started flurrying again. She stopped spinning, pulled down her scarf, and stuck her tongue out to catch snowflakes. And she laughed. Brooke walked over to us, kicking the snow with her duck boots as she went. "Is that hot chocolate I see? Where'd you get it? Don't hold out, freshman." I pointed her over to Olivia. "Awesome, thanks!"

"Hey. Uh. Mia?" I turned, startled to hear my name. It was Max. He was beside me with a toboggan behind him. "You wanna take the first run with me? We can smooth out the path for everyone else."

Sophie stopped spinning. "Yes, yes, she would like that very much," she said, pushing me toward Max.

She was happy, and I felt secure leaving her. I turned to Max. "Okay. Let's go."

"Great." He walked toward the hill with the long wooden toboggan trailing behind him. I followed quietly, not knowing what to say, feeling my cheeks redden again.

We got to the top of the hill and he stopped and turned around. "I actually really like this place. I think it's awesome that you can see the entire town from here." He looked at me with his bright blue eyes, then turned back to the view. "Sometimes I sit up here at night and stare out at the lighted windows, wondering what everyone is doing in their own lives, then I look up at the stars." He turned his face toward the sky, allowing snowflakes to settle on his eyelashes. "And I think about how small we are, yet at the same time, so gigantic." He took another look at me, then I felt his gloved hand grab my woolen-covered one. "Do you want to come up here with me sometime? Just to talk about the universe."

Hot. My face was hot. I'd never been asked out before. I didn't know what to say or how to react. So I simply went with, "Yes."

"Cool. Cool. Okay. Cool." He was smiling.

He let go of my hand and grabbed the rope to the toboggan. "Get in the front. I'll get on behind you."

I said nothing. I just sat toward the front of the sled. He handed me the rope. He sat behind me and ran his legs beside my body on each side. He wrapped his arms around me and moved in close so that I was leaning against his chest. Then he took the rope from my hands.

He nestled his chin on my shoulder and asked, "Before we go, can we get a selfie?" *WHAT?*

"Sure. Can I take one too?" I could not believe I was really there with him, on a sled, talking about selfies.

"Cool. Here's my phone. Take it for me?" I took the phone, took off my glove, set the screen for maximum brightness, and held the phone above and in front of us. All I could see was his eyes because his mouth was resting against my puffy jacket, very close to my neck. I took the photo and handed it back to him without really looking closely, then fumbled to get my own phone out of my pocket. I smiled for the camera, but I noticed on the screen that he had his nose nuzzled into my neck. I got goosebumps and shivers all at once. I took the second photo and a few more just to be sure. Then I put my phone back into my pocket and got my glove back on.

"You ready?" he asked.

"Yes."

He pulled me in more closely to him than I was before and used his arms to get us started. And off we went. I couldn't concentrate on sledding, all I could think about was how close I was to him, how close he was to me. His body kept me warm while the cold air whipped by my face. This was heaven. Then, out of nowhere, we hit a rock and were thrown off the sled. We fell sideways, but he never lost his grip on me. When we landed, we both laughed.

"Are you okay?" he asked.

"Yeah. Let's do it again!"

He laughed at my suggestion. "I would love to." He let go of me and we both lay there on our backs, just staring up at the snowflakes falling on top of us, breathing heavily. He grabbed my hand again.

We didn't notice, or maybe he just didn't care, that Everly and Victor were about to fly right past us on their sleds, just a foot away from our heads.

They stopped and got off. "What the hell! Clear the path! We could have killed the both of you," Victor yelled.

Max and I just looked at each other and started laughing.

"What the hell?" Everly said, standing over us.

"Nah. Don't be crazy; it's not like that," Max said and got up. He held out his hand to help me stand. "Just friends having a good time." He looked at me, "Right, Mia?"

My stomach fell. "Oh, right." My smile vanished.

We turned and started our trek up the hill with Victor and Everly following us. "So, um. What was that about?" Everly asked me. "It looked like the two of you were becoming comfy."

"We were just having fun. No big deal," I said back. Max kept his eyes forward, not looking at me at all. What was the most romantic moment of my life, up until that point, swiftly became the most awkward. Was I really that bad that he didn't want to acknowledge what just happened? What was so wrong with me? I bit my tongue and refused to cry.

When we got to the top, Sophie ran over to me. "What happened?" Before I could answer she took my arm and pulled me aside. "It looked like you were nestled tightly into him." She was smiling from ear to ear, but it didn't feel right, like the smile was fake in some way.

"Yeah, I guess we were." But I didn't tell her any more than that. I didn't want to talk about it.

"You look frozen—here's some hot chocolate." She handed me the little disposable mug she was drinking out of. "Warm up."

"Are you going to try to sled?" I asked her.

"Nah, I probably couldn't get up the hill again if I did. I'm just having fun watching everyone."

"Well, I think I'm done now." I looked at her, trying to hide the fact that I was embarrassed. "Do you want to stick around some more, or are you ready to go?" I asked, hoping she would say she was ready to go home.

"Yeah, we should probably go." She nodded, then she dug her inhaler out of her pocket and took a puff.

"Heads up!" I felt a hard icy ball of snow hit me in the back of the head. "Sorry. I warned you, though," Everly yelled. I turned slowly to look at her, trying not to show I was holding back a tear. Everly was standing there staring at me, not laughing like everyone else. I was sure she had meant to do that.

"No big deal. It was an accident," I choked out. I was done. I looked at Sophie. "Can you walk home? Or should we call your parents?"

"Hang on." Sophie looked around. "Hey, Max?!"

I died a little bit inside.

"Max," she yelled again, trying to get his attention. He was too busy talking to Alex and Leo to notice her, and her voice was becoming more and more quiet.

"Sophie, stop. I'll call your parents."

She looked at me, her lips drawn tight. "No, don't call them." She took a deep breath in and yelled louder, "MAX!" then broke down in a strong cough, followed by a series of smaller coughs that carried a bubbling sound with them. He turned, not at her yelling but at her coughing, and ran over to us.

"What's up?" he asked. Sophie continued to cough.

Everly noticed what was going on. "Sophie, are you okay?"

"No, she needs to go home," I answered. "We were wondering if Max could take us home."

"Why'd you bring her here? You shouldn't have. She's going to be sick," Everly said.

"No." Sophie waved her hand in front of her face. "I'm fine. I just want to go."

I added, "She wanted to come. It wasn't my decision. Her parents okayed this."

"Obviously, she's not okay."

"No, really. Everly. I'm fine."

"I'll drive you home. Don't worry," Max said.

Everly squinted her eyes at me and turned around, not saying another word.

"Thanks," I responded to Max. Then turned to Sophie. "No, seriously, are you okay?"

"One-hundred percent."

We followed Max to his truck. He opened his door. Sophie stood aside and told me to get in first. I shook my head no. She gave me a dirty look and gestured for me to get in. So, I climbed up into the large red beast. As soon as I was seated in the middle of the front seat, I reached around and grabbed Sophie's hand to help pull her up, while Max helped her step up. Once she sat and he closed the door behind her, she looked at me and gave me a sly smile. Then she patted my knee, cleared her throat, grabbed her phone from her pocket, and started texting. The driver's side door opened and Max heaved himself into his truck, slamming the door behind him.

"Ladies, give me a minute to get this engine revving then I'll get the heat on." He turned on the engine to a loud purr.

I looked at Sophie who was furiously tapping away. "Who are you talking to?" I asked.

"Ryan," she said with a small giggle.

"Oh cool. He's able to break away today?"

Ryan was her boyfriend. He went to a private boarding school in Maryland. He didn't get to call and talk often, so when he did, she dropped everything. Even me.

"Yep. He messaged me while you were sledding."

"Wait… Is that why you wanted to leave?"

"Well. I mean, yeah, I wanted to get home so I could call him."

I rolled my eyes. "I thought that you weren't feeling good."

"Well, I'm not, but since when has that ever stopped me." She put her phone on her lap and turned her head to look at me. "I'm sorry. I wasn't thinking. Did you want to stay?"

"No. no. I'm good. I was ready."

I had been worried that being out in the snow was too much for her. I was relieved it was about Ryan. I wasn't going to complain, especially after the awkwardness of the sled ride.

Max relaxed as his truck heated up. He slouched a bit and blew air into his hands to try to warm up. "Did you ladies have fun?"

"Yeah. It was nice being out," Sophie answered. I said nothing.

His thigh was against mine. We were touching… again. Not as closely as on the sled, but still. But I guess all he wanted was a new friend? I was confused.

"So, you really wanna come to the movies with me next weekend?"

"Oh. Um. Sure?"

"Ok." He aimed the truck for the exit and started driving. We drove in silence all the way to Sophie's house, while she tapped on her phone screen.

- Chapter Six -

We barged in through the door of Sophie's house, ready to warm up. We took off our boots, coats, and everything else, then left them in a pile by the front door and flopped on the couch.

"Hey, girls! Have fun?" Lisa asked.

"Yeah," Sophie answered.

"So… not gonna put this stuff away? Maybe hang it on the line in the laundry room or something?" she said, pointing to our discarded wet winter clothes.

"Sorry," I replied, getting up to do just that.

"No, it's okay. Enjoy this time. I'll do it." She walked over to our pile, heaved it up into her arms, and carried it off to the laundry room.

"Do you mind if I go upstairs and call Ryan?" Sophie asked me.

"No, not at all. Go. I'll just sit here and relax."

"K. Thanks." She bolted up off the couch, and walked up her steps, texting as she went.

I sighed and grabbed the remote to flip through the channels on the TV. Finding nothing interesting, I got my phone out of my pocket and started flipping through the normal photos people post on social media of dogs in the snow, snowmen, selfies with snowflake-encrusted hair.

Then I saw it. Just one photo. One amazing photo. Max must have posted it right after he dropped us off. I couldn't believe it. In it, my cheeks are bright red. People will probably think it's because of the cold, but it's because I was shocked to be so close to him. I didn't realize it at the time, but he was smelling my hair in the picture, not smiling at the phone like I was. It looked like he was taking in my essence. I lowered my eyes to read the caption. It read, "The best sled ride I've ever taken." I gasped, then clicked the heart under the photo. I cradled my phone in both hands and then held it up to my chest. I thought he didn't like me after the sled ride. But I guess I was wrong.

With the phone nestled close to me, its ringing made me jump. I hoped it was Max, but it was actually my father. "Dad?"

"I'm just calling to check in. How are you and your mom doing through the storm?"

"I'm actually not at home. I'm at Sophie's."

"What? I didn't know that." He took a pause and a deep breath in. "Your mom was alone during the storm?"

"Yes."

"Mia was that—"

I cut him off. "Dad, she kicked me out of the house—in the storm."

"What? Why? Who came to get you?"

"Because Sophie and I were too loud this weekend when she slept over. No one came to get me."

"What do you mean by no one?"

"Dad, I walked."

"In the storm?"

"Yes."

"No, something more must have happened. How loud were you?"

"Not really loud, just laughing. I keep telling you that she treats me differently when you aren't home."

"I can't believe this."

"Dad, she also wouldn't let me grab my hat, gloves, or scarf. Not even my boots. I had nothing."

"Mia, you should have called someone. You should have called me!"

"Dad, she took my phone."

"What do you mean?"

"I don't know how else to say it. She would not let me take my phone with me."

"Was she drinking?"

"No, Dad."

"How was she the day before?"

"Dad, I don't know. I try to keep an eye on her, but it's better if I just stay away from her when you aren't home."

"I'm going to come home early."

"She was fine last night. She was able to drive through the snow and bring me my things. She even talked to Sophie's parents."

"What did she say to them? What did YOU tell them?"

"Dad, I had nowhere else to go. I had to come here. And, of course, they asked questions."

"Okay, I'll clean it up with them."

"Dad, she's never kicked me out before. What's going to happen next time?"

"Mia, I honestly don't know what's happening. Things are always perfect when I'm home."

"Of course they are. You are only home one week a month."

"Don't talk back to me. How do you think I pay for everything for you and your mother?"

"Dad. I didn't mea–"

"Are you sure you aren't the one causing the problems?"

"Dad!" I cried.

"Ok. Look. I'm sorry. I'll change my schedule around and come home this week."

"Then she'll act like a loving mom, and you'll leave, and it will start all over again. It means nothing, Dad."

"I'll be home tomorrow," he said with a sigh. "I'll come to pick you up and fix the situation."

"Ok."

He hung up the phone. I could tell he was furious, but I couldn't tell if he was mad at me or my mother.

All of the dread I felt the night before came back. I felt a lump grow in my throat. No one understood what I was going through. My dad didn't want me to talk to Sophie or her parents about it, but who could I talk to otherwise? Either something was extremely wrong with my mom, or there was something seriously wrong with me. Either way, I couldn't handle this on my own.

I could hear Sophie laughing on the phone up in her room. Laughing, then coughing, then laughing again. She was happy. She was so very happy. She was always happy. How could Sophie, who was so sick all the time, be the happiest person I knew while I was healthy and miserable?

Sophie's mom came back from the laundry room. "I hung the coats and put everything else in the dryer. They'll be ready for your next sledding trip," she said, looking around. "Where's Soph?"

"She was able to talk to Ryan. She's up in her room."

She stopped and looked at me. "Do you like him? Ryan?"

"I think so. He makes her laugh."

"Well, that's important. Ok. I guess I just worry. First heartbreaks are the worst."

"I wouldn't know about that yet." I laughed, trying to hide my real feelings.

"Yes, well, as for you, Miss Mia. Be careful. Max is a junior. Protect your heart. Keep your head about you. Okay?"

"What are you talking about?" I asked.

"I saw the way he was looking at you in the diner. Also, don't think I missed that he asked you out. Seriously though, he's a Junior. They have different ... expectations."

"Ewwwww!" I put my hands over my ears. "I can't talk about this with you."

"Yeah, well, I don't think you can talk to your mother about it either. Listen, I promise you, you CAN talk to me. Even if it's awkward. Okay?"

"Okay."

"Promise?"

"I do."

"Okay. Want hot chocolate?" she asked.

"Yeah, can I come help you make it?"

"Absolutely. Want to make some chocolate chip cookies too?"

"YES!"

- Chapter Seven -

I tried to sleep that night, but I just couldn't. My mind raced. My dad was supposed to pick me up after school. I knew my mother would act as if she missed me. She would hug and kiss me, and it would all be fake—like nothing happened at all. I would never be able to bring it up again because it would be too upsetting for her. I would have to bury the memory and never talk about it again because, as I was always told, I could never, ever upset my mother. I lay there staring at the light coming in through the window from the streetlight, but I wasn't all there. My mind was replaying all these things that had happened in my life. Things with my mom, each playing over and over again in my mind. From all the times she slapped me across the face, to the times she got back from the pharmacy, complaining about the cost of medicine, yelling that she wished she'd never had me. I was to blame. She knew it. I knew it. What could I have done differently? My father always tiptoed around her, so when she blew, it had to be something I did myself. But what? Sophie's mom never blows up at me. I don't want to upset anyone. Why do I upset my own mother? Why did she even have me?

I wasn't prepared to face my mom again. She'd stand there hugging me, crying, telling me that she loved me and that she was so, so worried. That's what she always did in front of my father... or anyone, really. She'd never kicked me out before, but I knew the reaction that would be waiting for me. She would never admit to what she'd done. Round and round the memories swirled in my brain until the sun rose and Sophie's room lit up. She stirred just as her alarm started playing music.

Sophie sat up and stretched. "Did you sleep okay?"

"No, not really."

"Worried your father is coming today?"

"Yeah." I nodded.

"You still have my rock?" she asked.

"Yeah."

"Keep a hold of it. Actually, hold it in your hand when you see her tonight. Got it?"

"I will. I'm not sure how it will help."

"It will help. I promise."

Lisa came in and started working with the vials of medicine, squeezing fluid into the top of the nebulizer. "Mia, why don't you get your shower while Sophie does her treatment," she said, handing Sophie the mouthpiece. "You don't want to be late for school. There's no two-hour delay today."

That's when the tiredness hit me. My brain started feeling foggy. The memories exhausted me. I had held too much fear about going home to sleep at night, but with the day starting I just wanted to curl back up and go to sleep. Instead, I got up, put my feet on the cold wooden floor, and tiptoed my way to the bathroom. I could hear coughing behind me as I closed the door.

I turned on the shower faucet, put my hand in the stream of water, and recoiled at the coldness. It reminded me of that walk through the woods when I thought I was going to die. I stood back and waited until I saw steam coming from the streams, then slowly put my hand in the water again. This time, it was hot, probably too hot. I got in anyway. My skin felt like it was melting off, but I craved the searing heat. It took me out of my head and let me just feel.

I got out of the shower and went back to Sophie's bedroom. Her mom was doing percussions on her back. She looked at me and said, "Want to finish up so I can go get breakfast made? I want you to have some good food for today."

"Okay."

As she rose from her spot next to Sophie, Lisa signaled for me to take over, then left the room. I sat on the floor next to Sophie's bed.

"Ready?" I asked, cracking my knuckles.

"Yep."

I cupped my hands and started hitting her back to the rhythm of songs the both of us liked.

"Okay. My turn to do you."

"What do you mean?"

She got up off her bed and sat on her knees facing me. I turned toward her and sat the same way. She stared at me for a long moment, then reached her hands up to me with her palms perpendicular to my body. Something in me made me reach my hands out too. I held my hands up to hers, our palms almost touching. We sat there for a moment, feeling the energy move between our palms.

Sophie liked to do all sorts of spiritual things, but this was new. As I sat there my hands got hotter and hotter as I felt our energies grow together like a flexible ball of power suspended in the air between us.

Sophie opened her eyes slowly,."Do you see it?" she whispered.

I looked into her eyes, wondering what she meant. "See what?"

"The light, silly." Her eyes traced an outline around my body.

"What light?"

"You don't see it? I see it. It is going through me and into you."

"Sophie! No!" I sat back quickly. I knew she was trying to give me positive energy, but she needed all her energy to stay healthy.

"What?" She took a deep breath.

"You need your energy," I said.

"I'm fine. I slept. I could feel that you were tired. Anyway, it isn't my energy." She cocked her head sideways. "You didn't sleep. You were up worrying."

"How do you know?"

"I can feel it. Duh." She waved her hand in front of her face as if what she could do wasn't anything strange. "Besides, the energy just passes through me. It's not mine: it's meant for you."

I looked at her through squinted eyes. I knew to never question her; there were things about her that just couldn't be explained. To be close to her meant accepting those things. "Fine." I held my hands up again.

"Awesome, but you can put your hands down."

I let them drop to my side.

She started speaking in a quiet, calm voice. "Unclench your muscles; it's like you have a wall up. I can't help you unless you relax." I could hear faint bubbling in her lungs, but she didn't cough. She was focused. "Close your eyes." I did as she instructed. She continued. "Start by relaxing your fingertips. Let the calm move up your fingers to your palms. Then up your arms, to your shoulders. Now concentrate on your shoulders, let go. Now loosen your back and your pelvis. Now your legs." Her voice cracked as she spoke.

She held her hands above my head, then moved them ever so slowly above my body, from my head to my toes. She didn't touch me, not even once, but I could feel her. Even with my eyes closed, I knew exactly where her hands were. The warmth from the energy felt like love. It was like I was surrounded by angels. She let out a breath and asked me to open my eyes.

"How do you feel?"

"Okay. I think?"

"Maybe it gave you some energy. Let's wait and see. This was the first time I ever tried it."

"What was it?"

"I'm not sure; it just felt like the right thing to do."

"And you tried it on me instead of yourself? You need it, not me."

"I mean, of course I tried it on you. You are the one who needs it."

"Girls, come eat." We both jumped when we heard her mother yelling up the steps.

We looked to the door as if we were doing something wrong, then got up and quickly went downstairs to eat breakfast.

- Chapter Eight -

The only thing I could think about all morning was the feeling of love I had felt from Sophie's hands. I sat behind her in English class and just sat staring at the back of her head, wondering where she came up with the stuff she did. I drifted off into a daydream. It looked like light started shrouding Sophie's body. The light held all sorts of colors like it was shining through a prism. The light filled the entire room until it was almost blinding. Then I jumped and found myself staring at an empty classroom, with Sophie standing beside me, trying to get my attention.

"Mia! What's wrong with you? Come on, we'll be late."

"Oh, right. Sorry."

We emerged into the hallway where I felt like I was taller than normal. I had energy, but the feeling was different. I felt otherworldly. I felt like I could … fly. I didn't understand and there was no way I could explain the feeling.

"Mia."

Sophie and I both turned, startled. "Max, you scared me."

"Sorry. I just thought I would say hi," he said. His hand lightly grazed mine.

"It's okay."

He pulled his hand away and ran his fingers through his hair while looking down at me. Then a smile spread across his face. "Hey, want a piece of gum?"

"Sure."

He reached in his pocket and pulled out a pack of cinnamon gum. "Here you go," he said and held it out to me. As I grabbed it, our fingers touched briefly. I felt my face go hot. I was blushing, but so was he.

"Thanks."

"Cool." He smiled, then looked like he had an idea. "Oh hey, can I text you later?"

"Maybe. I'm going home tonight. I'm not sure what my parents have planned." I didn't want to tell him what was really going on.

"Okay. Well, if you can't talk, just don't answer back. Kay?"

"Okay."

He walked away as quickly as he had come.

"So, this is getting serious," Sophie said.

"I don't know about that. What Junior wants to date a freshman?"

"Apparently Max."

We both laughed.

"I hope so," I nodded.

At lunch. we found our normal spot to sit and eat. Sophie and I got out the lunches her mother made for us. I didn't usually get to eat homemade food at lunch, so this was a treat. Sophie was the opposite. She always wanted cafeteria food, but her mom would never let her.

The gang crowded in the seats around us. Emma and Lily were first, always together, always fighting. They grew up across the street from each other and shared a bond like no one else.

"Whatever, Lily," Emma snapped.

"Oh, so you're hurt?" Lily stuck out her tongue and laughed.

"Oh, shut up."

"Ladies!" Lily said, her eyes trained on the two of us. "What's up?" She flung her backpack under the table.

"Oh hey. We're gonna hang out in the parking lot and wait for the guys after basketball practice. Wanna hang with us?" Clearly, whatever Lily and Emma were fighting about wasn't serious, or wasn't a fight at all. It was hard to tell with the two of them.

"We can't. Mia's dad is picking her up at my house right after school," Sophie answered.

"Okay. Maybe we can go to the movies this weekend."

"Sounds great!" I said.

Then Sophie laughed and said, "Oh my God, you guys, Mia is going to the movies with Max this weekend. I almost forgot."

Lily and Emma whipped their heads toward me. "WHATTTT?" Emma asked.

"I knew it!" Lily said, smiling.

I couldn't believe Sophie had said anything. "Oh, did you, now?"

"Well, one thing is for sure," Lily said as she sat down. "This explains the Instagram post."

"Yeah. We were wondering about that," Emma said. Her tone was sly as she leaned in closer. "Is this serious?"

"I don't know. Probably not," I answered without shifting my eyes from the sandwich in my hand.

Madison and Olivia dropped off their backpacks without saying a word, then got in line for pizza. Next came Everly who pulled a chair out, sat, and looked straight at me. "So, uh. Max?"

"I guess so, but it's not a big deal."

"It is. How'd you get his attention?" Everly produced an apple from her brown bag and took a bite. Juniors never sat with freshmen. I wondered what she was up to. "Seems strange that he's into you, but whatever." Everly was always bold, but she was probably saying what everyone was already thinking. She didn't give me time to answer before she said, "Hey, Soph, you feeling okay after sledding? I noticed you guys left early." She may have been talking to Sophie, but Everly kept her eyes trained on me as she spoke.

Sophie was busy eating. Not looking up to answer Everly, she said, "Yeah, I was fine. No big deal."

A loud argument started across the cafeteria. I turned to see what was going on. It was the seniors who eat lunch at the same time as us. THE Luke Stewart, the guy everyone the guy everyone loved (or loved to hate) was being screamed at by his ex-girlfriend, Reagan. "I told you to leave me alone. Go mess with those little girls over there." She pointed to our table, all freshmen. "That's what you like, anyway."

"Larkin?" He looked at the girl next to Reagan.

Larkin shook her head. "Oh, I'm the last person you want to bring into this."

"Whatever, you are both bitches anyway," he said, then he walked away.

The senior girls drew in close to each other, rolling their eyes and laughing. Then Reagan got up and walked across the cafeteria toward our table.

"Reagan's coming. Who knows what she'll say," Emma whispered to Lily.

"Nah, I think she's changed," Sophie said. Sophie always gave people the benefit of the doubt.

"We'll see," whispered Emma.

"Hey, girls." Reagan approached our table. "I'm sorry to drag you into that. It was unnecessary. Just. Just stay away from Luke."

"Why?" Everly asked, her eyebrows raised in a challenge.

"Oh, you know why," Larkin said with a hand on her hip, then she turned to me. "Because he'll take your virginity then laugh in your face."

I felt like the air was being sucked out of the cafeteria. Everly looked straight at me. I had no idea what Reagan meant.

"And you, Mia. Remember, Max is a Junior, and he's friends with Luke. Be careful."

I was shocked. I finally felt a tiny bit of happiness. Why couldn't people just let me enjoy it?

Everly cursed me with her eyes, but at the same time, it was weird. She looked sad and panicky.

Larkin spoke up from behind Reagan. "Reagan, come on. Don't scare them." She grabbed Reagan's hand. "Sorry ladies. Enjoy lunch." Larkin walked with Reagan back to their seats. Marco was there. He gave Larkin a quick kiss on her forehead. I saw her close her eyes while he did it, and it looked like she inhaled. That was what I wanted in a relationship, to have someone love me so much, that they just want to inhale my essence. That was everything I had ever dreamed of … a relationship like they had.

We ate and talked about everything–everything except for Max.

***

That afternoon Sophie and I had just started the trek to her house when Larkin's blue Scion pulled up behind us. Marco was driving.

Larkin poked her head out of the passenger side window. "Hey, ladies, want a ride home?" She looked at us expectantly.

Sophie and I turned to each other, stunned. It wasn't every day that two of the most popular seniors noticed you and offered you a ride. "Sure!" Sophie yelled. We climbed into the back seat and shut the doors behind us. "Thank you."

"No problem," Larkin said. She held Marco's hand as he tried to drive one-handed. "I just noticed you guys left early from sledding, so I thought maybe Sophie wasn't feeling well." She looked back at us. "I didn't want you guys walking all the way home."

"Oh, I'm fine. Today is better," Sophie said.

"That's good," Larkin and Marco said at the same time.

Larkin looked at Marco and smiled as he drove over the hill and past the cemetery. "Also, one more thing. Don't worry about Reagan. She wasn't trying to be mean."

"She sure can get loud," I said. My voice sounded small. I was nervous to be talking to her at all.

"Yeah, but she worries. I don't think Max is Luke, though. I think it's fine."

"Larkin, I'm not sure anyone in Luke's crew is fine. I mean, just saying."

She spun to face Marco. "Marco, stop."

"What, I have opinions." He shrugged.

"Sure. I think what he means is that Luke likes freshmen," she said, turning back to me. "So, I guess we aren't so sure what Max is up to."

"I'll be okay." I didn't think anyone could hurt me as badly as my mother had. I wondered if Larkin had picked us up specifically to warn me about Max. *Weird.*

"I mean, I'm not trying to be in your business," Larkin said then turned back around to look out her window.

Sophie's phone vibrated. She reached into her backpack to pull it out. I could tell by her smile that it was Ryan. Her face turned bright red.

"You okay?" Marco asked Larkin.

"Marco, yes! I'm fine. Chill!" She snapped her head toward him, then took her hand away.

From what I had heard, Larkin had some sort of accident at the beginning of the school year that had ended up in the hospital. No one knew exactly what had happened, but she did seem much healthier now. Marco was a doting boyfriend. He always made sure she had enough food and checked on her all the time. I was surprised to see her reaction. I looked out the window embarrassed by witnessing whatever had just happened. Sophie was so busy texting that she never even noticed the tense situation. She even took a selfie at one point. I may as well have been alone in the backseat.

Marco wasn't able to drop us off right in front of Sophie's house because my father's car was parked on the road, so he pulled up in front of the house next door.

"Thank you!" I said to Marco.

"You're welcome. Take care!"

Sophie didn't say anything; she just kept her face in her phone.

Obviously, she was not as impressed with our ride home as I was. Once Sophie and I were on the sidewalk, Marco pulled away.

"So, you didn't think that was cool?" I asked.

"Oh, yeah, yeah, yeah. I just. I'm worried about Ryan getting freaked out about my health again," she said. "But it's fine." She waved the notion aside and looked up at the sky.

We were walking up the perfectly shoveled sidewalk when Sophie decided to step off the walkway into the pure untouched snow. The snow went up to the middle of her shin.

"What are you doing?"

"I want the world to know I was here, right now, at this time, with you." She pulled her other foot over into the snow and stood there, laughing. "Come on. Let the world know we are here."

I laughed and jumped into the snow next to her. We clasped our hands and flopped down together onto the white covering. It caved in around us.

"Isn't it beautiful?" she asked.

"It is! It really is."

"How did you feel today?"

I answered without much thought, "Perfect. I felt perfect. In fact. I felt like I was taller."

Sophie got up and held her hand out to me to pull me up. Once up, I squeezed her hand and asked, "What did you do to me this morning." I let out a little nervous chuckle. "I couldn't get it out of my mind all day. I felt supercharged." Then I remembered that she was the reason I felt that way. "Were you okay? After that?"

"I think it felt the same for me as it did for you. I've been feeling like my head is in the clouds." She let go of my hand and started to spin ahead of me with her arms held high in the air and her head turned to the sky. Then she stopped and laughed. "I feel strong."

The word strong was big coming from her. Happy, yes, but strong? She never said that she ever felt strong.

"What are you girls doing?" We heard her neighbor's voice. He was an old man who loved being a grump.

"Nothing, Paul. Just enjoying the snow!" Sophie called out to him.

"Ruining my pristine snow-covered lawn is what you're doing." He glared at us, then said, "Sophie, you best get on home now. You don't want to catch yourself pneumonia."

"Yes, Paul." Her voice sounded shocked and sad at the same time.

"Let's go."

She looked upset. I know she just wanted to be healthy. She hated when fun moments were cut short because she was sick. She hated the reminders.

"You okay?"

"Absolutely!" She took a few steps back onto the sidewalk and then flung her hands in the air. Smiling towards the sky. "I'm just fine." And she started spinning. The thing she did when she wanted to feel free.

That's when I started spinning, too. I was never the spinning type, but it just felt right. I didn't even let the comments about Max get me down the way I normally would have. I just flung my arms in the sky and spun around. Just me and Sophie, in the middle of the town, spinning for all we were worth. And I felt free. Everything about that moment was light, heavenly, and just exactly right. As I held my arms lifted to the sky, I let go of the worry I felt about going home with my dad. I let go of the fear of my father blaming me for my mother kicking me out of the house. I didn't think about what my mother would do the next time I made her angry. I just spun. And for a fraction of a moment, I was free.

When we finally stopped spinning, both of us stumbled as we tried to regain our balance. We threw our bodies back down into Paul's yard. The coldness of the snow and the rigidity of the first layer of ice broke us from our trances, but still, we lay there, staring up at the sky. "It's special, you know?" Sophie finally said after catching her breath.

"What's special?" I asked.

"All of this. It's beautiful, but it's also scary." She paused to take a breath. "I mean, two nights ago you were scared you were going to die because your mom kicked you out in this, and now we are acting like it's magical." She grabbed my hand. "It's amazing to me that something so treacherous can also bring joy."

I understood what she was trying to say. "Sometimes, the bad stuff makes us understand beauty so much more. Right?"

"Yeah, kinda. But I mean. I'm sick, but because I'm sick I'm forced to see all of this—every single minute detai—as something beautiful." We stayed there a little while longer, holding hands. "It's really just another way of breathing, you know?"

"I mean it, ladies. Flop around in your own yard," Paul yelled out to us again.

"We're fine Mr. Murphy. What's the point in having all this snow if you never enjoy it? As for pneumonia, well, that wouldn't be anything new to me," Sophie said laughing, then coughing. "You should come out here and flop with us!"

"Go home." He waved us on. "Silly girls," he said to himself as he turned to go back into his house once again.

We slowly got control of our laughing—and Sophie's coughing—and got up and headed for the house. I was so happy to get those laughs out; it felt cleansing.

Then I remembered my dad was inside Sophie's house waiting for me. My heart sank.

"Soph, I don't want to," I said. My voice sounded small and far away.

"Mia, you'll be okay. We've got you. We are only a phone call away."

"Yeah, if she lets me keep my phone."

We walked in silence. Halfway up her walkway she reached out and grabbed my hand. Nothing more needed to be said.

As we approached the door we heard yelling.

"You can't let her stay there with Kim anymore. This needs to change." It was Lisa.

"Kim is her mother." My father's voice boomed.

We stood stock-still in front of the door. Sophie squeezed my hand and looked at me. "Together?"

"Together." I nodded. It was a comforting thought, but I knew this was something I had to do alone. Just like Sophie's illness. I was there with her through it all, but ultimately, she was the one who had to go through it on her own. We were the same in that way, the same but very different.

She took a step forward and grabbed the door handle, then turned it slowly. The door came flying open as if by itself. My father was standing there, red-faced, looking deflated.

"Princess," he said, looking relieved. "Come here." He grabbed me and pulled me into a hug. I knew he was trying to deal with everything too, so I fell into his hug with sincerity.

"Hi, Dad." I backed away from the hug to put my backpack down by the door. It had been three weeks since I had seen him last. Traveling for work wasn't easy on the family, and I think he felt guilty for it. No, I was sure he did. "Are you taking me home?"

"Yes, yes I am. We will work through this as a family."

"Okay."

"Will you be strong for me?" he asked.

"Yes."

"How strong does a child need to be? Honestly!" Lisa said under her breath.

"Lisa, don't," Sophie's dad interrupted. "Let Mia and her mom work this out."

"Fine!" Lisa said, giving him a dirty look. "Girls, let's go upstairs and pack Mia's things." She gestured toward the steps. "Let the men talk a bit."

Sophie and I went up the stairs, but I turned around to look again. When I did, I saw our two dads standing perfectly still, eyes locked in a stare. It gave me the shivers.

In Sophie's room, I noticed Lisa had already packed my things. "You packed me up already?" I asked as she walked in the door behind me.

"Of course, dear. I just needed this time to talk to you." She pointed at the bed. "Sit down. Both of you." We did as instructed. "First, Sophie, Dr. Thomas got in touch with us, and he wants you to go into the hospital tomorrow."

Sophie looked out the window. I grabbed her hand. This was nothing too unusual. With Cystic Fibrosis your lungs tend to fill with gunk. Sometimes it gets stuck and you have to go into the hospital for a few days. But this time she seemed a little worse, and I was a bit more freaked out than normal. The gurgling sound was new.

"Mia, that is the only reason I'm not fighting your father right now." Lisa took a long deep breath. "Your father promised that he would be home for a week. And that during that week he would make sure you all talk to someone about your problems. Your mom needs help and she's not getting it now."

"Okay. I know." I said in a small voice. "But," I said a little louder, "Why does this hospital stay seem different?"

"It might be. We just don't know yet. But don't worry about that right now."

Sophie kept staring out the window. When I looked to see what she was looking at, I realized there was a cardinal sitting just outside the window, staring back at her. It gave me hope. After all, it was the cardinal that had helped her breathe when we were walking in the snow; I was sure of it. But Sophie's face looked different now, and one tear was forming at the corner of her eye. I squeezed her hand tighter, which broke her trance. She looked at me and smiled. "I'm fine. It's going to be fine," she said. I nodded and she quickly wiped the tear away from her eye.

"Yes, it will," Lisa agreed. "Mia, I don't feel safe leaving you without somewhere to turn, so I bought you this phone." She pulled a phone out of a bag sitting next to Sophie's bed. It doesn't have a lot of minutes on it so it's only for emergencies. Just make sure to keep it to yourself. And, keep it charged. Our numbers are already programmed into it." She handed the box to me. "If your mother does anything like that ever again or tries to hurt you, please use it. We will find a way to get to you no matter what. Do you understand?"

"Yes, but I don't think it's necessary."

"It is. Also, if your father doesn't get therapy for all of you, and especially for your mother, I will have to make some hard decisions. But I can't do that this week and I don't want you in the system."

I got chills when she said that: the system.

"We just can't do anything about it this week, because we need to be at the hospital." She placed a hand on my shoulder. "It's going to be okay. We love you. Know that, okay? We all love you." Her voice shook as she spoke.

"I love you guys, too. But right now I'm more worried about Sophie."

"Don't," was all Sophie said. She wiped a tear from her eye and straightened her back. "I'll be fine; I always am. This is nothing. The same as always."

"Promise?"

"I promise."

"Okay, girls. I'm going to give you a few minutes to chat before Mia leaves with her father. Don't worry, okay?"

"Yes."

Lisa got up and left the room, closing the door behind her.

The sunlight was shining through Sophie's window in rays, beautiful rays that I just couldn't stop looking at. The bird maintained its vigil, watching Sophie. Its shadow was apparent on the wall.

"What's going on? Why does this seem different?"

"At my last appointment with my pulmonary specialist, they told me I was getting worse." I gasped at her words. She quickly added, "No, don't worry. With so many new treatments now, they are probably going to explore some of those this week." She squeezed my hand. "I feel positive about it all. Please don't worry about me."

Her phone buzzed in her pocket. She took her hand out of mine to grab it. "It's Ryan. Look. He sent me a whole screen of hearts!"

"You guys are so cute. Does he know you are going into the hospital?"

"No. I don't want him to know. You remember what happened last time?"

The last time she was in the hospital, Ryan had been so worried that he kept saying over and over again that he didn't think he could handle it. It hurt Sophie, but she was never good at letting anyone see when she felt weak.

"I do remember. That scared me. I don't want him to hurt you."

She sat spinning the promise ring he had given her around on her finger. "He won't," she said, nodding. "It will be okay." She gave a little laugh. Then got up and started spinning again. "It will all be okay." She stopped spinning and pointed at me. "and, you'll be okay too." Just then the cardinal flew away. His wings flapped against the window as he pushed off. "And we will go to that camp this summer, and it will be the time of our lives." Her smile was spread across her face. It was hard to not smile when she was smiling at you.

- Chapter Nine -

The ride home was quiet and awkward. I have to believe my father knew that taking me back to the house was a bad idea, but I'm not sure he knew what else to do. He couldn't quit his job, and he couldn't take me on the road with him. I was thankful when my phone started vibrating.

Max: Is this Mia? It's Max.

I was excited to see his text.

Mia: Yes! Hi, Max.
Max: Oh good, I'm glad it's really you.
Max: I just wanted to say hi. And tell you that I had a lot of fun on the sled ride with you yesterday. I wish you could have gone on another ride with me.
Mia: Me too, but I needed to get back with Sophie.
Max: I get it.
Max: So, I know I brought this up already, but you wanna pick the movie for this weekend?

This was going to be my first date ever, and I lost my breath a little bit when he brought it up.

Mia: Sure. I would love to. Any preference?
Max: No, just no super-girly movies, okay?

I laughed out loud.

"What's so funny, Princess?"

"Nothing, Dad," I replied, then I realized that I never said anything to my dad about going out this weekend. I needed to before he made plans for us. "Do you mind if I go to the movies sometime this weekend?"

"Sure. What day? Do you need a ride?" He seemed happy to offer.

"No, I have a ride. Hang on."

Mia: When do you want to go to the movies?
Max: How about Saturday night? I'll pick you up at 6:30?
Mia: Perfect.

My smile was huge. I couldn't hide it. "Saturday evening. That okay, Dad?"

"Sure." Then he looked at me and noticed my smile. "Sophie will be in the hospital. Who are you going with?"

"I have my first date," I said, bouncing up and down in my seat.

My dad let out a big sigh and muttered, "and so it begins," under his breath.

"What's that supposed to mean?"

"It just means that you're growing up. Is this guy picking you up?"

"Yes."

"I don't know how I feel about that. You're only fifteen."

I couldn't believe he was worried for my safety. Who was he kidding? "Dad, Mom just kicked me out of the house during a snowstorm, without a winter coat, boots, or my phone. I hardly think Max is the one you have to worry about hurting me." I looked directly at him, trying to burn a hole through his skull so he would wake up and see what was happening.

He took a deep breath before he spoke. "I know this is hard and not fair for you at all." His eyes left the road briefly to look at me. I was still staring with intent. "Look. I'm going to deal with it. I'm going to get her help."

"Dad, she's had help before. It's just getting worse. And yet you still leave me alone with her."

"Mia, it's difficult." He flipped on the turn signal to the private dirt street heading up the mountain to our house. "Look, I've been thinking about something. I'm going to look for a new job."

My eyes widened. "Really?"

"I think it's for the best. I'll start looking at job boards tonight."

"Thank you." I was sincere. "But, dad, she really does need help. Her personality changes so quickly." I hoped that he was listening to me. "We need to do more. You aren't around enough to see it happen."

"All right, look. I will NOT be raked over the coals by my teenage daughter. I'm doing the best I can to keep a roof over your head. And now, because you pissed off your mother so much that she kicked you out in a snowstorm– I have to– Goddamned ungrateful, is what you are." His face was bright red.

I walked right into that. I should have realized I was pushing too hard. I should have known. All conversations about my mother landed me here. I looked out the window, trying to shield my feelings from him. He would be understanding, to a point, then snap back like a rubber band.

"You don't understand what we go through. It's not like you were wanted anyway."

And there it was.

He was driving fast over the mountain road. Too fast, hitting bumps at full speed. I refused to give him the benefit of seeing me hit my head on the window. I was sitting strong. At last, we were in front of the house. He stopped the car with a jolt. I opened the door as quickly as I could, slammed it behind me, and ran to the house. I'm not sure what I was running toward. I knew that what was through the door was no better. But I also knew that after the mess she caused, my mom would be sweet as sugar to me while my father was home. At least for a few days.

I held my breath and grabbed the doorknob. Maybe she would be asleep. What I needed was to just make it to my bedroom without having to talk and without being smothered with fake kisses while my father stared daggers at me. I could never win. I would never have everyone happy with me all at once.

I stepped through the door quietly while my father got my bag out of the back of his truck. My mother wasn't asleep. She was pacing around the living room and wringing her hands together looking nervous.

"Baaayyyyybbbeeee. There you are!" she said, wiping a fake tear from her eye. "I missed you so much." She ran over to me and grabbed my arms. She held me at arm's length. "Let me look at you," she said, producing actual tears. "Why did you run off like that? You gave me such a fright?"

"Mom, you–"

"Mia, just let your mother be happy? Keep your mouth shut and let her take you in." My father slammed the front door shut. "She was worried."

Normally, I would have started to doubt myself and to question what reality was. But this time was different. This time I knew I hadn't done what I was accused of. I knew my mom had kicked me out for no reason. I knew I hadn't run away. Maybe, in the past, I was rude or talked back, and maybe that made my mother freak out. But this time? No, I was just eating ice cream when she kicked me out into the snow.

I stayed silent. I didn't say one word. I was only fifteen, what could I do? Not much.

She finally let go of me. Her mascara was smudged under her eye. "Baby, let me make your favorite dish." She turned to walk into the kitchen, then turned back toward me. "What was that again? Your favorite dish? I can't remember, it changes so often."

"Shepherd's pie, Mom. Shepherd's pie. It's been shepherd's pie since I can remember."

She laughed nervously. "Oh. You stop. It has not!"

I took a quick glance at my dad. He said nothing, just stared at me.

I went with it. "Well, I just love your Shepherd's pie so much, how could I ask for anything else? You've been doing something new with it, haven't you?"

"Oh yes! I've been using Colby-Jack cheese mixed with cheddar. I'm so glad you noticed. You want to come and skin the potatoes for me?"

And just like that, I was forced into the charade again. I had to play the game to make living bearable. "Yes, I would love to help," I said

My dad let out a deep sigh of relief. "Good, you girls get cooking. I'm going to get Mia's bag upstairs and unpack my own suitcase."

My phone vibrated. It was Sophie.

Sophie: Is everything okay?

Mia: Yes. Everything is the way it always is when my father returns home.

Sophie: And you accept that?

Mia: It's all I can do.

Sophie: Ok. Mom wanted me to remind you to charge the phone.

Mia: I will. Tell her, thank you.

Mia: Are you ready for the hospital tomorrow?

Sophie: Of course. It's not a big deal.

Mia: Okay, I just want to find a ride to visit you. I'm going to try my hardest.

Sophie: I would like that, but

My mother grabbed my phone from my hand. "I said you were sup-posed to peel potatoes, not text with Sophie." Her wicked voice chilled the air. Then she smiled. "Come on. Cooking together will be fun—just what we need to get reacquainted." As if I had been gone for years instead of just two nights.

"Mom, Sophie's going into the hospital tomorrow. Can I at least tell her goodnight?"

"Honestly, I don't know why you are friends with that girl. She's loud, weird, and her situation is"– she waved her hand around –"depressing." I could not believe she said that. I wanted to punch her. "Now get in the kitchen and help me. You'll thank me later." She handed the phone back to me.

"I have to go to the bathroom. I'll be in the kitchen in a minute."

"Hurry, the potatoes won't peel themselves."

I didn't answer her. I just walked to the bathroom.

"No texting!" she called after me.

I closed the door behind me and stood against it for a moment, then pulled out my phone.

Mia: Sorry about that, my mom grabbed my phone.
Sophie: I was saying that it's okay if you can't come. I know things
are tense right now.
Mia: I want to bring you junk food and sit with you, like normal.
Sophie: Yeah, it wouldn't be the same if that didn't happen. Okay. I'll
allow it.
Mia: So, I will work it out.
Sophie: I would love that. Do you still have your stone?

I reached into my pocket and pulled out the rock. I held it in my hand and smiled at it. I didn't understand what was so special about it, but it made me smile just the same.

Mia: I have it. I'm holding it in my hand right now.
Sophie: Good, keep it with you, okay?
Mia: I will.

Like I said, I never questioned these things, I just went along with them.

Sophie: Okay. I'm off to bed, we have to be on the road by six.
Mia: Kay. Love you!
Sophie: Love you too, night.

I put the phone back in my pocket, took a deep breath, turned, and opened the door to help my mother peel the potatoes for my special meal.

- Chapter Ten -

My mother and I sat in silence while my dad outlined his plan for finding a new job. My mom sighed and snapped her tongue repeatedly. She held her wine glass near her face grimacing as if she was smelling something horrendous. Once in a while, she would roll her eyes and say, "I just don't understand why this is necessary."

I kept my eyes on my plate of mashed potatoes and peas as much as possible.

"I just think it's time. I've been traveling for four years."

"Mia and I are just fine."

"I'm not sure about that. Look what happened in the snowstorm," I said.

My mother shot me an evil look. I wondered if she was capable of murder.

My phone started vibrating on the table. I reached for it when my mother slapped it out of my hand with such fury that her ring slashed my knuckle. I pulled my hand away quickly and grabbed a napkin to stop the small amount of blood that was seeping through the scratch. She picked up the phone and slammed it beside her. I looked at her wide-eyed. She'd done things like this a million times before, but never in front of my father.

"Kim! What in the world?" he bellowed.

"She's rude. Did you see the way she reached for the phone like it was her God-given right?"

"It's her phone!"

I sat there saying nothing.

"We pay for it. She doesn't need to be on it during dinner." My mom was obviously taking the news of my father leaving his job out on me.

"And now - NOW - Dennis, you have to change your job, and our entire lives, for this child we didn't even want."

My eyes left the peas and potatoes. I held my breath. The napkin in my hands provided a better focal point. I twisted it and balled it up, then twisted it again. *Didn't. Even. Want.* She had said this many times in the past, and it was the second time I was hearing it today. I hadn't taken a breath when she grabbed the phone and threw it past me, then pushed her chair back. I felt the sting on my cheek before I felt the danger. Before I saw the fury in my mother's eyes as she loomed above me, her hand positioned to strike another blow.

I screamed, "STOP!" while my lungs filled with air.

"Mia, get upstairs," my father yelled.

"YES! Go! Just get out of my face," my mother screamed and turned away. The resulting silence was terrifying.

I bent down, picked up my phone, then pushed my chair back and stood, all while holding my cheek. I turned and walked step by careful step through the living room, up the stairs, and to my room. I didn't run. I was too scared to do that. I wanted to, but I knew better.

My parents remained silent as I walked to my room, and I was glad. I didn't want to hear anymore. I didn't want to be there anymore. I closed the door quietly. I wanted to slam it, but I was afraid. The screaming started almost immediately. My room wasn't really safe, but I could make it more of a sanctuary. I walked over to my computer, turned on my external speaker, and cranked my music as loud as I could. I wanted to disappear. I just stood there for a while, holding my cheek with one hand and my phone in the other. Standing. Processing. My phone vibrated again.

Max: I just wanted to say hi. What are you up to?

I didn't answer him right away. I had no words—true or made up.

Max: I guess you are busy. I can't wait to see you tomorrow.

I took a breath and sat at the edge of my bed.

Mia: No. I'm not busy.
Max: Can we FaceTime?

I stopped breathing and stood up to look at my face in the mirror. The side of my face was a little red, but nothing serious. I pulled my hair over the redness to try to hide it. Luckily, I hadn't cried. I had been too stunned to do that. My eyes were fine. I turned down the music.

Mia: Sure! You can call.

The phone buzzed almost immediately. I took a deep breath, lay down on my bed, and positioned the phone so he could see my face.

"Hi, Max!"

"Hey," he said, then looked at me with squinted eyes. "I'm so glad you texted me back."

"Of course." I tried to smile. I didn't want him to know I was upset.

"I was just thinking. Can I pick you up for school tomorrow?" He looked at me, his dark brown eyes laser-focused as he waited for my answer.

All I could think was, please come pick me up now. But I didn't say that. Instead, I said, "I would like that."

"Cool," he said, nodding. He cocked his head to the side and then said, "Is everything okay? You look different."

"Oh yeah. I'm just tired," I said.

"Are you happy to be home?" he asked.

"I guess. I just"– I stopped myself from saying more, but I wanted to. I needed to tell someone what just happened. I didn't though. –"I'm just worried about Sophie."

"Why?"

"She's going to the hospital tomorrow."

"Oh no." His brows furrowed.

"It's okay. I mean, she goes at least twice a year, so she's used to it. This time just seems different to me."

"Oh, right. She has some sort of lung disease, right?"

"Yeah, Cystic Fibrosis. I don't know. I just worry."

He raised his eyebrows. "Can she have company there?"

"Yeah."

"Are you going to go see her tomorrow?"

"I'm not sure. My parents are being weird right now." That was putting it mildly.

"Oh man, I know what that's like. You know, if you'd like to go, I can take you. Would that be okay?"

"Oh my God. Really?"

"Yeah, I mean. I know you two are like sisters and stuff. You guys probably need to be together."

"I would like that. A lot. Thank you."

"Maybe we could get pizza, or something, after?"

I was pretty sure I was blushing. I never wanted this FaceTime to end. "I would love to get pizza."

This was perfect. This meant I didn't have to have dinner with my parents. And maybe I could get away without seeing my mom altogether. Maybe this would put enough space between the two of us so she could calm down.

I would really like that," I said with a smile.

The skin beside his eyes crinkled a bit and his dimples appeared when he smiled back. "Okay. I'll pick you up at seven tomorrow morning, then again at five? Maybe?"

"Perfect."

"Oh. Since I'm taking you to school," he said, then stopped and bit his lip like he was nervous to ask, "can I bring you home too?"

We still didn't know much about each other, but he wanted to make plans. I could tell by his voice that he was nervous, and I thought that was cute.

"I would like that very much," I said, nodding, maybe a little too much.

"Okay. It's a date—or. Um. Is that okay to say? I mean, a ride to school and a hospital trip isn't really a date, but …"

"It's a date. An odd date. But a date."

Now he was blushing. Blushing and laughing. "I mean, it's what we have, so I'll take it."

"Agreed." I nodded. Seeing him laugh helped to lighten my mood. I allowed myself to laugh along with him. The tension started to melt away. That's when I remembered the rock Sophie gave me. It was still in my pocket. Knowing it was there made everything a little bit better. It was calming for me; I could breathe without the restriction of stress.

"You look beautiful," he said, quickly. "I'm sorry. It's just. When you answered you looked stressed. But now - now? No, just beautiful."

Instead of talking, my mouth hung open. My eyes were wide. No one had ever told me I was beautiful before. No one. And I didn't know how to process it. I didn't feel beautiful. I felt clunky and clumsy. I looked away from the screen. I didn't know what else to do. I didn't know how to react.

"Hey, I have to get going. I'll see you tomorrow morning, okay?" he asked.

"Uh. Um. Yes."

He ended the call, but I still sat there holding the phone. A new emotion took over. It felt like everything was in extremes. My mother had thrown my phone and slapped me, and Max told me he thought I was beautiful. Sophie was in the hospital, and I was trying to figure out who I was. All of a sudden I was both a terrible daughter and someone who felt beautiful for the first time in her life. How could this be? I started crying. Was it tears of sadness or happiness? I don't know. Both maybe. All my emotions were coursing through my veins, and I couldn't figure out how to manage them.

I stood up to reach into my pocket and grab Sophie's rock. I pulled it out and held it in my hand. It was small and smooth. It had probably tumbled through the river for eons. It looked like any rock that you would just toss into the water. But the moment I held it in my hands I became calm. It made no sense.

I closed my fingers around it and grasped onto it as tightly as I could. Then I closed my eyes and inhaled slowly and deeply. Over the music, I could still hear my parents screaming at each other, but I couldn't understand what they were saying, and somehow it didn't matter. I was somewhere else, somewhere deep in my soul, and I felt at peace.

I raised my arms and started spinning the same way Sophie always did. It wasn't a decision I made, my body seemed to just do it itself. I imagined the problems with my mom just flying out of my fingertips, flowing far, far away from me. As I slowed, dizziness set in. When I flopped down on my bed, the room spun around me, flowing as if I had never stopped spinning. I closed my eyes until I regained stability.

I heard someone stomp up the steps. My breathing stopped. I wasn't ready to see her. I needed a moment to get myself back together. Thankfully, no one came to my door. I knew it was my mother, but she went into her room. I held my breath, then heard the sound of things being thrown at the wall that separated our rooms. The sounds became louder and louder. Each time something hit, I would jump, then cringe. I stood and stared at the wall, glad that it existed and that she wasn't actually throwing things directly at me. After a while, the throwing stopped and a door slammed. I heard my mom stomp down the steps.

I was startled sometime later by a small knock at my door. Even though it was small, I jumped and my breathing stopped again. The door opened ever so slightly. I tried to make my body as small as possible. My father stuck his head through the crack. My breathing became short and shallow.

"Can I come in?"

I didn't answer. I didn't move.

He came in anyway and closed the door behind him. "I wanted to let you know, I told your mother to go stay with your grandma for a bit." I couldn't believe what I was hearing; I thought he didn't believe me. "I know this is a shock, but it's for the best. She will be leaving tonight." He sat down next to me on my bed, turned to me, and placed a hand on my shoulder. I sobbed. I couldn't hold it in anymore. "I'm sorry that I didn't believe you all this time." He pursed his lips together. "But seeing it tonight. Mia, I believe you."

I said nothing but he hugged me anyway. Finally, I wrapped my arms around my father and cried uncontrollably into his shoulder.

- Chapter Eleven -

After my father left the room, I locked the door behind him. My mom tried to get into my room twice over the next hour, screaming at me from the other side, calling me horrible names, telling me I would pay for what I did to her. At one point, when they started screaming at each other outside, I peeked through the window. My mother got into her car, slammed the door, and revved her engine. She pulled away so quickly that she skidded on the ice that was still in patches on our dirt road. Her car regained traction and sped off. I watched the light move farther and farther away until it disappeared.

I couldn't sleep that night. I just kept tossing and turning. Every time the heat turned on, I would jump, the sound making me think my mom was back. I knew she wasn't there, but my body had a mind of its own, continually jumping at every little sound.

Finally, the darkness lifted. I sat up and placed my feet on the cold wooden floor, pausing a moment before I stood. A beam of sunlight was coming through my window. Everything just felt weird. Off. But the sunlight was the same as it was every morning, and as always it gave me comfort and let me know that I would, eventually, be okay. I had a headache from crying the night before. I tried to stretch to loosen my tight muscles, then walked to the door. I opened it for the first time since the fight and crept to the stairs, hoping not to wake my father. Dishes clanked in the kitchen. I froze. Someone was there. What if she had come back? I thought about hiding, but what good would that do? Instead, I tiptoed down the stairs and walked as quietly as I could to the kitchen. Sunlight filtered through the window, and there was my dad, wearing an apron, flipping pancakes.

"Mia! I'm making you breakfast. Come sit at the bar while I finish up."

I laughed a little bit to release the tension I was holding throughout my body, then walked to the kitchen bar, pulled out the tall stool, and hopped up.

"I have a lot of meetings today, so I'm not sure I'll be here when you get home from school. Will you be okay?" he asked, putting three pancakes on a plate for me.

"Yeah. I'll be fine." I sat staring at him. I hadn't had one of my dad's breakfasts in a very long time. "I'm going to visit Sophie in the hospital."

He stopped wiping the counter, "I forgot about that. I can move my stuff around and take you. Would you like that?"

"No, it's fine. Max is going to take me."

He stared at me, not saying a word.

"Is that okay?" I asked.

"Um. Yeah. Yeah, it's fine. I just. I'm not ready for you to grow up like this." He started moving again, handing me my plate. "Um. I'm not sure of the right questions to ask here. So bear with me." I took the plate from his hand. He grabbed another plate for himself. "How old is he?"

"Seventeen."

"Seventeen. Okay. You're fifteen."

"Yes, Dad. I know. I'm fine. He only just turned seventeen. Besides, he's a nice guy."

"Right, they all are," he whispered under his breath.

"Is this what life is going to be like now?"

"What? Me worrying and questioning you?"

"Yes. Mom never did this," I replied.

"You never had a boy pick you up before."

"True." I nodded. My mother would have been sure to make a spectacle in some way. Either in outrageous love or anger.

"Yes, this is what it's going to be like now," he answered.

I smiled and laughed. "I'm looking forward to it."

"Me too. I should be able to find another job quickly. I already have a few promising leads."

"That's great, Dad!" We talked like that while we ate, never once mentioning what had happened the night before. My mother's anger hung in the air, but we didn't speak about it.

- Chapter Twelve -

I rushed to the window at the sound of a car driving up our road. Max or my mother? I held my breath. It was Max! He really was picking me up for school. It felt like a dream. I ran down the steps, grabbed my backpack, and practically leaped out the front door. Max was pulling up to the house as I bounded down the porch steps.

He jumped out of his car and held his hands out in front of him. "Hang on! Hang on!" I stopped in confusion. He ran around to the passenger's side of his car and opened the door for me. For some reason, I didn't know what to do next. So I just stood there.

"You coming with me? Or have you changed your mind?"

That knocked me out of my spell. "Oh, oh, yeah. I'm sorry," I said, smiling. I unstuck myself and walked toward the car. When I got to the open door I said, "Thank you," and climbed in.

He ran back around, swung his door open, and jumped in the driver's side.

I couldn't help but laugh.

He looked at me suspiciously, "What's so funny?"

"Nothing, this was just unexpected, is all." I held my hand up to my mouth to stop myself from laughing any further.

"Are you saying that I am—"

"Oh, no. I would never— okay, maybe a little?"

"Well, get used to it. I plan to make you laugh at me as much as possible."

"I like that!" I wasn't lying. He was making a fuss, something I wasn't used to from anyone other than Sophie.

He turned the ignition on. Music blasted from the speakers. I jumped and grabbed my ears. "Oh crap, I'm sorry." My headache spiked. He reached over quickly to turn the music down. I always got headaches when I cried. I had forgotten it was there for a moment. "Are you okay?" he asked. "Your eyes are red."

"Oh, yeah. I'm good," I lied.

"I'm sorry. What I meant to say was that you look beautiful."

I let a tiny smile peek out from behind my pounding head. "Thank you."

We drove down my bumpy road. Most people were not used to driving it and he was one of those people. He grunted a bit.

"There's a big hole just up ahead on the right, you'll want to swerve left."

"Thanks. I just didn't realize."

"No, I'm sorry. No one does. I should have been guiding you." I held my breath a bit, feeling a lump grow in my throat. I grasped the side of my seat waiting to be yelled at. My body tensed and I held my jaw so tight, it hurt. Like he was going to yell at me at any moment. I felt a lump grow in my throat, getting ready for it. I looked out the window, willing myself to not look at him. My body was tense, jaw clenched.

"It's okay. I have eyes, I could have spotted them." He reached out to grab my hand, then ran his thumb over my pointer finger. "I was just concentrating on you." He gave a little laugh. "So, wanna eat lunch with me?" I glanced at him quickly and caught his eyes, then looked away. "Or no. I could just sit at your table with your friends."

When he glanced at me the second time, his eyes were narrowed and he looked a bit sad. I realized he was reacting to the way I was holding myself. The tension was obvious. I took a deep breath to clear the worry away. After all, he hadn't yelled at me.

"Or, I could just eat at my table. It's fine. I don't want to take you from your friends," he said, obviously reacting to my breath.

He really did want to spend time with me. "No, no. That's not–" I stopped myself and refocused, "Yes, yes, I would love to have lunch with you."

"I'll look for you then."

I couldn't believe this was happening. I had had a crush on him since I was in middle school and he was in ninth grade. I had gone to as many soccer games as I could, just to watch him play. I never even understood soccer that well.

"I would like that."

"I'm not like Luke."

"What?"

"Nothing. It's just well, someone told me about what Reagan did at lunch yesterday. And I wanted you to know, I'm not Luke."

He was referring to the senior who cheated on and took advantage of every girl he came into contact with. Even so, all the freshman girls loved him just the same.

"I didn't think you were," I said in a small voice. I looked at him. Even though his eyes were on the road, he smiled at that exact moment. "You have been respectful. Completely respectful."

"I just wanted you to know that." He fumbled with the steering wheel with his thumb. "I really like you. I don't want to hurt you." He bit his lower lip. "I know I'm friends with him, but that doesn't mean I like what Luke does."

"I understand."

"And. I really like you," he said. We were stopped at a red light about to turn onto the road that led to the school.

I smiled and looked out the window. I didn't know what else to do. I didn't know how to react.

"I hope you like me too?" he said.

I pulled my lips inside my mouth and bit them a little. The palms of my hands were suddenly sweaty. I dried them on my pant leg while trying to figure out what to say. I went blank. I just couldn't get anything out. What did people say in these situations? What if I said the wrong thing? I wanted to scream. YES! OF COURSE I LIKE YOU. AND, I CAN'T BELIEVE YOU EVEN LIKE ME AT ALL! But I didn't. I stayed quiet. Too scared to speak.

He started fidgeting.

I needed to say something, but, I didn't.

"I mean. Do you?" he spoke up again.

I nodded. He didn't see me nod though. I was so terrified; my nod wasn't large enough for anyone to notice.

We turned into the school parking lot. The silence was killing me. My silence. Still, I said nothing. I was just THAT awkward. I knew I needed to say something, anything, but I had no words. I was trying to will myself to speak when he pulled into a parking spot.

He turned to me. "Mia. I need to know. Am I wasting my time here?"

Because he was looking at me, he could see me shake my head 'no,' ever so slightly.

"Are you nervous?"

I nodded yes.

He smiled. "Are you into me?"

I nodded slowly. Biting my lip. Scared that I would do something wrong.

"You are? Please say something. Anything?"

I let out a small whisper, "Yes."

- Chapter Thirteen -

I absentmindedly threw my backpack under the seat between Emma and Olivia and walked up to the food line in the cafeteria.

"I saw you got a ride with Max this morning."

I turned around to see Everly standing behind me.

"Yeah, he picked me up."

"So it's official now?" she asked, looking me up and down.

"I don't know." My stomach dropped. I didn't know what was going on, but the way she was looking at me definitely made me feel uncomfortable.

Max walked into the cafeteria and scanned the room. When his eyes hit me he smiled and started toward me, then stopped mid-step when he noticed Everly. His smile disappeared. I looked at Everly wondering if some sort of message was being passed between them. There wasn't; she didn't even look up at him.

"You know he was with someone else for a while, right?" Everly said.

"No, I've only just started talking to him." I watched as Max approached. "Who was he with?"

"Me."

"Ladies! Hello." Max approached slowly.

"Hey, Max," Everly said. "So tell me, is this who you left me for?"

"Everly," he said with a sigh. He didn't say any more than that.

"Right, whatever." She rolled her eyes and turned her back to Max.

He leaned in close to me. "So, Mia. How's your day?" I could see out of the corner of my eye that Everly was angry and getting angrier. He wrapped his arm around my back and pulled me close. It reminded me of sledding, but it didn't feel the same. He put his arm around me, but all I could think about was how angry Everly was.

"Sure, cut in line. Why not?" Everly snapped.

I started to sweat.

"Ignore her," he whispered into my ear.

I couldn't though. I couldn't ignore her.

After Max and I finished eating, he reached out his hand to lightly touch mine. Everly stared. No one else seemed to notice.

"Hey, I have to run and talk to Coach before lunch is over." Max smiled at me. "I'll catch up with you later. And if I don't, I'll meet you at your locker at the end of the day."

I couldn't say anything. His hand was touching mine. One touch and I was speechless. His hands weren't sweating at all. Mine, on the other hand, were embarrassingly damp. I just nodded and tried to imagine how I could secretly wipe my hand off without removing it from his.

His smile grew even wider and he squeezed my hand, then let go and got up. The warmth of his hand lingered on mine even after he had walked away. I just kept staring at my hand. Then I was broken from my trance.

"You're just a plaything to him. He'll come back to me. Don't worry."

Instantly my hand went cold. I didn't say anything.

"You know, Everly. Maybe you should stop acting so jealous," Lily blurted out.

"Whatever, freshman. You are all so naive." Everly slammed her hands on the table and stood up.

"You're the one sitting with us 9th graders," Emma said. I was shocked. Emma never says anything to upset anyone. Well, almost never. I could tell she was fuming.

Everly looked at Emma and then back at me before she huffed and turned, stomping away like a toddler.

"Well, I'm glad that's over. What the hell?" Lily asked.

"She's still in love with Max, apparently," I replied.

"Good riddance," Emma said.

- Chapter Fourteen -

I stood at my locker fighting to pull my winter coat off of its hook when I felt a tap on my shoulder. Taken by surprise, I jumped.

"Whoa, I'm sorry. I didn't mean to–"

I turned quickly. He wasn't expecting my reaction. Most of my friends know not to sneak up on me, but he had no idea. I didn't want him to. I didn't want to explain how or why it was my instinct.

"–you okay?" Max asked.

I forced myself to laugh and put my hand over my heart to calm the anxious beating. "Yeah, yeah, I'm fine. You just startled me."

"Sorry. Are you ready?"

"Absolutely," I replied.

He already had his jacket on and his backpack slung over his shoulder. Lockers slammed around us as the mad rush to exit the building began. Max stepped closer to avoid being trampled. My face was so close to his chest that I could smell fabric softener. I looked up at him just as he turned his head to watch the crowd passing us by. He put his arm around my back and moved in closer. I couldn't help but smile. He made me feel safe, a welcome change from being startled just a moment before.

I needed to turn to pull my coat out of my locker, but I didn't want to move. I never wanted that moment to end. The hallway was loud. Some were yelling and chatting. Some were running through the halls so they didn't miss the bus. Others were milling around without a care in the world. But Max and I? We were frozen in time, standing there against each other, my head against his chest.

The crowd of students thinned out, but he still stood there, holding me. And I stood there, smelling him.

He took a step back. "Let's get going. I bet you missed Sophie today."

I smiled. "I did miss her."

"Then let's reunite you two." He took a larger step back. I turned and began pulling on my coat again. "What are you doing?" he asked.

"My coat is stuck."

"Apparently. Scoot back. Let me try." I stepped back. He came forward and tugged lightly on my coat which was clearly stuck. He had to stick his head halfway into my locker to release the coat. Finally, he pulled it out and held it for me. I turned and slid my right arm, then my left arm into it. He pulled it up, then reached around to zip it for me. "Don't want you to get cold," he said, his voice cracking.

I could feel the heat rise from my neck to my face. I was sure I was bright red, so I grabbed a quick glance in the mirror on my locker door. Yes, I was absolutely bright red. I turned back toward the inside of my locker to grab my books and hide my blushing. I shoved my geometry book into my backpack and turned around. Everly was standing across the hallway from us with her back against her closed locker, her arms crossed across her chest. Max took my backpack and zipped it, ignoring her. He slung the bag over his other shoulder, grabbed my hand, squeezed it, then looked at Everly and said, "Hey, Everly."

We started down the hall, walking hand-in-hand. I could feel her eyes staring a hole in the back of my head. It made me nervous. Everly had a reputation, and I didn't want to make an enemy of her.

But I wanted to know. "So what's that all about?" I asked.

"Honestly, nothing. We dated this summer. Stuff happened and now she thinks she owns me."

I turned my head around to see if she was still standing there staring. She was. "It seems like she's a bit obsessed."

"Yeah. but don't worry about her." He looked at me and winked. "I'm here with you."

"I won't," I said, but inside I was being torn apart. I hated pissing people off. It scared me. I was always afraid they would act out against me. We turned the corner, and I started feeling better just knowing she was no longer watching me from behind. I shifted my focus to concentrate on his hand in mine. How comfortable it felt.

"So, you want to eat before or after we see Sophie?"

"Let's eat after. I have her homework. I want to make sure she has it quickly."

We walked a little more.

"They make her do homework when she's in the hospital?"

"Yeah, well, it gives her something to do."

"Seems evil."

"Probably, but she's used to it."

We walked out of the building and toward his truck. Once again, he opened the door for me, but before I got in, he grabbed me in a tight hug.

"I know it's hard when she isn't here for you," he said. Then he kissed me on the top of my head, and let his arms go to my side. "Let's get going."

I had the chills.

- Chapter Fifteen -

The warm air hit our faces as the hospital doors opened wide. Max flinched and wrinkled his nose. The smell of bleach didn't bother me; I was used to it by now. Sophie was always on the same floor, so I bypassed the information desk. I knew exactly where to go.

I led him down a hallway with shiny white floors and fake marble walls. A faded painting of Mary holding a baby Jesus hung on the wall at the end of the hall. I took Max's hand as we made our way to the elevators. I stopped at the panel of buttons and pressed four. We waited. His hand was sweaty, but I didn't let go.

"She's here a lot, isn't she?"

"I guess, maybe like twice a year."

"I've not been in a hospital since…" He stopped talking, then took a deep breath. He shifted his weight back and forth from one foot to the other.

The door finally opened and we walked in. As the door slid shut, the scent of antiseptic took over the bleach smell that had overwhelmed the lobby. The stagnant air was almost suffocating. Max's eyes darted around the elevator, his palm still sweating into my hand. The elevator buzzed and stopped. When the door opened someone pushing a cart of food squeezed beside us. All of the platters were covered, but the smell coming from the cart was putrid. The elevator jolted as it resumed its upward climb. Max squeezed my hand, then cleared his throat and gave me a weak smile. I probably should have prepared him, in some way. The hospital didn't really bother me much, anymore.

We reached the fourth floor and the door slid open. I could see the ride had been much longer for Max than for me. He nearly leaped out of the elevator with me in tow, still holding my hand tightly.

"You okay?" I asked.

"Yeah, sure. Of course." He gave me another small grin. He looked a bit green.

"Do you want to wait in the car?"

"No, no. I'm fine."

"Okay." I looked at him with my eyebrows raised. "I need to go to the nurses' station to find out what room she's in this time." I began walking away, but he didn't let my hand go. He just stood there, keeping me next to him, holding my hand tight. I squeezed his hand and gave him a small, caring smile. "I have to go over there," I said pointing to the nurses station. "I'll be right back. Okay?"

He nodded and loosened his grip.

I approached the station, smiling to myself. The reaction he had? It was endearing. Sweet. Vulnerable. I liked him even more.

A nurse remembered me. "Hi, Mia. She's in room 405 this time."

"Oh great! She has a view of the river!"

The nurse winked at me. "Of course she does. You know how I take care of our girl."

"Thank you!" I turned to walk back to Max. He grabbed my hand immediately.   I led him to Sophie's room. She was sitting up, scrolling through her phone. As usual, she had a nasal cannula tube in her nostrils and a few leads coming out from her PJ top, leading to a heart rate monitor. She hadn't noticed us yet, but she was frowning a bit. Not much, but enough to make me concerned.

I squeezed his hand once more, gave him another caring look, then held up my finger telling him to hang on a second. I wanted to make sure everything was truly okay before I brought him in. Soph and I would usually lie in her hospital bed together and watch TV.

He whispered, "I'll stay here. I understand."

"Thank you," I whispered back.

I took a deep breath and skipped into her room. Then I held my hands up in the air and said in a sing-song voice, "I'm here for you now." I made sure I had the biggest smile I could. When I visited Sophie in the hospital, I always tried to radiate happiness. It helped get rid of the yucky energy of the hospital, as Sophie would always say.

She laughed. "I was wondering when you would get here."

I plunked myself down on the bed right next to her. "What's the news? Is this a normal trip?"

"No, I don't think so. They are all so serious this time. I'm not sure what's up yet." She set her phone on her hospital tray. "My parents are coming tonight, and the doctor is going to swing by."

"I'm sure it's fine. They always make something of nothing."

"True." She nodded, then looked at me.

I swung my arm up and over her shoulder and pulled her tight.

"So, what's going on with your parents?" she asked.

I looked out the door to see if Max was listening in. He was playing a game on his phone, not listening to a word. I felt safe to tell her without him hearing. It was all heavy. I didn't want him to know that much about me, at least not yet.

"What 'cha looking at?" she said, not noticing Max.

I pointed my finger to where he was standing.

"Oh my God! He brought you to see me?"

I bit my lip and nodded.

"GET OUT!"

"I know."

"How'd that happen?" She looked at me wide-eyed.

"He asked if he could bring me, and I said yes." I chuckled. "Okay, enough about him. I want to tell you what happened with my mom before he checks on us." I gestured to him with my thumb.

"It sounds serious."

"It is. When you were texting me last night, she hit–"

"WHAT?"

"Shhh," I said, holding my finger in front of her mouth. "And she did it in front of my dad too." I looked Sophie straight in the eye. I knew she always worried about my dad not believing me. "He finally saw it. There was no denying last night."

"Did she hit you hard? Are you okay?"

"No harder than normal."

"What did your dad do?" she asked, clearly concerned about me but smiling because she knew it was good he had seen the hit.

"He sent me to my room and kicked her out of the house."

"WHAT?" she yelled again.

"Shhhh, you have to stop doing that."

"Are you OKAY?"

"You're still yelling!"

She lowered her voice to a whisper. "I mean, how do I not yell at a time like this? Are you okay?"

"I am? I haven't had time to think about it, I guess?" I looked up to the ceiling trying to figure out how I was feeling. "I mean, I'm trying not to think about it and what it means. She's my mom."

"Why didn't you use the phone my mom gave you?"

"Honestly, I didn't think about it." I said, looking at the floor.

"Okay." Sophie looked away, took a deep breath, then looked at me again and said, "She's horrible."

"Yeah. But still," I answered, "she's mine." Confused at myself, I started feeling things I wasn't expecting. Dread. Sadness. Guilt.

Max cleared his throat.

"We'll talk about it later," I whispered.

She nodded back at me then yelled out the door, "Max, come on in!"

He walked in slowly, wide-eyed at the wires Sophie had attached to her.

"Um… hey. Is it okay that I'm here?"

"Absolutely," Sophie said, waving her arm for him to come in. She spoke loudly, with a happy voice. She always turned on the charm when someone was apprehensive about visiting her in the hospital. "Get in here!"

"Oh… okay," he said sheepishly.

I got up, walked up to him, and grabbed his hand.

"Sit down on my bed," Sophie said. "We can share some of my snacks and talk about the day."

He sat, back straight, limbs rigid.

I decided the best thing to do was to just start talking to Sophie as a way to ease the pressure off of him. Not everyone is good at being in hospitals, even just to visit.

"Oh, Soph. I brought your homework," I said.

"Yuck. Fine. I was hoping you'd forgotten."

"If I forgot, your mom would kill me." I laughed. I opened my backpack and got out a folder of papers. "Mrs. Lingle said she loaded some stuff up on the network for you to access with your computer. Did you bring your computer?"

"Of course."

"Okay, then you are set," I said. "When are your parents coming?"

"In about an hour."

"Do you want me to go get you some food?"

"No, it's fine."

"Do you have the hot doctor? Dr. Stewart?"

"Oh yeah." She nodded, eyes wide.

Max laughed. "Crushing on the doctor?"

Sophie laughed, then said, "I mean, yeah. You haven't seen him. But no. I have my boyfriend."

"Oh, is he coming to visit?"

"I wish," she said, waving her hand in front of her face. "He's in boarding school in Maryland."

"Wow. How does that work?"

"He lives near here normally. He comes home for the summer and holidays. It's not a big deal."

"Does he know you're here?" I asked.

"No."

"You didn't tell him?" I probably shouldn't have pushed, but I did. I didn't like the way he had handled her being in the hospital the last time.

"No." She looked at me, then to Max. "Sorry, you're about to hear girl stuff." She turned back to me. "No. You know I'm afraid he'll break up with me."

"Sophie, he knows you are sick. If it bothered him, he wouldn't be with you anyway," I answered.

Sophie started spinning her ring on her finger. It was a small opal ring he had given to her for her birthday. She loved that ring. But soon after he gave it to her, he broke up with her for the first time.

"So, Max."—Sophie was obviously trying to change the subject. "What are you planning on doing with my friend tonight?" she said.

Max relaxed his back and took a breath. "Spending time with you, then taking her for pizza."

"Oh, sounds good. Thank you for bringing her to me. Can you do it every night?"

"I– I– w– ww– would love to–" he stuttered.

"It's okay. I'm joking," she said, punching him lightly in the arm. "No, but seriously, what are your intentions for her?"

He straightened his back again. "Um. I just want to get to know her."

"Are you going to kiss her tonight?"

"Oh my God, Sophie!" I leaped off the bed.

"Well, it might be a possibility," he answered.

"WOW! Really?" Sophie just about shouted.

I could feel my face turn hot. I knew I was blushing. I tried to look away and bite my tongue. I'd never been kissed, but I wanted to be.

"I mean. We'll see. But I do like her a lot," he said, then gave me a small glance.

I didn't say it, but I wasn't sure that I wanted my first kiss to be after visiting my best friend in the hospital. On the other hand, I couldn't help wondering what it would be like. My lips puckered ever so slightly at the thought.

A nurse wheeled a portable computer desk into Sophie's room, snapping me out of my reverie. The nurse asked if she could get some vitals.

"Sure!" Sophie said.

Max asked, "Should I go?"

I hadn't thought about the fact that watching medical stuff being done might be awkward for him. I was used to sticking around.

"Well, it's up to Sophie," the nurse said, "but I'm fine with you staying. Nothing gross is going to happen."

"Oh stop being weird, Max," Sophie blurted out. She was always bold like that and growing more so by the day. "I mean, she's just going to get my temperature."

"True. Temp, blood pressure, then I'll just mark it down and leave." The nurse stepped to Sophie's bedside, pulling the computer with her.

"Okay," Max replied and lowered his head.

I grabbed his hand and squeezed again. Then stuck my tongue out at him as a way to make him laugh and cut his tension. I realized that I did not want to keep him there for much longer. He was NOT comfortable.

The nurse took the thermometer and scanned Sophie's forehead with it. It beeped and she typed the temperature into the computer. Then she wrapped a cuff around Sophie's arm. Max flinched every so slightly as a mechanical whoosh sound came from the cuff as it put pressure onto Sophie's arm. He flinched the same small flinch again when the cuff began deflating. The nurse marked those numbers on the computer as well.

Everyone was quiet. The air was thick. This was not normal. Max's discomfort was making everyone else uncomfortable.

"Okay, all done here." She smiled. "We'll text Dr. Stewart when your parents get here. Dinner will be here in a few."

Sophie nodded. "Sounds good."

I caught Sophie's eyes. They were looking intently at me, boring into my soul. I could hear her voice in my head. *Go! He's making me sad,* the voice said. I looked back at her. She smiled and touched my hand softly. I knew. He was too freaked out. I needed to get him out, and quickly.

"Hey, Max?"

"Hmm?" He said, turning his eyes toward me.

"We should get going. Soph's food is coming, then her parents and her doctor." I smiled at him. "It's too much Let's let her rest."

"Okay, sure." He stood up.

"Have your dad bring you tomorrow?" Sophie asked.

"Of course!"

"Thanks for bringing her, Max." She nodded. "I'm sorry it's a busy evening." She was lying, of course. She was used to having a lot of people. The problem was Max. Max just wasn't prepared to be there. That was my fault, completely. I felt terrible.

"It's okay," he said, standing in front of me, shifting back and forth on his feet. He held out his hand to help me get up. When I grabbed it I noticed it was still wet with sweat.

I turned toward Sophie, who was still propped up on her bed, and hugged her. I whispered in her ear, "I'm sorry."

I heard in my mind, *It's okay.* I didn't know if I was imagining it, but it seemed real, maybe too real. I stood and backed away, furrowing my brows. I pointed to her and mouthed, "Did you?" She gave me a quick wink. I was confused. I stood looking at her for a bit, my legs shaking. She gave me a sideways smile. I know she did. It wasn't in my imagination.

"You guys should get going. You're both probably hungry," she said, waving her hand to shoosh us out the door.

- Chapter Sixteen -

Max and I walked out of the hospital hand-in-hand. As soon as we got outside, he started to breathe easier, and his palms stopped sweating so much. I was still shaky. How did she talk to me like that, in my mind? I couldn't figure it out. Had Sophie really spoken to me in my mind? Is that even possible? Maybe she whispered it and I just thought she was speaking in my brain? *So weird.*

"Where do you want to eat?" Max woke me from my thoughts so abruptly that I jumped a little. He looked at me. "You okay?"

"Oh yeah. Sorry. Just thinking about Sophie." I nodded. "Actually, are you okay? You didn't seem okay in there."

He took a deep breath. "Yeah. I guess I just wasn't expecting the smell, then to see her there with wires sticking out of her. It just brought back some memories." He shrugged.

"I'm sorry. I guess I'm just used to it," I said, feeling sheepish.

He wrapped his arm around my back and pulled me close. "Remember, I offered to bring you, and I was happy to be a part of this." We slowed our pace toward the parking garage when he leaned down and kissed me on the top of my head. The pressure of his lips gave me chills. He took his arm away from my back and held my hand the rest of the way to his car.

We drove to the pizza shop in silence. He seemed as lost in his thoughts as I was in mine. A few times we looked at each other and smiled. He fiddled with the radio. I stared out the window. My thoughts shifted between the fact I had heard Sophie in my mind, to feeling bad over Max being uncomfortable, to him kissing my head. I felt stupid for bringing him, but if I hadn't brought him, he wouldn't have shown his vulnerable side. I loved that vulnerable side. My hair still tingled.

We pulled into The Pizza Grill, which was more upscale than your average pizza joint. "I didn't realize we were getting gourmet pizza," I said.

"I mean, what did you think I meant?" He looked at me. "I wasn't going to take you to just any pizza joint. This is a date."

I didn't know what to say. All I could manage was a small laugh.

"Is this okay?" He ran his fingers through his hair, his eyes anxious but soft.

"Yes. I've just, well, I've never been on an actual date." I bit my lip a little. "I mean, okay. No. I've never been on any date and this feels like a big moment and I'm being stupid." I swiped my phone like I was checking the time, then swiped it again to check the weather. *Like I cared about the weather!* I couldn't think with my heart racing.

"Hey," he said, "look at me."

I looked at him.

He leaned toward me. I closed my eyes and felt him move closer to me. *What do I do? What do I do? Oh God, what do I do?* His lips gently touched mine. I kept my eyes closed. When he backed up I could still feel his energy tingling around me. His face was inches away from mine when he whispered, "Was that your first kiss?"

I nodded, then opened my eyes.

"I should have asked first. Can I kiss you again?"

I nodded again.

He leaned in once more. His lips felt soft on mine as if he was just skimming my lips, not applying too much pressure. I was sure he was holding back, so I leaned in closer to him. He opened his lips ever so slightly. I followed what he did, mimicking his kiss, then our mouths closed. We stayed there for a little longer, with our lips barely touching. Then he backed away and took my hand in his. He pulled my hand up to his lips and kissed my fingers softly.

"I know you're nervous. So, I thought I would just get that out of the way early. Is that okay?"

I nodded. I didn't know what to say. I was trying to process what was happening, but at the same time, I wanted to jump out of his truck, get on top of it, and yell to the world that I, Mia Stanoslovski, just had my first kiss! I wanted everyone to know, but, I managed to contain myself.

I tried to stop myself from asking, but I couldn't. Instead, I just blurted it out. "Are… are we… are we a thing now? Like. Are you my boyfriend?"

He laughed. "I really like you, Mia. I would be thrilled to be your boyfriend."

I simply nodded, yet again.

"Yes?"

"Yes."

"Would it be okay if I kissed you again?"

Again, I nodded.

He leaned into me. I closed my eyes. I could feel his lips lightly touch mine again. *He was kissing me!* I kissed him back. Not just a light kiss, but a real one. I started to open my mouth to his like I thought I was supposed to. I felt his tongue lightly graze my bottom lip and then, nothing. He closed his mouth and slowly pulled away, picking up the part of my hair that was hanging out of my coat as he did so. He lifted my hair to his nose and inhaled.

"I'm sorry. I have to pump the breaks here. You just had your first kiss; let's wait just a little bit before we do anything else."

My stomach fell. "Did I do something wrong?"

"No, no, not at all. I just like everything about you. And I don't want to freak you out."

"No! Freak me out, please?" I could not believe I said that.

He laughed. "There will be more time for that. I just want to hold onto you as long as I can."

"Really, I'm fine." I wanted another kiss.

"No, I've made this mistake in the past, and I'm not going to do it with you." He raised his hand to my face and stroked my cheek.

"What? What does that mean?"

"Don't worry about it." He looked at me softly. "Let's just go in and get something to eat."

- Chapter Seventeen -

As we drove up the bumpy dirt road to my house, I directed him away from all the large holes in the road. Unpaved mountain roads are no joke. The darkness had settled by the time we got home. We had no streetlights or anything like that, so I'm sure my father noticed our approach. Max pulled up beside our garage and turned off the lights. The darkness was heavy with anticipation. The wind whipped around Max's truck. My grandmother used to tell me that wind brings change. If she was right, this time change was on its way, and fast. We could feel the truck shake with its howling. The porch light snapped on, but my dad didn't come out.

Max reached out and grabbed my hand, then turned his head toward me. "I'm sorry I was weird at the hospital. It wasn't a good look. Was it?" His voice was so soft that I could barely hear him.

"You were fine. I forget sometimes that regular people don't spend that much time in the hospital. I'm used to it in ways most aren't," I said with what I hoped was a reassuring smile. "I'm sorry. I should have talked to you about it first." I sighed and looked out the front window. "It was incredibly kind of you to bring me to see her. That's what counts. That means the world to me."

"I know you two have a special bond, so I thought it was important."

"We do. We're sisters."

"I can see that. I've been watching. You two really are like sisters," he said.

"You've been watching me?"

He stroked my fingers with his thumb. "Yeah," he said in the lightest voice possible. "I'm sorry if that sounds creepy."

A wave of heat formed in my cheeks then moved down my neck, down my arms, giving me goosebumps. I wanted nothing more in that moment than a kiss. A real kiss. A heavy kiss. I wanted to be in his arms. But we just sat there with our heads leaning back into the head rests, heads turned, staring at each other.

Suddenly, there was a knock at the driver's side window. We both jumped. My dad was standing there in his housecoat. I threw Max's hand away and grabbed the door handle. It wouldn't open. I nearly screamed. I pulled again. The door opened and I jumped out, trying to act casual. It's not like we were doing anything wrong at all, but I had thought the thoughts, enough of them to make me feel guilty.

"Dad! Hi!"

"Hey, pumpkin. I just wanted to come out and meet this Max guy." He pointed to Max who was getting out of his truck.

As soon as they were face to face, Max extended his hand.

My father looked at Max sternly, then, apparently satisfied, took Max's hand in a firm grip and shook.

"Oh, um, Dad. This is Max. Max, this is my father, Dennis."

"Mr. Stanoslovski," my dad corrected.

"Right, sorry, Mr. Stanoslovski," I said.

"So, Max, thank you for taking Mia to see Sophie. It's appreciated."

"You're welcome. I know how important Sophie is to her."

"Right. So, how old are you?"

"I'm seventeen, sir."

"Senior?"

"No, sir, I'm a Junior," Max said.

"You understand that Mia is a freshman? She's only just turned 15."

"Yes, sir. I do. I promise you that I am trustworthy."

"What are your intentions for my daughter?"

"Dad, stop. He's safe."

"Mia. Let me do what dads do." My father's voice was stern.

"Fine," I said. I crossed my arms over my chest and stomped my foot, then stood staring directly at my dad, barely blinking.

"Sir, I promise, I have no ill intentions. I understand that she is younger than me and I respect that." Max shifted back and forth on his feet. I could tell he was nervous. "All I really want to do is to spend time with your daughter. If that is okay with you?"

"Who are your parents?"

"Sir, my mother is a second grade teacher with the school district, and my dad is a civil engineer for the state.

"Hobbies?" my dad asked.

"Soccer, sir."

My dad stood there nodding. "What are your plans for the future?"

"I plan on following in my dad's footsteps by going into engineering."

"Good, good. Do you go to church, son?"

"Dad, we don't even go to church," I interrupted.

"Yes sir. I attend First United Methodist with my family every Sunday."

"Pumpkin, I'm just trying to gauge the type of person you are dating."

Dating? I couldn't help but smile. I looked at Max. The hint of a smile formed on his lips. His eyes twinkled. I smiled wider.

"Okay. I approve. But listen to me closely. Mia is my only child. Do you understand me?"

"Yessir. I do."

"Okay. I'll leave you guys alone." My dad took one last look at Max. "Take care of her." He turned to walk back to the house. At the doorstep he said, "I mean it. Mia is my baby," then walked inside.

I turned to Max. "I'm so sorry."

"No, no, it's good. I would be the same way if I had a daughter." He leaned against the truck.

I took a step toward him. "I guess this kind of ruined the mood."

"Maybe a bit. Come here," he said.

I took another step toward him. He reached out his arms, put his hands around my waist, and pulled me right into him. The wind whipped around us, but with his arms wrapped around me and my head nestled against his chest, I felt warm. We stood there quietly for what seemed like half the night. Every once in a while he would kiss the top of my head and smell my hair.

"What do you use in your hair, you smell intoxicating."

"Strawberry shampoo."

"I love it."

I buried my face into him and closed my eyes.

"Um, Mia?"

"Yes?"

"Your dad is blinking the porch lights. You should probably go in," he said, loosening his grip on me.

"Grrrr." I took a deep breath. As soon as I backed away, I realized how cold it was outside. Without his warmth, I shivered. "Call me tonight?"

"I will."

I turned to walk away, but he grabbed my hand and pulled me in for another quick hug. It felt like heaven again, even if just for a fraction of a second. As I pulled away, he grabbed my waist, put his hand under my chin, and kissed me on the cheek, ever so softly.

Chills.

- Chapter Eighteen -

I floated into the house, my steps as light as my heart. I closed the door and stood against it to catch my breath, then walked over to our living room bay window. I watched the truck lights as they snaked down my driveway and onto the dirt road. I stood there until his lights disappeared, then I watched for a little bit longer, daydreaming.

Hearing footsteps, I turned to look at my father as he entered the living room. I couldn't help the smile I had across my face.

"Did you have a nice time?" he asked.

"I did, Dad."

"Good. He seems nice."

I laughed a little bit. "Did you have to scare him though?"

"Yes, yes I did." He sat on the couch and then he patted next to him, signaling that I should sit. My smile disappeared at the look on his face.

I walked over and sat at the edge of the couch. We hadn't talked about my mom since everything that happened the night before, so I knew he didn't want to just catch up.

"Mia. First, I want to apologize to you for not being there for you all these years." He paused to look at me. "And, more importantly, you tried to tell me over and over again. I'm sorry I didn't believe you."

I didn't speak. I barely breathed. My heart felt like it was constricting and traveling to my throat. I had ignored the intrusive thoughts about my mother all day. No one at school knew what had happened and I was glad because that meant I didn't have to talk about it. I bit my lip. I didn't want to cry.

"I need you to know that your mother showed up while you were with Max. She is not well. She's going to try to seek full custody of you."

My tears started rolling. I thought I was safe, but I should have known better. At the same time, I loved her. I loved her so much. I didn't want her to hurt. I didn't want to be the cause of the hurt. I couldn't live with her, though. I just couldn't.

"Mia, I'm trying my hardest here." He tried to assure me.

My tears flowed freely. "I can't deal." My voice was barely a whisper.

"I know, princess." He hugged me. My tears changed to sobs. He sat holding me and rocking me just like he had when I was a little girl.

When I finally stopped crying, he said, "But there's not much I can do if I don't find a job here. If I go back to traveling, no one is going to allow you to stay with me. Our options are limited."

The living room was warm, but my dad's words brought the cold in from the outside. I shivered, feeling the chill air return—only this time Max wasn't there to keep me warm.

"I've already gotten two interviews for Friday. They feel promising." He took a deep breath. "If I don't get one of those, I'm not sure what we'll do."

I couldn't take it anymore. I couldn't have this discussion. My emotions were a mess—fear, guilt, anger, sadness, confusion—I had to get up.

"Dad, you don't understand. I miss her. I love her. And I hate her." I turned and ran up the steps, leaving him alone in our empty home. I slammed the door behind me and sat down with my back against it, my knees against my chest.

- Chapter Nineteen -

I finally wiped my tears and stood up. I looked at myself in the mirror. I had caused this. My parents were splitting up because of me. If only I hadn't tried to pick up my phone at dinner, she wouldn't have hit me. None of this would have happened. If only Sophie and I hadn't been loud that night, my mom would have gotten her sleep, and I wouldn't have had to walk in the dark through a storm. None of that would have happened. It was my fault. I angered her. It was always my fault.

My phone buzzed.

Max: Thank you for tonight.

I took a deep breath and focused.

Mia: No, thank you for taking me. And for taking me out to dinner.
Max: Can I pick you up for school tomorrow?
Mia: I would love that.
Max: Perfect.
Max: I just want you to know that you are beautiful.

I didn't know what to say, this was a stark contrast to how I was feeling. I looked at myself in the mirror. My mascara was halfway down my face, my eyes were red and puffy, and my hair was a mess. Beautiful I was not. He had no idea.

Max: You still there?
Mia: I am.

Max: Did I embarrass you?
Mia: A little.

I wasn't embarrassed at all. I just didn't know what else to say. There was so much going on that he didn't know about. He had no clue and I didn't want to give him one.

Max: Don't be. I like you, Mia.
Mia: I like you too.

We texted back and forth for the next hour. We talked about everything from what teachers I should avoid to our favorite songs. Our texts were nice and light, exactly what I needed. Then my phone rang. It was Sophie.

Mia: Hey, I gotta go. Sophie is calling.
Max: I'll pick you up tomorrow morning.
Mia: :)

I answered my phone. "Hello?"
The line was quiet. Then I heard sniffing.
"Soph? What's wrong."
"Mia?"
"Yeah. What's going on?"
Silence.
Sophie wasn't speaking. Sophie always talked to me—even when she could barely breathe—something must be wrong. "Are you upset at me for coming there with Max?"
A small voice spoke up, "No, not at all." I heard more sniffing on the other end. "That's not it."
"What's going on?" She was never like this. It scared me.
"My parents just left. We talked to the doctor."
"Okay?" My stomach lurched. I couldn't imagine what was wrong. She always had hospital stays. It was never a big deal.
"Mia, they want me to have a lung transplant."
"WHAT?" I said. "You aren't that bad yet. Why?"
"They said it would take a long time to get to the top of the list, so I need to get on it now."

"If it takes a long time, why didn't they put you on it sooner."

"I wasn't sick enough." More sniffles. "The doctor said that because I'm older than 14, I could have a say."

"You're going to do it, right?"

"Mia. Sometimes people don't survive lung transplants." Her voice crackled. "And, my lungs are so small, I would have to get a young child's lungs."

I began to understand.

"Which means a small child has to die in a car accident, or something, for me to be able to live." She started crying louder. "I can't do that. I don't want a dead child's lungs, Mia."

"What happens if you don't go on the list?"

She said nothing.

"Sophie. What happens? What can they do?"

Still nothing.

"Sophie. What's going on?"

"Mia. They don't think I'll make it to my 18th birthday."

I started shaking and crying all over again. Silent tears this time. I didn't respond. I couldn't trust myself not to make things worse by sobbing out loud. Sophie needed my strength—not my grief and certainly not my terror.

"My parents want me on the list."

All I could say was, "Do it."

"Mia, I could die during the surgery. And, if I survive, the protocol afterwards is hard to deal with, I would have to be on anti-rejection meds."

"Sophie. Don't leave me." I broke down and started crying out loud, no longer able to disguise my pain. "You are all I have. You are mine. Don't leave me."

"I don't know what to do," she said, through sobs.

"I don't know what you should do."

"This is too big."

We talked for a little while longer, weighing out the pros and cons. I tried to stay calm, but it was next to impossible.

The range of emotions from the day was too much. I ended up collapsing in bed. I don't remember falling asleep.

- Chapter Twenty -

In my dream, Sophie was next to me in a hospital bed with more wires and tubes coming out of her than usual. She looked so weak and so skinny. Her eyes were sunken into her head. Next to her stood a beautiful angel, stroking Sophie's hair. The beeping of the machines bothered me, but the angel kept smiling at me, then looking down at Sophie, then smiling at me again. The angel said nothing at all, but its light was filling the entire room and growing brighter by the moment. I told the angel that I would give Sophie my lungs. Both of them. I cried and begged the angel to take mine, to take my lungs. I told the angel that I wasn't any good, that I had no reason to live, that all I did was upset my mother. Sophie was special. I was not. I begged and pleaded with the angel to rip my lungs out of my chest and put them in Sophie. But the angel just kept smiling at me and shaking its head back and forth telling me, "no"–all the while growing brighter and brighter. I screamed and woke myself up. The bright morning sun was hitting me in the face, and I had a splitting headache. I had been crying in my sleep. I heard a soft knock on my door.

"Come in."

The door opened and my dad walked in with some hot chocolate.

"You had a restless night. I could hear you tossing and turning. So, I thought you might need something sweet to drink this morning."

My dad handed me the mug. "Thank you."

"Are you okay? Are you sick? Do you want to stay home from school?" His questions were coming like rapid fire. He had never dealt with any of my childhood illnesses; he always seemed to be on the road. I knew he didn't know what to do.

"Dad, no. I'm fine. I just didn't sleep well. I kept having nightmares."

"About your mother?" he asked, innocently.

"No. About Sophie. She had some bad news yesterday and…" I had to stop talking, I was about to cry again. I placed my mug on my side table.

"What's going on?"

"They want her to have a lung transplant."

"Isn't that good news?"

"Not exactly. And she doesn't want to do it."

"Why not? Don't her parents have a say?"

"Yes, but she also has a say because she's older now. And she doesn't want to do it."

"That's not right."

"I know."

"If she doesn't have it, what will happen?"

"They don't think she'll make it to her 18th birthday."

My dad didn't respond.

"I can't lose her. I can't lose her and mom."

"I know." He wrapped me in his arms and cradled me again, stroking my hair.

"I can't do this. All of this is too hard. All of it. Why does life have to be like this?" I didn't want to deal with this. "It's too hard. It's all too hard. Is this what life is like? Is this it?"

"Mia, no. There are good times. Think about this, you and Sophie have had so much fun together. And you still have time."

That didn't help. That didn't help at all. He was trying though, so I nodded and tried to get control of myself. I let go of him, put my feet firmly on the floor, and stood. My headache spiked and I put my hands to my temples to try to stop the pain. My dad rushed to my side.

"You're going to stay home today," he said.

"No, Dad. Max is going to be here in about an hour to get me. And I just want to see him."

"Princess, I think you are sick."

"I've been crying. I cried last night before I went to sleep. I've been crying in my sleep, and now I'm crying again." I looked at him, willing him to let me go to school. "I'm fine. I'm just sad."

"Okay. Okay, fine. But if you get worse, I won't be able to get you. I'll be talking to potential employers all day."

"I'm fine; I won't need to call," I assured him.

"I'll let you get dressed then." He got up and gave me another kiss on the head. "Sophie will figure out what she needs to do. I'm sure she'll ultimately listen to her parents and doctors."

He didn't seem to understand that Sophie could die in the surgery, but I didn't want to go into that. I didn't want to think about it at all. So I just nodded and gave him a weak smile.

He turned and left my room, closing the door gently behind him. My mother would have found a reason to yell at me over all of this, but he was trying to be understanding. Still, I missed my mom. It made no sense, but I missed her anyway.

I walked to the bathroom to get my shower. The shower was my sanctuary. My mom always screamed at me when she heard me crying, so I would hide in the shower. But I was out of tears. So I just stood there, limp, not moving. I didn't even wash my hair. I just stood there with water cascading around me like the tears I could no longer shed.

After a while, I got out and started to get dressed. I wanted to look good for Max, but I didn't have the energy to actually put myself together. Ultimately, comfort won over fashion. I threw on a gray pair of sweatpants and a black hoodie. I didn't even dry my hair; I just threw it up in a bun. I couldn't put makeup on because touching my eyes hurt and they were sticky from crying, despite the fact that I had showered.

I looked at myself in the mirror and contemplated taking my dad up on his offer to stay home from school. I looked like hell.

My phone buzzed.

Max: Hey. I'm on my way. Can't wait to see you.

I looked at my phone but didn't answer. If I wanted to stay home, I needed to tell Max right then. I wanted to see him very badly though, so I decided to go to school.

Mia: Okay.

- Twenty-One -

I sat by my bedroom window waiting to see Max drive up the dirt road. There was absolutely nothing special about me. I was just wearing a hoodie and sweatpants. My hair was piled on the top of my head in a messy top knot. I had on no makeup at all. I hadn't even tried. But I was going to school, and he was picking me up, and that was something. I heard a knock at my door just before it opened.

My dad stuck his head into my room. "You didn't come down for breakfast," he said.

"I don't feel like eating."

"You have to. I brought you some toast." He approached me slowly, almost as if I were a wild animal. In his hand, he held a small plate.

Two pieces of cinnamon sugar toast, I could eat that. I took the plate. He stood there awkwardly and watched me eat.

"You still look sick to me. I'm not going to be home to come get you from school. Are you sure you're okay to go?"

"Yes, I promise." I took another bite of toast then asked, "Why won't you be home?"

"I have an interview. I just got the call."

"Really? Dad!" I swallowed my mouthful. "Dad, that's great! Where?"

"Just a business in Harrisburg. Doing procurement. We'll see what happens."

I got up and hugged him. "I know you'll do great."

"I hope. I can't leave you at home alone. And if I go back out on the road again–"

"Wait! Have you heard from Mom?" I backed up from our hug.

"No, she's been very quiet. I'm concerned." He looked out the window. "I know you miss her. I do too."

At first, I got a little angry, but then sad. I had to admit that I did miss her. For the first time in years, though, I didn't feel on edge at home. "I do, but you're not going to let her come home, are you?"

"No, I can't." He started pacing the room. Then he stopped, turned, and looked at me. "I'm so sorry I didn't believe you. All those years on the road, I just didn't think it was possible that she would hurt you. I thought you were being dramatic."

"It's okay."

"No, it's not. How she behaved the other night startled me."

"Dad, it's okay."

"I have an appointment next week with a lawyer. I want to make sure she can't take you away from me."

"Is that a possibility?"

"Anything is. She convinced me. She could convince the judge the same way."

My heart started beating out of my chest. "Dad?"

"I'm sorry. You are safe." He reached out to hug me again. "You're safe. I promise."

The dresser buzzed. My phone was sitting on top. My father let me go. "I guess that's Max?"

"Yeah."

"It's not too late to stay home."

"No. I need to go."

"Okay. Can I take you to see Sophie tonight? I could drop you off around four and pick you up at six?"

"I would like that. Thank you."

After he left the room, I gathered my homework that was sitting next to my computer.

On the way out, I stopped to look at myself one more time in the mirror and thought, "Well this will have to do." With that, I left the safety of my room and walked down my steps.

"You sure you're okay to go?" My dad sounded anxious.

"Dad, I'm fine. I'm not sick, just upset." I put on my coat.

"Okay. I'll see you tonight."

I wasn't prepared for the cold wind that hit me when I opened the front door. Part of me wanted to turn back, but I took my step onto the porch. The wind stung. I clung to the porch railing and to the idea of Max. The rail was cold, but Max's smile was warm. He jumped out of his truck, ran around the front of it, and opened the door for me.

"Thank you," I said as I reached him. "I didn't realize it was this cold out today."

"It really is. But the truck is warm for you."

I got in. He was right. He had the heat on full blast. It felt heavenly. I had only been out in the cold for a few seconds, but I was carrying a lifetime of cold within me. He shut my door, then ran around the front and jumped in. I tried not to look at him. I didn't want him to know how upset I was. Sophie always told me it was much easier to attract people while smiling, but I didn't feel like smiling.

"Hey," he said, after closing the door.

"Hey," I replied without looking at him.

He didn't start driving. I could feel him staring at me. "Are you okay?"

"Yeah. Why do you ask?"

"Um, because you won't look at me."

I turned my head and he grabbed my hand.

"Seriously, what's wrong?"

"Sophie. She just got some bad news."

"Do you want to talk about it?"

"Not really. I'm sorry."

"It's okay." He looked deeply into my eyes, then took his hand and smoothed out the fly-away hairs coming out of the bun on the top of my head. When he held his palm against my cheek, I gave him a small smile. "We don't have to talk about anything at all. It's fine."

"Thank you."

He drove carefully down the dirt road, expertly avoiding the potholes he'd struggled with the day before. I was silently thankful that he was able to make the ride off the mountain smooth. I'm not sure I could have given directions if he'd needed them. As soon as we got to the stop sign that separated our road from the rest of civilization, he turned on the radio.

True to his word, Max didn't speak again until we were pulling into his spot in the school's parking lot. Then he said, "I'm here for you, okay?"

I nodded.

"Stay here for a sec." He turned off his truck, got out, and once again ran around the front. It actually made me laugh that he kept running around the front like that. He got to my side of the truck and opened the door for me. I hopped out and he shut the door. Then we walked hand in hand into the school building.

- Chapter Twenty-Two -

Something always felt like it was missing when Sophie wasn't at school, but holding his hand made it just a bit better. I held my head up and even allowed myself a small smile. No one was looking at us today; the gossip about us had already waned. That was fine with me. I didn't want the attention. Sophie always attracted everyone's attention so much that I was used to falling to the background. In fact, I kind of liked it that way.

We rounded the corner and saw Emma at the end of the hall standing against her locker with Alex leaning in next to her. He was twirling her hair between his fingers. I had always longed for something like that. I smiled to myself thinking that, just maybe, I finally had it.

Emma turned her head just in time to see me. She whispered something I couldn't hear, then broke away from Alex and bounced over to me. Max let go of my hand.

"Hey, Mia!" She hugged me. "How's Soph?"

I didn't know how to answer. Sophie hadn't told me not to tell people, but I also didn't think that she was ready for the world to know. "She's okay."

"Okay, cool. So is it just her normal stay?"

I couldn't believe she said that so nonchalantly as if someone going to the hospital every few months is normal. Rather than try to explain, I opted for the easy-out. "Yeah, basically."

"Cool, cool," she said, nodding.

I smiled at her.

She took my elbow and led me away from Max. "So, um. What's going on here?"

"Here?"

"How serious is it with you and Max?"

"I don't know. We are just getting started. Why?"

"Oh, nothing. Nothing. It's just that Everly was angry as hell yesterday. I had a feeling it was about you two." She wagged her finger back and forth from me to Max, who had already found his friends and was joking around.

"Oh." I had no idea what else to say. I had never had a boyfriend before, let alone one who had someone like Everly who wanted him. Everly scared me. She wasn't afraid to go after people. My palms started sweating.

"I'm sure it will be fine. Don't worry." Emma waved her hand in front of her face as if none of it meant anything. "But let me just ask this"–she looked me dead in the eye and winked–"are you going to sleep with him?"

"What?" I was shocked. I hadn't even thought of that. I was just happy to hold his hand. People always told me I was naive, apparently they were right.

"I mean. I'm just saying–to keep a guy like him you're going to have to."

I just stood there stupid with shock. I tried to think of something to say, but I literally had no words.

"Look. Why do you think Everly feels so attached to him? She slept with him. He was her first." She did the hand wave thing again and said, "Don't worry. I didn't think I was ready either, but it'll be okay." She glanced lovingly at Alex.

"Wait, are you...?" I asked.

"Oh yeah. I mean– yeah." She started stumbling. "You didn't know?"

"No."

"You might have to sleep with him. You realize that, right?"

"No, I haven't really thought about it."

"It's not as bad as you think it would be." She nodded, deep in her own thoughts. "Well, maybe at first." She looked at me again. "Anyway, it's import-ant to know." She nodded. "Plus, he's really cute. So."

Outwardly, I nodded, at least I think I did. But inside I was terrified. I wasn't ready for that. We had only kissed a few times, and I liked that. I wasn't ready for anything else. I just wasn't. I thought Max was safe. Maybe I was wrong. What was I going to do? I stood there lost in shock, barely noticing when Emma turned and walked back to the arms of her boyfriend. When he saw her leave, Max walked back to me and reached for my hand. I suddenly re-alized how sweaty my palms were. I pulled my hand away. He looked confused.

"What was that conversation about?" he asked, crossing his arms across his chest.

"Oh nothing, just girl talk." I took another look at Emma. She saw me and winked, then turned and kissed Alex.

"Alrighty. Well. This is my next class," he said and pointed to the door next to me. "Do you want me to walk you to yours? Orrrr should I see you at lunch?" He stumbled over his words.

I couldn't even look him in the eyes. I was embarrassed. "I'll just see you at lunch."

"Okay. Cool." He handed me my backpack and then left me standing there as he walked into his classroom.

I sighed and looked around. Was this what everyone around me was doing? Were they all having sex? Most of my friends were with someone. I wondered if I was the only one who had never had sex. Was I the lone virgin? I looked down to the ground and realized I was alone in a crowd of shoes. Someone tapped me on the shoulder. Startled, I jumped.

"Hey, girl. What's up? We gotta go." It was Lily. "If you keep standing here like this, you'll get run over."

"Oh. Right. Yeah." I shook my head to bring myself back to reality and started walking with her to history.

"Lily?"

"Yeah?" she answered, looking at me oddly. "Girl, you are acting weird."

"Can I ask you a serious question?"

"Of course."

"Have you had sex?"

She laughed. "Look, I don't even have a boyfriend. What do you take me for?"

"Okay." I sighed. "What if you had a boyfriend? Would you?"

"Hmmm. Maybe?" she said with a shrug. "But then again, I don't even know what I like. No." She looked at me and asked, "What's gotten into you?"

"I was talking to Emma."

"Oh. Yeah. That makes sense," she said, nodding. "That girl is boy crazy. She would do anything to keep Alex."

"Do you have to sleep with a boy to keep him?"

"I have no idea. None. At all. I'm sorry I can't help you," she said. We reached the door to the history classroom. "But one thing I can tell you is that you shouldn't do anything you aren't ready for. And if he breaks up with you because of that? Then he sucks."

I didn't respond, sure now that Max and I were through. We just didn't know it yet. The only thing I took from what she said was that he would probably break up with me. That's not what she said, but it didn't matter. It didn't make me feel better. I knew. I would be thrown away if I didn't do what he wanted. That's how it was with me. Sophie was the only one who wanted me, and she was dying.

Once Alex walked away, Emma came up behind Lily and put her arm around her. They were like twins, the type of friends who will stay close forever.

"Sup, slut?" Lily said.

"Slut? Yeah, well. At least I get some." Emma laughed.

"Why'd you tell little Miss Virgin that she had to put out?"

"Wait, is that exactly what I said?" Emma asked, pointing at me.

"Ummm. Yeah. You did." Lily answered.

"Well. She likes him, right?" She held her hands up in the air.

They both looked at me. All I did was nod.

"Well, friend, then you know what you have to do," Emma said, looking at me.

Lily rolled her eyes. "Let's just go in. The middle of the hallway is not where we should make major life decisions."

"What's so major about it?"

"Oh my God, whore."

"Don't slut shame me." Emma stomped her foot. "This isn't 1950."

They both started laughing, then grasped hands and walked away. I was left there wondering if I would even be able to keep Max.

- Chapter Twenty-Three -

"Mia Stanoslovski, please come to the office."

I glanced around the classroom, surprised to hear my name over the loudspeaker. Twenty sets of eyes looked back at me. I'm not someone who is ever called to the office. The message repeated. I froze, eyes fixed on the loudspeaker.

"Go ahead, Mia. Go see what they want," Mrs. Stewart said to me.

The room was still and silent. I dropped my eyes to my desk, then cringed at the sound of my backpack as I zipped my books inside. I didn't have to look around again, my scalp tingled a warning that everyone was watching me. I forced myself to stand slowly, walk down the aisle, and leave the room. Once in the hall, my mind raced into overdrive. Did something happen to my dad? What if something had happened to him? Did he have an accident on the way to his interview? My luck wasn't that bad, was it? No. It had to be something else. Maybe something had happened to my grandmother? Kids always got called to the office when their grandmother died. What if it was my mother? Maybe she was in the office waiting for me. Should I even go to the office? If my mother was there, I definitely did not want to go. But what if it was Sophie? What if Sophie was in trouble? I had to go to the office. But too much was happening. I just wanted to be back in my bed. My dad was right. I shouldn't have gone to school.

I walked down the steps, worrying. From there I could just make out the "Main Office" sign at the end of the hall. I squinted my eyes to see if anyone from my family was there, but I couldn't see anything. Then it happened. A door opened to my right and Everly walked out of her classroom. What had I done to deserve this? It wasn't even lunchtime yet. I could escape through one of the side doors, but that would trigger the alarm. Then I'd be in for it.

Ignoring her was my only option. I walked past keeping my eyes on the floor.

"Hey!" Everly said.

I kept my head down and walked.

"I said, hey!" she said again.

Visions of my mother hitting me ran through my mind. I didn't want to turn around, but if there was one thing I knew, you didn't ever turn your back on someone who was mad at you.

I turned around slowly. "Yes, Everly?"

"What are you doing with Max?

"We're dating. Why?" I reached into my pocket to find comfort in the stone Sophie had given me. I pulled it out and balled up my hand so Everly didn't know I had anything. I ran my thumb over it.

"You know he's mine. Right?"

"Oh, I thought you broke up?"

She glared at me, her glowing red face telling me I'd made a terrible error.

"Oh, did you?" she snapped.

I put my head down and tried to start back on my path to the office.

"Excuse me. Did I say you could go?"

"Sorry." I pointed my finger at the office. "I was called to the office." I took another step down the hall.

"You're lucky."

As I turned back around to face her again, a slow sneer spread across her lips. I willed my feet to keep moving toward the office, but instead they froze, keeping me in place. "Why do you say that?" I said, my voice steadier than I felt.

"Because you won't get your ass beat right now."

"Excuse me. But are you still dating Max? Is there something I should know?" I asked.

"He was about to come back to me until you stepped in. As far as I'm concerned, you did this to me."

"Okay. Well. I didn't even know you had ever dated him, so you should take that up with him."

"Like I said, you are damn lucky." She pointed at me. "I'm watching you. Whore."

I laughed. Bold laughter right in her face. Probably not my best move, but I couldn't help it. Everly calling me a whore? After the conversation I just had with Emma?

"What the hell are you laughing at?"

"Nothing." I shook my head. I was no stranger to being hit, maybe that's why I didn't back down. I bit my lip. It was time to stop giggling. I could taste blood on the inside of my mouth.

Everly backed up a few paces, then held her left arm out, pointed her finger at me again, and said, "Watch yourself."

"Right. Okay." I started to turn around.

"Bitch, you wanna go now?"

"No. No. That's not necessary. Plus the office is waiting for me. So." I turned completely and walked away quickly.

"Get back here."

I ignored her and kept walking. I think she must have kicked a trash can because one went flying past me. She didn't realize that was something I was used to. So used to, in fact, that it didn't phase me one bit.

As I got closer to the office, I could see a woman standing near the window. My stomach dropped and I started shaking.

- Chapter Twenty-Four -

I stopped walking, not wanting to move forward, towards her. I checked behind me to see if Everly was still standing there. She wasn't, so I felt like it was safe to stay still for a moment to get a hold of my thoughts. All at once, I felt like I wanted to run into her arms and beg for forgiveness. Beg for her to love me. Like, really love me, not the act she put on in public. I wanted her to love me at home, for real, not an act. I wanted to know why she didn't. I wanted to know what I did to make her hate me. I wanted to beg her for love. But I also wanted to run, far, far away. I had known I would see her again, I just didn't think it would happen right then and there in the school office.

I watched her through the glass. There she was—my mother—standing there wringing her hands, speaking words I couldn't hear. Then her tears started and I knew which mother I would be getting. The secretary stood up, walked around the front counter, and hugged my weeping mother. My weeping mother who practiced crying in front of a mirror. My weeping mother was putting on a show.

Yes, I knew exactly which mom I would be getting. She was there to make my dad look bad, to make it look like I was ripped from her loving arms. Standing there with this knowledge, I didn't want to take another step. I willed the floor to open up and the world to swallow me whole. Why couldn't she just be real? No, that was a stupid question. If she were real, she would have walked into the office, slammed the door, thrown things against the wall, and threatened violence. She couldn't be like that in public. In public, she needed to look like the most loving mother ever.

I took a deep breath. There was no turning back. I had to walk through that door and face her. At least she would hug me. I just had to grin and bear it. She wasn't going to give me the love I craved. I took a step. Then another.

As I approached, she saw me through the window and came rushing out of the office door to greet me.

Her face was a mess, just the way she liked it. Mascara streaked and wet with tears. Even her red lipstick was smeared. She often liked to do this, wear too much makeup when she knew she'd have an audience for her theatrics. She planned for the mascara to streak in just the right way.

"Oh, Mia." She clasped her hands to her face. "Come here, baby."

I looked at the secretary watching us from the window. She was crying as well. I furrowed my brows at her until she moved away from the window. I assume she meant to give us our space.

My mom gave me a look like she was saying, "Do your part, girl." Then pulled me into her arms. I did not wrap my arms around her, but I allowed her to hold me in her grasp. She squeezed tight and began wailing. In the middle of my school. Wailing, loudly. I couldn't see past her poofy hair to know if anyone was watching what was going on, but I'm sure they were.

"Babyyyyy, I've missed you soooooooo much. I can't believeeeee he tooooooook you from meeeeee."

"Mom. Mom. I'm fine. It's fine."

"Noooo, it's never fine. I just love you so much."

I wrapped my arms around her and gave her a small hug. What else could I do?

"Yourrr my babyyy."

"Right mom. Okay." I pushed her off of me. "What are you doing here?"

"Whatever do you mean?"

I looked up and down the hallway to see if anyone was watching the show. There were a few, luckily most of the students were still in class. I took her hand and pulled her into the office. As I walked, in I noticed the secretary staring at us, dabbing her eyes.

Right.

"Mom. What are you doing here?"

"Oh, baby, I just couldn't be apart from you any longer. And I just knew your FATHER wouldn't let me see you."

"But he would have. He would have just wanted to be there."

"Oh no, you don't understand the painnnn I've been innnnn."

"Mom. Do you remember what happened?"

"Oh shush. It's not important now." She fanned her face.

"Um, excuse me." The secretary stuck her head out of the office door. "Can I open an office for you guys? You know. For privacy?" she asked.

"No," I said immediately.

"Yes," my mom said over me.

"No, really. It's fine. We can catch up later. But right now I have a test in history. I can't miss it."

"Oh, isn't that just Mia?" she said, looking at the secretary. "Always so worried about her grades." She was nodding. "All mothers should be so bless-ed."

My mom was spreading it thick, that much was sure.

"Right," I said, backing away from her. "So, I'll call you and we can go out to dinner or something." This whole conversation was just for show.

"Oh yes, I would love that," she answered. "Just don't let that father of yours get involved." She turned to the secretary. "I swear, these men of today. They have no idea what it's like to be a mother."

The secretary nodded.

My mom turned back to me "Look here, Sweetie," she said to me. "Don't let that man get between us. He doesn't understand our bond."

"Okay." I nodded. "Bye, mom." I walked to the door.

"Aren't you going to give me a hug goodbye?" Her words were rushed, a look of panic overtaking her face.

I walked up to her and tried to give her a quick hug. She pulled me in tight and whispered into my ear. "Remember something. I'm your mother. You would die without me. I can end you."

And her true self came out.

I broke from her grasp and walked out the glass door. I didn't turn back around to wave goodbye. I just kept my head down and headed straight to the girl's bathroom. The farther I got from her, the more and more I felt like I was going to cry. I quickened my step to try to make it there before I burst out in tears. I didn't want to give anyone more of a show than they'd already seen. I didn't want to see Everly. I didn't want to see Max. Now that I knew what he expected of me, I had to think of what to do before I saw him again. The bell rang. I threw my body into the door of the girls' room just as the students flooded the hall. The smell of bleach smacked me in the face. I threw my backpack in the corner and slammed into the first stall. I pushed the door shut behind me and leaned against it. I could hear the rush of students outside the bathroom door. There weren't many classrooms near the office, so I felt tucked away. I didn't expect anyone to come in. I breathed in relief. Then the tears started. I couldn't control them. I tried deep breathing, hoping to gain composure, but the more I breathed, the more images started flashing through my mind. They didn't come in any sort of order, just flashes.

Sometimes the flashes were of my mother telling me she loved me after she hit me. Other times they were flashes of her actually hitting me. Then kissing Max slipped through my brain, and I smiled a little until Emma's voice cut into my memory, *you'll have to sleep with him to keep him.* I saw images of Max breaking up with me. Then, my mom's slap across the face. I felt my hands grow cold, like when I was walking down the mountain in the snowstorm. Then I saw myself as a little girl standing at a window of my house watching my dad drive away, both of us crying. I felt my mother pull my hair as she screamed at me to stop crying. Then, finally, my mind's eye took me to a gravesite with Sophie's name on it. Above Sophie's grave was a large ball of light. In that light, I felt love. I wanted to be sad envisioning the gravestone, but I couldn't be. In the bathroom, my tears stopped and I couldn't hold back a smile. I whispered, "I love you, too, Soph."

As soon as I whispered her name, the door to the hall opened. The wind from the door emphasized the bleach smell which brought me back to reality. Two separate laughs fill my ears. I didn't want to be found, so I stayed as still and quiet in the stall as possible. But they were too busy laughing to realize anyone else was in the bathroom with them.

"Honestly, can you believe it?" I couldn't figure out whose voice it was until I heard, "Why would he want a freshman?" and that's when I realized. Everly.

"It's insane. He'll be back. She's just someone for him to play with before he gets serious with you." Now that I knew it was Everly, I recognized the other person as Taylor, another Junior.

I looked at them through the crack in the door. They were fixing their hair and touching up their makeup.

"Right? I think all I need to do is scare her a little, and she'll give up." Then Everly laughed. "Hell, I may have scared her already."

"And what if you didn't?"

"Then I'm going to have to kick her ass. He's mine. She needs to know."

"Wouldn't he get mad at you?"

"Please, he doesn't really care about her. Are you kidding?"

"True," Taylor said.

They left the bathroom together. I felt waves of heat coming over me. I put my head in my hands. I knew I had to end it with Max. There was nothing else I could do. First, I wasn't ready to sleep with anyone, so I might as well break up with him before he broke up with me. Second, I didn't want to piss off the whole junior class. I didn't need it. I just didn't need it.

Finally, I took a deep breath and looked up at the fluorescent light blinking above me. A tear rolled down my cheek.

I whispered, "What's it matter anyway. I'll never get what I want." I took one more deep breath of bleach air, then left the stall. I looked for my cell phone to call my dad and beg him to pick me up. I didn't want Max driving me home. I dialed my father's number, but no one answered. That's when I remembered that he was in a job interview. So I texted him.

Mia: Dad, can you come get me?

He didn't respond.

Mia: Dad, mom came to the school. Can you please come get me?

Nothing. No reply.

I leaned against the wall. What could I do? I didn't want to go to my next class. I didn't want to go to lunch. I just wanted to go home. Could I stay in the girls' room all day? Maybe I should just wait here and take the bus home? But I was hungry. I needed to eat. And I was developing a headache from the stress. I hoped my dad would call me back.

Then again, maybe sleeping with Max wouldn't be so bad. I could do that. After everything I had gone through with my mom, maybe being that close to him would make me feel better. And he would love me if I did it. I needed him to love me. Everly was a problem, but she wouldn't be that big of a deal, right? I could handle her. It would be fine. I could do it. I could sleep with Max. I could make sure he wouldn't break up with me.

I walked to the sink, looked at myself in the mirror, turned on the water, bent over and washed my face. Hands and face clean, I straightened my back, raised my head, turned, grabbed a paper towel, and dried my face. I left the bathroom, sure of my decision.

- Chapter Twenty-Five -

The hallway was almost empty. I was going to be late for class. I was never one who wanted to get in trouble so I looked into the office window to make sure my mom was gone. No sign of her, so I took a deep breath and proceeded.

I opened the door. The office was much brighter than the bathroom had been. The walls were glass. Anyone walking by could see me in there. It smelled of paper and ink. I quietly stood at the counter until the secretary noticed me.

Finally, she stopped typing on the computer and looked up.

"Oh, darling. I want you to know that I know how hard this all is." She jumped up from behind her desk, practically ran around the front counter, and hugged me. "Those men, ripping their children away from their mother's arms. It's unconscionable." She backed away from me and looked into my eyes. "Are you okay?"

No clue. She didn't have a clue. Plus, I'm pretty sure she wasn't allowed to be hugging me.

"Well, there's a lot more going on than that."

"Oh. I'm sure. I'm sure." She nodded. "There's always something, isn't there. Someday these men will treat us right." She tapped her long pink nails on the counter. The rhythm annoyed me.

"I was in the bathroom clearing my head, so I'm late for class," I said, watching her nails as they tapped. "Can I have a pass?"

"Oh, of course. Don't you worry about anything." She stopped tapping, walked back to her desk, grabbed a pad of notes, and scribbled something on it. As she handed me the note, she said, "You know, dear, If you'd like, you can just hang out here. All of this must be so traumatic."

"It's fine. I'm just going to go to class." I took the note from her hand, turned quickly, and got out of there before I had to suffer through any more of her pity.

At the office door, I turned right, trying to get to class without running into Everly again. Once I was out of the secretary's sights, I stopped and pulled out my phone to text Sophie.

Mia: Just checking in. How are you?
Sophie: Mia! You can't have your phone out in school like that.
Mia: It's fine, I won't get in trouble today. Trust me.
Sophie: kk.
Mia: How are you?
Sophie: Ok. Fighting with my parents. They don't understand.

I wasn't going to talk to her about it through text. I couldn't handle it.

Mia: My dad is dropping me off after school.
Sophie: Good. I need you.
Mia: I need you too. You'll be ok. Right?
Sophie: Yeah. They are just being weird.
Mia: Promise?
Sophie: Yes.
Mia: Ok. I have something to talk to you about then, something about Max. Oh, and my mom showed up at school just now.
Sophie: WHAT? Oh no.
Sophia: Is the Max thing good?
Mia: Time will tell. Ttyl.

I put my phone in my back pocket and walked to history.

- Chapter Twenty-Six -

As I was walking out of history with Emma and Lily, I noticed Max standing by my locker.

"Ooooo, look at him waiting for you." Lily pointed to him.

"He wants you. You gonna do it?" Emma asked, just as Alex came up behind her and took her backpack.

My face felt hot. I knew I was blushing. Max looked incredibly hot standing there, leaning against my locker, waiting for me. I couldn't help but smile.

"You are. Aren't you?" Lily asked.

I gave her a coy smile. "Maybe," I said.

"Girllll. We need to talk about some stuff," Emma said.

"What are you talking about? What are you going to do?" Alex asked then kissed Emma on the top of the head.

"NOTHING," I snapped. I didn't want things getting out.

Alex laughed. "Oh, ah. I see."

Emma elbowed him. "Shh, don't say anything."

"Oh my God, is it that obvious?" I asked.

"Yep," Alex responded.

"Seriously, Alex. Don't make this awkward," Emma said.

"I'm not saying a word, babe."

By this time we were a few steps away from Max. Alex let go of Emma's hand, walked around us, and fist-bumped Max. Then they went in for a man hug. I walked up next to them, and Max reached for my hand.

As we intertwined our fingers, Emma gave me a look. Max noticed. "What's that look about?"

Emma walked up to Alex, kissed him, and said, "Oh nothing."

"Y'all should get rooms," Lily said.

"We need to get you someone, Lily," Emma replied.

"Nah. I'm good. Come on, let's go get lunch."

I looked at Max as we walked, hand in hand. Was he the one? I never dreamed I would lose my virginity this young. But I didn't care. I wanted stability. He noticed me looking at him, squeezed my hand, and winked. My face felt hot again. He had no idea what I had decided, but I knew he would be happy. And that was all that mattered to me.

- Chapter Twenty-Seven -

We walked into the cafeteria with Lily leading the way. The guys decided to sit with us instead of with their friends. My gang was already at the table. Everly was there too. She noticed us coming in together and sneered at me. I looked away from her and focused on Max. We threw out backpacks under the table and got in line.

Emma and Alex were in front of us. Kissing. Is that what I needed to be doing, kissing in line? Is that what Max wanted? He looked perfectly happy just holding my hand, but I couldn't risk it. I couldn't risk losing him. I leaned up on my tiptoes and kissed him on the cheek. I heard someone's chair push back loudly, then, "Oh, whatever." It was the same voice that had threatened me earlier, Everly.

I went down flat-footed again. Max took his arms to pull me tight to his body. He smelled like heaven. Then he bent down and kissed me on the top of the head. This would be okay. I could do this. I needed to keep him. Being a virgin had to end sometime.

Lily jumped up behind us and tapped me on the shoulder. "Hey," she said.

"I just wanted to ask if you heard from Sophie?"

"Yeah. I just texted her. I'm going over after school."

"Okay. Cool."

We stood in line a while longer, then got our food and went back to the table. As I sat, Everly picked up her tray and slammed it down hard and loud.

"Bitch!" she screamed.

Max didn't say a word. Everly turned and stomped out of the cafeteria. I looked at him begging for some sort of answer. He had none to give.

The entire cafeteria was quiet after that. All eyes were on me. I just looked down at my food. Not eating. Not talking. Not looking at anyone.

- Chapter Twenty-Eight -

I pushed my way out the front doors of the school to find my dad sitting in his SUV waiting for me. He waved as soon as he saw me. I ran up to the passenger's side door, opened it, and got in. He was playing cheesy 80's ballads, so I turned the volume down. I didn't want anyone to hear.

"Hey, Dad."

"Hey. How was school?"

"Did you get my text?"

"You texted me? I didn't. I was in that interview all day."

"All day?"

"Yes. It's a long process."

"Do you think you'll get it?"

"I don't know. I hope so. It was a pretty good interview."

"And you won't be traveling?"

"Well, we'll talk about that later. Tell me about your day."

It didn't really register what he had said. "Mom showed up at school. Which is why I texted."

"She did?"

"Yeah. She did."

"Why?" He didn't seem shocked at all.

"I don't know, Dad. She said you were keeping me from her."

He got really quiet.

"Dad, what's going on? You're acting weird."

"Nothing. You want to go through the drive-thru before I drop you off at the hospital?"

I knew to not ask again.

"Sure. Can I get something for Sophie?" I asked.

"Sure."

He drove up to the McDonald's menu board and ordered two chicken nugget meals.

"Aren't you getting anything?"

"No. I'm going to drop you off and go get something on my own."

"Okay."

We reached the window and food was handed to my dad, who promptly handed it to me. I held the two sodas in my hands and the food on my lap.

"Do you want a french fry?" I asked.

"No. it's okay," he stared straight ahead, not really saying anything. I did the same.

He drove through the hospital parking lot and up to the main doors. He held the sodas for me while I gathered my stuff. "Thanks," I said. "Thanks for bringing me here."

"I'll be back in two hours."

"Okay."

With full arms and Sophie's backpack slung over my shoulder, I got out, pushed the door closed with my foot, and leaned up against it making sure it was shut. As I walked toward the double doors at the front of the hospital, it occurred to me that more was happening with my dad than I knew about. My father was never at home much, and it had been great having him around. But the car ride shook me, there was something more going on. I could feel it.

I approached the desk to get a visitor pass, then turned and walked toward the elevator. The hospital lobby was quiet. I stood waiting. No one was getting on the elevator with me, and I was fine with that. There was this ominous feeling of dread I couldn't shake. I needed to get out of that frame of mind before seeing Sophie. That was the last thing she needed. The elevator doors opened and I stepped inside. I pushed the number four with my elbow. The doors slid shut. A deep breath shook my entire body as I tried to lose the dread. I could see my reflection in the door, so I looked myself in the eyes and said, "You are going to be okay." Just before the door opened to the fourth floor, I nodded at myself. I got out and turned. At the nurses' station, they were tapping away on computers or holding charts. One of the nurses nodded at me as I passed. "Hey, Mia!" she called.

I waved hello but didn't answer. She lowered her head back to her files.

I stood off to the side of Sophie's door to commit myself to positivity before walking in.

I turned the corner. Sophie was sleeping. I quietly shut her door behind me. Then sat at her bedside and watched her for a bit. She looked so peaceful. Sure, she was hooked up to IVs, and tubes were pushing oxygen into her nostrils, but she was breathing more clearly. I could only detect a faint wheeze. I hoped this meant she was okay, that all the talk about transplants would go away. I opened my McDonald's bag and started to eat my nuggets. I was starving. I had been too worried to eat during lunch.

Sophie stirred and opened her eyes. I put my nuggets down and stood by the bed.

"I thought I smelled nuggies," she said quietly with a smile.

"I thought you would like them." I grabbed her food for her from the bag.

She sat up, ready to eat. "Thank you. I've been starving."

Sophie generally needed to eat a lot, but she rarely gained weight. Cystic Fibrosis affects the digestive system along with the lungs. She could always eat so much more food than I could. I never saw it as fair, but I kept my mouth shut.

I put her food on her tray, then pushed it in front of her. I opened the containers, dumped the fries into the nugget container, then put a straw in her soda. I pulled my chair right next to the bed and started eating my nuggets again.

"Any news?" I asked.

"Not really. I'm just bored at this point." She shoved a few fries in her mouth, then took a drink. "I don't want to talk about hospital stuff. What happened at school today? Your mom showed up?"

"Yeah." I nodded.

"What did she do?"

"You know what she did."

"Made a scene and cried over you?"

"Yep."

"How bad was the makeup running down her face?" Sophie asked.

I started laughing so hard that I choked on a fry. I tried to regain myself by taking a quick sip of soda. The choking stopped, but not the laughing. "I'm not going to lie. It was pretty bad."

Sophie giggled. I chuckled a little louder. Then the two of us just let go and broke into rolling laughter. We laughed until our eyes were streaming. Sophie started coughing through her laughs, until finally, her face became bright red, and she was full-on hacking. I stopped laughing and stood up. She was struggling to get a breath in. I screamed for the nurses, but they were already running into the room.

One of them grabbed her hand. "Sophie, look at me." The nurse started taking loud, exaggerated breaths, in and out, as a way to get Sophie to copy her. Sophie tried to mimic the nurse but her lips were turning blue. She was trying so hard to catch her breath that I found it hard to catch mine. The other nurse covered Sophie's mouth and nose with an oxygen mask. I couldn't believe what was happening. We always laughed. Crazy laughter, but she had never had a problem before.

"Can you try coughing some of it up for us?"

Sophie nodded.

Once Sophie was breathing a bit better, I asked, "What happened?"

"Well, she's had a lot of gunk in her lungs," the nurse said, smiling at me. "So this laughing attack may have loosened up some stuff." She nodded at Sophie, then touched my hand that was clasping the bed's handrail.

"But it's never happened before." I was on the verge of tears.

"Well, she has a lot more gunk in there than usual. That's what the IV is for."

"Oh."

Sophie sat there, trying to cough sputum from her lungs.

I looked at the nurse and asked, "Is she going to be okay?"

She waved her hand nonchalantly. "With a friend like you, how could she be anything but okay," she said.

That annoyed me. I didn't like being treated like a child but I kept my mouth shut because she was trying to comfort me. Plus, Sophie needed her, and I didn't want to make the nurse angry.

Sophie continued coughing and spitting into a container. She was going back and forth between the oxygen mask and spitting up this thick, beige sputum from her lungs that was tinged with blood. It was gross, but it was coming up, which was good. She finally finished coughing and sank back down, exhausted. One of the nurses wet a washcloth and wiped Sophie's face.

"See? I told you she'd be okay."

I just nodded.

They left the room and Sophie looked at me. "Yeah, I'm fine. You know, you actually probably did help me out by making me laugh. They were trying to loosen up some of this all day. It just wasn't happening." She closed her eyes for a moment. I grabbed her hand and she opened them again. "So I think laughing helped."

"I still feel bad," I said.

"No way, I can't go home until I get it all up. It's really thick this time."

"Okay."

"Let's change the subject. So what's going on? Is your mom coming back home?" Sophie asked.

I hadn't considered that thought before, but after she said it, I thought about how my dad was acting. Like about how he hadn't asked what my mom wanted, almost like he had known she had been at the school.

Sophie noticed my body shake at the thought. "What's wrong?" she asked.

"It's just that… Well, I can't be sure. But my dad was acting weird when he picked me up from school."

"Weird?"

"It's probably nothing. Honestly, I would rather hear about you."

"That's stupid, you know how boring it is here. I want to hear what's happening in the real world."

"Fine." I sighed. "He had a job interview today, when I asked him about it, he wouldn't tell me anything. Then he was super quiet. When I asked if it was a job where he'd be able to be at home. He said nothing at all."

"Oh no."

"Yeah." I nodded. "And he didn't seem surprised that my mom came to the school."

"Do you think something's going on?" Sophie asked.

"I'm not sure." I stared at the floor.

"Remember. If she comes back. I'm sure my parents would let you move in with us."

Sophie always hoped for that, but I knew that taking in another child would be too much for her parents. I just smiled at her.

"Oh. Also, Everly cornered me."

"WHAT?" Sophie sat up a bit taller. "What do you mean by cornered?"

"She's pissed."

"At you?"

"Apparently she and Max had a thing this summer. They slept together," I said.

Sophie put her hands up to her mouth. "Does she still want him?"

I nodded.

"She threatened you?"

"Yup." I nodded again.

"What did you do?"

"I didn't have to do much. I was down the hall from the office, so she was too afraid to try anything."

"Oh my. I mean. Thank God for small favors."

"Right?" I smirked. "So, anyway. Now I know he's not a virgin, so I have decided to sleep with him." I said the last part really quickly.

Sophie coughed a little bit. I stood.

"I'm fine. I'm fine. Just—What?" she stammered.

I looked away from her, out the window. From the window, I could stand and look down at the river. I could see the rush hour traffic. The bridges were all full of cars. Some dedicated runners were passing the sculpture garden through the snow. An ambulance zipped past. I looked to my right to see the Blue Mountain range that the Susquehanna River cut through.

"Hey. Come back to me here," Sophie said loudly. "You can't just say that then turn your back!"

I took a deep breath, trying to gather my thoughts.

"I'm going to sleep with him."

"You've only been together a few days."

"I want to keep him."

"Mia. He likes you. Why rush?"

"Because that's what I have to do to keep an older guy."

"Okay. Can you think about it for a little?"

I nodded, but I was already thinking about what I was going to do. I looked her in the eyes and said, "Will you help me figure this out? My mom never told me anything about all this. I have no idea."

"So... wait."

"Never mind, let's just change the subject."

"Really?" she snapped. "What are you trying to prove?"

"Nothing." I looked down at the tiled floor. "You're right."

"I don't believe you."

"No. Drop it," I said, with a slightly louder voice.

"Mia!"

"DROP IT!"

She had no idea how much I just needed something to cling to. How much I needed someone to choose me over everything else. Max was always nice to me. Always.

"Changing the subject." I grabbed her backpack and opened it. "Here's your homework folder. Let me know if you need help. They didn't send much for you this time."

"That's good, I guess?"

"Yeah, so I can get you caught up if you'd like."

"Mia! Stop. We need to talk about this."

I flopped into the chair next to Sophie's bed. "There's really nothing to talk about. You wouldn't understand."

"Oh, I wouldn't. Really? Remember, my boyfriend is attending a boarding school that is nowhere in this vicinity. You don't think I feel that pressure?"

That was the first time she ever mentioned feeling pressure about sex. She loved swooning over kissing him.

"Mia, think about it. I'm always sick. You know he's had problems with that. I've thought about doing it to keep him."

My mouth fell open. He would often break up with her because he was scared and couldn't deal with her illness. It shattered her when he did that, but they always got back together.

"I'm sorry. I didn't think."

"It's fine. I just think we should both talk about it."

I looked at her and didn't say a word.

"You have time. I don't. I feel like I should just get on with it."

"Sophie, you have time."

"No. I don't think so. There's been a lot of whispering between doctors and my parents. Something's going on."

"Isn't the whispering normal?"

"Not with my mom crying, it's not."

"Does this have to do with the transplant?"

Her face grew red. "I'm not doing it. I can't."

"Why, Sophie? I want you around longer."

"I can't imagine someone dying so I can have new lungs."

"It would be someone who was in a car accident or something like that. It's not like you would be the cause of the accident."

Tears started running down her cheek. I stood up and stretched out beside her on the bed.

"That's not it, Mia. Don't you understand? I have the body of a 10-year-old. I'm tiny."

"Right? What does that have to do with anything?"

"Mia. Don't you get it? That means I would need a child's lungs. A child would have to die for me to have a transplant. I can't." Tears started streaming heavily. I held her more tightly.

"I get it. I do. But you wouldn't be causing the child's death."

"I'm not doing it."

"Don't you think your mom will make that decision?"

"I can refuse. The courts could get involved, but I don't think my parents would put me through that."

I said absolutely nothing. I didn't know what to say, so I just held her.

"Don't pressure me. I'm sure I have time to make this decision."

"Are you sure? I need you."

She wiped her tears. "Yeah. Yeah, I am sure. I have time. I'm okay."

"You better be." There was no way I could comprehend what she was going through. "Soph?"

"Yeah?"

"I'm sorry. I didn't fully understand what was going on. I shouldn't have snapped at you."

"We both have a lot going on. It's okay. I love you."

"I love you too." I grabbed a tissue and handed one to her, then patted my own cheeks with the other. "Have you heard from Ryan?"

"Yeah, we've been texting."

"Does he know you're here?" I asked.

She started using her thumb to play with the promise ring he'd given her.

"Sophie?" I said with a soft voice.

She still didn't answer.

I lay there next to her, waiting for her to tell me.

"No. He doesn't know," she finally admitted.

"Why?" I'm not sure why I asked. I already knew the answer.

"You already know. He can't handle this."

"Why are you with him?" I asked.

She started laughing. "I'm addicted. I don't know."

"Soph. You have to tell him."

"Why?" she asked.

"Don't you think he'd be worried?"

"I don't know." She sniffed through her nose. "What is with us? Good lord."

I hugged her closer. "I know, right?"

We started laughing again.

The nurse yelled in from the hallway, "Am I going to have to run in there again?" which only made us laugh more.

Sophie gave a small cough, then said, "No, I'm in control this time."

"I don't know what's going on with my dad or my mom. I just want to come live with you."

"YES! Please? I can't imagine my parents would say no."

Ever since we had been little, Sophie and I daydreamed about what it would be like to be sisters. It's something we always talked about when she was in the hospital. I think it made us feel closer to each other at a time when we both needed it.

- Chapter Twenty-Nine -

I woke up to Sophie's mom shaking my leg. "Mia, honey," she said, quietly. "Your dad is outside waiting in his car. He looks upset. He said you were late and he's been trying to call you."

I sat up slowly, trying not to wake Sophie. "Thank you."

She gave me a small smile. I got off the bed as carefully as I could. I grabbed for the McDonald's trash, but Sophie's mom stopped me.

"Don't worry about it; I'll clean it up." She took the trash from my hands. "Just go out to your dad. He didn't seem at all happy."

"Oh." My phone vibrated on the window sill. "Crap. Okay. Thanks." I grabbed my phone, threw on my coat, and hugged her. Then I walked over to Sophie and kissed her gently on the forehead. "Um, how long will she be here this time?"

"We aren't sure."

"Okay. I'll try to come back again this week. Oh, and the school sent some homework."

"Thanks, Mia. Now get going."

I left the room, still in a bit of a sleep stupor. My head felt dizzy. I almost never fell asleep in the hospital with Sophie. I had sat and watched her sleep many times, but I had never fallen asleep myself without intending to. The prior days had been a lot for me. I guess I had just needed to collapse someplace where I felt safe. And I felt safe with her. Sophie was my home.

I walked past the nurses' station and waved at them, then got on the elevator. Once again, I was alone, staring at my reflection in the elevator door. I looked just as tired and red-eyed as Sophie's mom. I shook my body, trying to wake up.

The lobby was more crowded than it had been when I arrived. At the gift shop, a line of people was waiting to buy flowers. The coffee cart was doing good business, too. I thought about stopping to get a coffee for my dad and me, but then my phone vibrated again. I pulled it out of my pocket.

Dad: Mia, are you coming? I've been waiting a while.

No coffee then. I left the hospital. My father was parked in front of the doors. He was fuming. His knuckles were white where his hands gripped the steering wheel. His face was held tight. My stomach sank.

He turned toward me but didn't smile as I climbed in the passenger door. The seat was uncomfortable. Suddenly I wished I'd asked Max to pick me up.

"Hey, Dad! Sorry, I fell asleep with Sophie." My voice sounded small. I was waiting for the yell.

"It's fine." He started the car and pulled out with a screech.

We drove in silence until I spoke up. "Dad, I'm sorry. Things have been hard, and I just collapsed."

"Mia, I don't have time for this. I'm trying very hard here."

"What do you mean?"

He took a deep breath. "They won't hire me unless I take a traveling position."

"Oh. So you'll be looking for another job? I'm sure something will pop up."

"No, Mia." His jaw was clenched so tightly, I could see it. Hell, I could sense it.

"No?" I looked at him intently. "What do you mean, no?"

"I had to take the job they offered. I wasn't prepared for that. We don't have enough money saved. I had to take the first job offered to me."

"You don't have your old job? I thought you just came home on vacation or something."

"No, I had no leave. When I said I needed to come home they fired me."

"What? But we have no money? What happened?"

"I don't know if you know this, but it's expensive to raise a child. So, I'm sorry. But I have to take what I can get now."

I was holding my breath, too afraid to breathe.

"Mia. If I can't feed you–"

I cut him off. "Dad, you'll be away from home all the time, again. Am I supposed to just live by myself? I don't even have my license."

"Your mother will be moving back."

It was like he slapped me right across the face.

"What are you talking about? You saw what she did to me."

"Well. Mia. Come on. Stop acting spoiled and entitled. You need to be more understanding. Your mother is dealing with a lot."

My mother? There was another verbal slap.

"I've seen her lash out only one time in the fifteen years you've been alive. I refuse to believe it's like that all the time."

"What?!" I snapped. Loudly.

"She just had a moment. You should try to be a little more humble."

"Humble?"

"Understanding," he said in a tone that felt like a growl.

"Dad, I can't live with her. I'm afraid of her."

"Don't be ridiculous. She's your mother."

I stopped talking. My entire body was tense. I chewed my tongue to stop myself from crying.

"Just deal with it. You'll only be home for a few more years anyway."

I ignored him.

My phone vibrated in my hand. I looked down at it.

Max: Hey cutie. How's Sophie?

Mia: Can I see you tonight?

Max: Sure. Should I come over?

"Mia, we are talking. Get off your phone!" my father yelled.

"It's just Max asking how Sophie is doing. I need to answer him."

"Not right now you don't. Put the damn phone away."

"Fine."

I hated that I couldn't answer Max. I was worried he would get mad at me. I put my phone in my purse. It kept vibrating.

"Don't you dare touch it," my dad said.

"I'm not," I answered, my eyes wide. I thought I would appeal to the sweet side of my father. "Daddy, please don't let her move back in. I am afraid of her. I could have died when she kicked me out of the house in the snowstorm."

"Oh don't be dramatic," he spat. "You're always so dramatic. Do you have any idea what I went through with my own parents?"

"That doesn't excuse anything, Dad."

"Your generation? Your generation is producing a bunch of weaklings. That's what is really happening here. I got hit all the time and I turned out just fine."

"Did you turn out fine?" I didn't know what to do with this sudden change. Just a few days ago he had said he was going to protect me. Now this? Something must have happened in his interview.

"That's it. Keep your mouth shut."

I did as instructed for the rest of the ride home. In fact, I wouldn't even look in his direction. I kept my face turned toward the passenger side window. We drove all the way home in complete silence. Once we got up the mountain and to our garage, I jumped out of the car as quickly as I could. My father grabbed my arm, but I kept moving. I pulled my arm away from him, ran inside, and up to my bedroom.

My phone vibrated.

Max: Mia?
Max: You still there?
Mia: Yeah. sorry. Can you just come get me? Can we hang out at your house, or something?
Max: Sure. Give me an hour?
Mia: k

I turned to look at myself in the mirror and realized that I had spent the day in dirty sweats, hair in a messy top knot, and no make-up. This was NOT the way to attract him. I quickly walked to the bathroom and jumped in the shower. It was the fastest shower I'd ever taken. The water never even had time to heat up. I got out, wrapped myself in a towel, and left the bathroom. Back in my room, I ran a bit of leave-in conditioner through my hair, grabbed my blow dryer, flipped my head upside down, and started blowing my hair dry. It felt like it was taking forever, so I stopped halfway through. I ran to my dresser to find something that would be sexy, but also not look like I was try-ing too hard. I chose a light baby blue sweater, one that would come off easily without smudging my makeup, and a pair of jeans. The blue sweater matched my eyes, so I thought it was perfect. I had recently watched a YouTuber who talked about what turns men on. She said to wear things that compliment your best quality. That's why I chose the blue sweater. She also said to wear short skirts, but I didn't want to overdo it. Besides, it was freezing out, if my dad saw me going out in a short skirt he would stop me.

I opened my top drawer where I kept my make-up and repeated the words I'd heard on YouTube, "Go a little more dramatic than natural." Encouraged, I grabbed subtle make-up, remembering that she'd also said not to wear dark lipstick if you plan on kissing. A light pink stain should do it. It's supposed to stay on while kissing. That's what the ad says, anyway. Perfect. I ran my brush through my hair. Sure, it was still partially wet, but it was perfectly straight. It looked good. I spun around to figure out what shoes to wear, spotted my Vans checkered slides, and slid them onto my feet. I didn't want to have to deal with boots or shoelaces.

I took one more look in the mirror. I thought I looked good. Not sexy, but I didn't have time to plan sexy. Then I started questioning my choice. After all, he didn't even know what I was planning. What if he turned me down? What if he laughed at me? I didn't care. I had to try. I wanted to make him happy. If Emma was right? This was the only way to do it. I ignored the fact that he and Everly had ended up breaking up anyway. He would stick with me. I was different. This relationship was different.

- Chapter Thirty -

I heard my phone vibrate on my bed. I grabbed it and swiped to read the message.

Max: Just got to the mountain. I'll be there in about five minutes.

I put the phone in my back pocket. Stuffing chapstick in my purse, I had a thought that almost stopped me completely. Birth control: I didn't have a condom or anything. In fact, I had never had a condom. In fact, I wouldn't even know what to do with a condom. I looked at myself one more time in the mirror. I walked forward to look close up. I put my hands on my dresser and leaned in closer. I looked deep inside my eyes. I suddenly got nervous. I bit my lip and furrowed my brows at myself. Maybe I should text him and say that I couldn't come out. But I couldn't do that. He was driving up the mountain in the dark, and it just wouldn't be safe.

"No big deal," I told myself. If I chicken out, he'll never know because we've never discussed it at all. I took a deep breath and blew it out, blowing my hair away from my face in the process. Was this it? Would I be a completely different person when I returned home and looked in the mirror again tonight? I thought about his kisses and how they made me feel. How I wanted to be so close to him in the Pizza Grill parking lot that I had wanted to climb onto his lap. I had never felt like that before. I leaned back, picked my hands up off my dresser, ran my fingers through my hair, and nodded at myself. That was it. My mind was made up. I was doing it. I spun around, turned off my light, and left my room. My father wasn't downstairs; he was already in his room. He hadn't spoken to me since we got home, so I didn't think he wanted to discuss where I was going. After all, when push came to shove, he'd proven that he didn't really care about me at all.

When I saw Max's headlights shine through the front window, I grabbed my coat and put it on. I yelled upstairs, "Dad, I'm going to hang out with Max. I'll be home by ten." Without waiting for an answer, I opened the front door and left the house.

I was on the porch before Max even had time to park. He pulled his truck to a stop. I think the wheels were still moving a little when I opened the passenger side door and hopped in. I was ready, and I wanted to get on with it.

"Hey, beautiful."

"Hey." I leaned over the middle compartment to give him a kiss on the cheek, but he turned his head and my small peck landed on his lips.

"Well, hello." His warm breath touched my lips. He smelled like cinnamon gum. I felt dizzy. I leaned into his lips, opening mine slightly. He leaned into my kiss at the same time. I heard his breath change. Then suddenly, he pulled back. "Yeah, so. We should get out of here. Yeah?"

"Yeah." I had completely forgotten about my dad for a moment. And, I didn't care. After what he told me today, it was obvious my father didn't care either.

I had butterflies in my stomach as Max pulled his truck onto the dark mountain road. My hands were shaking. My lips felt hot. "So, where are we going?"

"Well, I guess that depends on you? We could go hang out with my little brother and play video games."

"Mmmm, nah."

"Didn't think so. Hmm, let's see. We could drive into town and get pizza."

"I already had dinner."

"Yeah, so did I."

"What else is there?" I wasn't going to suggest anything. I had no idea what to say or how to act. I just wanted to kiss him again, but I wasn't about to say that.

"Well. I know of this secluded area. It's a small road off the river right in town, but no one ever goes back there, no one lives in the house. We could go there and talk?"

That was my chance to have his arms wrapped around me again. To have his lips meet mine.

"Talking sounds good to me." I took a deep breath after saying that. Something inside of me wanted him to pull over immediately, but I needed to wait.

We came to the first stoplight off of the mountain. He turned to me, bit his lower lip, and said, "Okay." The red of the stoplight was shining off his face making his eyes sparkle. And the way he bit his lip? I was dying. "How long is this light?"

"Pretty long," I said, smiling.

He stroked my face with the back of his hand, then leaned over toward me. I leaned into him, and we kissed again. And again, the cinnamon breath hit my face. He leaned back in his seat and took a large breath in and out. I could see his jaw muscles flex as he chewed his gum. He put his hands back on the wheel and started tapping his thumb. His left leg bounced up and down. Was he nervous too?

We drove through town. I could see there was a gang hanging out at the pizza place. Everly was outside talking on her phone. Max had to stop at the stop sign in front of the restaurant. I tried not to look at Everly, but I couldn't help it. I glanced over. She was standing there with her mouth wide open. Once she noticed my gaze, she threw up her middle finger.

"Ugh, I'm so sorry," he said. "She's psycho."

"Did I tell you she stopped me in the hallway today?

"No. What do you mean?" He looked at me. "Did she try to hurt you?"

"No. Not exactly."

"Did she threaten you?"

"Well, yeah."

He had already started driving, but once he heard me say "yeah," he stopped the truck so quickly that it threw my body forward.

"Max, no. Don't worry about it. I'm not afraid of someone hitting me."

"No. It's not okay." He jumped out of his truck, with the motor still running, and walked over to her. I watched them in the side mirror. They were yelling at each other. I turned down the radio to try to hear them. I couldn't make out what they were saying, but it was obvious they were screaming. He was keeping his distance from her. She threw her arms out from the sides of her body and cocked her head to the side as if she was threatening him. He pointed to the truck, still yelling, his face red.

As he walked back to the truck, I heard her scream, "Whatever, dick-head."

By this point, he was on the driver's side of his truck. "Leave her out of this!"

She held up her middle finger again.

He got in the truck and slammed his door shut.

"I am so, so sorry that she's like this."

"It's okay. I'm used to psychopaths."

"What does that mean?"

"Nothing," I said.

He slammed his hands on the steering wheel, took a few cleansing breaths, and turned his head toward me.

"You're still in the middle of the road, you know?" I pointed out.

"Yeah." He smiled a thin smile at me, then began driving again.

Everly ran after the truck and actually threw a snowball at it, but we were out of range. After that, we rode in silence to the old abandoned road.

Near the river, he pulled onto a road that was so overgrown I hadn't even realized it was there. The road was bumpier than the one to get to my house, but he somehow avoided the larger holes in the ground as if he knew exactly where he was going.

"How do you know about this road?"

"I like to take photographs of the house. So, I'm here a lot. Not usually at night though."

He stopped in front of the house. To my eye, it looked haunted.

"Can you give me a moment?" he asked.

"Sure."

"K, stay here?"

He jumped out of his truck, keeping it running and the lights on. He walked a few paces out from the truck. I'm sure he didn't realize the lights were shining on him, almost like a stage spotlight. I watched him pace back and forth, running his fingers through his hair. When he knelt down and put his head in his hands, I took that as my cue to get out and go to him.

I climbed out of the truck, not even shutting the door, and ran to him. He was still kneeling, so I bent down and put my arm around his neck. I could feel the tension in his back.

"What's going on? She's not worth all this, is she?"

"No, no she definitely is not," he said. His head was still in his hands.

"So what's happening?"

"Nothing. She worries me."

"What do you mean?"

"She's psychotic. That's what I mean. I'm worried she's going to hurt you or burn down my house or something."

"Don't worry about me."

"I shouldn't have slept with her this summer. That's when it turned weird. She gets jealous of every person I talk to." He stood up and started pacing again. "She even tried to become best friends with my mom." He stopped walking and turned to me. "I'm sorry. I am so, so sorry. You probably didn't want to know that. That I went all the way with her."

He was right. I didn't want to know it. I wished he hadn't slept with her, that he'd waited for me. "No, I already knew."

"You did?"

"She told me today."

"So I have a stalker, who I slept with."

He really could have stopped at "stalker."

"But you didn't run away from me? You really aren't afraid of her?"

"I mean, I'd be stupid not to be. But I'm used to that."

"What do you mean by that?"

"Nothing. Just—I know how to take a hit. I'm fine." The fact that I said that out loud actually gave me chills. I was used to it. *How sick is that?*

He looked at me, then approached slowly. When he was about two feet away he walked faster until he grabbed me in his arms and held me tight. "Who hurt you?"

I pulled my arms up around him. He rested his chin on the top of my head.

"No one. It's okay."

He held me tighter. "Are you lying?"

"Yes," I answered.

"Do you want to talk about it?"

"No."

"Okay." He stood there holding me for a bit longer, then he took his chin off my head. As he pulled his upper body back, he took my face in his hand and tilted my head up. I faced him. Both of us had tears in our eyes. "I won't let anyone hurt you."

"That's something you can't promise."

"I can't let anyone hurt you. You are this beautiful precious flower."

"I'm tougher than you think."

He turned toward the side of the overgrown road and spit the gum out of his mouth. I went up on my tiptoes. He leaned down toward me. Our lips collided in a flurry of heat. One of his hands ran through my hair, the other splayed against the small of my back. He held me tighter. Our bodies matched. I thought the kiss was over when he pulled his mouth back from mine, but when he ran his lips across my neck shivers climbed up my body. I melted. This was it. Was this it? I pulled up the back of his coat and shirt, and put my hand on his back. His skin was warm. So, so warm. I shivered against the cold winter air and pulled myself closer. I wanted to be as close to him as I possibly could. What should I do next? I wasn't sure. Then he moved back to my mouth. His tongue danced with mine, sweetly, then more intense. So this was what everyone was talking about. This was kissing. Like, actual kissing. Everything about him told me he loved me, everything. Suddenly, I knew the difference between making love and having sex. With her, it had been sex. With me, though? With me, he'd be making love. Love that started with this amazing kiss.

Suddenly, he pushed me away.

I had to catch my breath. "What? What's wrong?"

He bent over and put his hands on his thighs. "We need to stop."

"Why?"

"We can't go further. We just can't," he said.

"Did I do something wrong? I mean, I've never done this before, I–"

"No. No. Not at all."

"Don't you want me?" I was shocked.

He laughed a little bit, then stood up straight. "Look. You are young. We can't do this."

He turned, walked to his truck, and climbed in, not shutting the door.

I stood there frozen in the beams of the headlights, my body illuminated in the same way his had been earlier. But he wasn't coming to me to comfort me, the way I had gone to him. He just left me there to feel completely alone. And exposed. Tears lit for all the world to see. Alone. Unloved. My worst fear. No one wanted me. No one. I felt like running after him, like begging him to want me. But I didn't. I just stood there. A shell of myself in the spotlight of hell.

Lights appeared in the woods. They reminded me of something, but I couldn't think what. They were getting closer. Then they turned red and blue. Flashing. They were flashing. Clarity struck.

"Shit," Max said. He got out of the truck and stepped over to me.

Two police cars approached. They parked in the back of Max's truck. The officers emerged and walked toward us.

"What are you two doing here?" the female asked.

"I just wanted to show her this house. I like to take photos here sometimes."

"At night? Doesn't seem like a good time to take photos.

"Well, no. We weren't taking pictures. I just wanted to show her," Max answered.

"You know this is private property, right?"

"Oh. I didn't realize."

"Can I talk to you privately, son?" the male officer asked.

"Yes sir."

Max approached the male police officer. The female officer approached me.

"Are you okay? Did he force you to come here?" she asked, trying to show concern in her voice.

"No, Ma'am," I answered honestly.

"We had a call from someone who said they saw you getting into this truck, then saw the truck turn down this road. They were worried you were in trouble."

"What? No. He picked me up at my house."

"Okay. Can you call your parents? I'd like to make sure that's the case."

My stomach dropped. "My dad doesn't know where I am."

"Well, then, I'm going to drive you home."

"No. Really. I'm okay. I have a ride. Max will take me home."

"How old are you?"

"Fifteen."

"Well, fifteen is too young to be with a guy alone in the woods. Go get in the squad car." She led me to her car. As she opened the back side door, she raised her voice so her partner could hear her say, "Jim, I'm taking her home."

"Okay. Sounds good," came the reply. "I'm going to send this one on his way."

I looked at Max and shrugged that I was sorry, then I got in the car.

I felt cramped in the back. My knees hit the back of the seat in front of me. Plexiglass separated me from the front. I felt squeezed. I tried to open the door before she started driving. I needed out. It wouldn't open. I was stuck.

The officer got in and turned around. "Look. You are far too young to be out here like this. It's not safe and trespassing is a crime." Her voice sounded strange through the partition.

I was shaking, scared, but numb too. "Am I in trouble?"

"Not with the police, but I am going to have to deliver you to your door."

I didn't say anything, but a different sort of panic set in. I had no idea how my father would react. I've never had any encounters with the police at all. And now I was being driven home by one? I was in serious trouble. I knew it. All I could think was that at least my mother wouldn't be home. I rode in the car quietly all the way to my house.

The officer did not have the red and blue lights on when she drove down my road. Small favors. When we got to the house she got out and released me from the back. My mom's car was parked in front of the garage. *No. No, please no.*

The officer walked me to the front door. I reached for the doorknob, but she stopped me and rang the doorbell herself. I felt like I was going to faint. Through the door window, I could see my mother walking casually to the door in a housecoat. Then she saw the officer. Her eyes scanned the yard, then landed on me. I saw a fleeting hint of triumph in her eyes just before she opened the door and burst onto the porch.

"Baby, my baby. Where have you been? We've been so worried." She grabbed me and held me tight.

Never mind the fact that she was in a housecoat. They weren't worrying at all.

"What happened to you? Are you okay?"

"Ma'am ..." the officer began.

My mom let go of me to let the officer speak.

"We found your daughter in the woods just outside of town."

"WHAT? How? What happened? Oh my God, was she abducted? Was my daughter abducted?"

"No ma'am, we don't believe that to be the case—"

"Then what IS the case?" my mother interrupted.

"Your daughter was there. With a boy."

My mother's tone changed completely. "A boy?" my mother snapped. "What boy? Was it that Max?"

"Yes Ma'am," the officer nodded. "They were alone, in the dark, at night. So I brought her home."

"Well, I mean. Didn't we all do that in our teen years?"

"They were also trespassing on private property."

My mother fanned her face as if she were about to faint.

"Mom, we didn't know it was private property." I tried to explain.

"Officer, is she under arrest?"

"No ma'am. I just wanted to get her home safely."

My mother thanked the officer, then turned to me and said, "Get inside, Mia." She didn't add, "Right this very minute or you're dead," but I heard it nevertheless.

"Have a good night, ma'am," the officer said, then returned to her squad car.

My mother slammed the door shut as she followed me into the house. My father flinched at the noise, his steps soft on the carpeted stairs as he descended from the second floor. I was relieved to see him until I noticed that he was wearing only boxers.

"What's going on?" he asked. "Was that a police car?"

"Yes. It was." My mother grabbed me by the hair, then dragged me to the kitchen and slammed me into a chair. Still holding my hair, she got up close to my face and spat at me. I tried to wipe the spit from my face, but as she let go of my hair, my head snapped forward and she grabbed my hand, hard. She squeezed it until my fingers went numb, then slammed it down to my side.

My dad's voice was a whisper compared to hers. "Kim, let's hear what happened," he said.

I had had enough. "No, I would like to know what's going on HERE," I screamed. "Are you two back together? It certainly looks like it."

My mom started laughing. Like, actually laughing. "Of course we are dear, you didn't think you could ruin us, did you? You are just a child. You understand nothing."

To my dad she said, "She went for a joyride with Max and ended up trespassing on private property. Is this what happens when I'm gone for just a few days? Did you not realize she left?"

"I thought she was in her room."

"Dad, I told you I was leaving with Max."

"No, no you didn't."

"You were in your room, ignoring me."

"Enough with the backtalk!" She slapped me across the face. "Get upstairs to your room. I don't want to see your face."

"Fine." I jumped up, not feeling the effects of the slap yet.

"No, stop. Give me your phone."

"Mom. I have to text Sophie. She's in the hospital."

"Well. You should have thought of that before taking off in the middle of the night with some guy."

"Mom, it's not the middle of the night. It's only 8:30."

"Give me your damn phone." She stood with her hand out.

I took my phone out of my purse and handed it to her. Then I turned and ran to my room. I'd managed to hold my tears, but once I got to my bed, all was lost. I cried before sobbing, my pillow my only friend.

- Chapter Thirty-One -

He was probably texting my phone. He probably thought I was ignoring him. Email. *I still had email.* I went to the computer. I had no idea what was going on, even before the police arrived, something odd had been going on. I mean, would Max even pick me up for school the next day? I had no idea.

I watched the screen, impatiently waiting to open my email. Nervous. My tears stopped. What was taking so long? My palms were sweating. I bounced my knee. Would he even check his email? He had to. If I didn't answer my texts, I'm sure he'd check his email. Right?

Finally, my desktop appeared and I clicked on my email. My email wasn't loading. I realized my internet was searching. A box popped up saying, "Parental controls are on." I stopped breathing. She had cut off my internet access.

I jumped up and ran downstairs. My parents were sitting on the couch, cuddling and watching television. I wanted to throw things. I wanted to throw things at them. *How dare they?* I walked up behind them.

"What the hell?" I boomed.

They both turned their bodies toward me at the same time.

My mother smiled, "What's wrong dear?" Then she laughed.

"Why did you turn off my internet access?"

She stood up, but I didn't cower. I stood up straight as she walked over to me.

"Oh dear," she said with a snark in her voice. "Well, if you get brought home by the police, you're going to lose some privileges. Internet access is one of those privileges." She said the word privileges like it was a knife.

I had to think on my feet. "Mom, I need it. I have homework."

"Well, you should have thought of that before going on your little joy ride."

"Really, mom. You're not going to give me access for homework?"

"No. Speak to your teachers. Tell them what happened."

"Mom, nothing happened! We were just talking."

She laughed again. She found this fun. "Now, why don't I believe you?" Then she pointed her perfectly manicured index finger toward the steps. "You should turn around and go back upstairs."

I huffed loudly, then did what she required. As I ran up the steps I could hear her laughing. My dad didn't stick up for me at all. He just sat on the couch with his eyes trained on the TV screen.

I stopped on the landing, turned around and squatted, and yelled down, "Mom, can I at least call Max? I have no idea if he's picking me up for school tomorrow."

"No, Mia. I'll be driving you to school."

"But, Mom, what if he drives all the way here for nothing."

"Oh, I'm sorry. Should I care?"

I got up and went to my room. I slammed my door, then leaned against it. I sank down into a fetal position, holding my hair. My scalp hurt where she had pulled it. I didn't know what to do.

- Chapter Thirty-Two -

I couldn't sleep at all that night. I kept replaying everything that had happened. I was ready to give Max everything, and he pushed me away. Why did he push me away? Didn't he want me? Did I read all of this wrong? Also, who called the police. The officers specifically said that a truck picked a girl up off the street. What was up with that? Then it hit me. Everly. So obvious, why didn't I realize it before? It was her. She was going to do anything she could to get him back and she didn't care who she harmed in the process. She really was a psychopath.

I tossed and turned. What else would she do to ruin my life? Did I need to be concerned? I got up and grabbed Sophie's rock. Somehow it made me feel better. Instantly better. Not all the way better, but that little piece of her helped me so much. I just wish she would be with me at school the next day, but that would take at least another week.

Finally, the morning sun peeked through my curtains. I rubbed my eyes, exhausted. I didn't want to face my mom at all, but I knew I had to. She was hell-bent on driving me to school. Hard to get out of that. Even though I was tired, I had to look good for school. I needed to keep Max's attention and show Everly that I wasn't phased by what she did. I needed to look like I had gotten a long night of sleep and was refreshed. Time to get moving with a cold shower to wake myself up. I prayed the cold water would get rid of my puffy eyes. It worked.

Back in my room, I chose a tight white sweater and a short pleated red skirt. Then I put on thick cable knit tights. It was still winter, after all. I grabbed my red Doc Marten boots. After I put on my makeup and made sure my hair was straight like a stick, I walked downstairs.

My mother was waiting there for me. I tried to go to the kitchen, but she stopped me. "Where do you think you're going? I need to get you to school."

"I was just going to get something to eat."

"No. There's no time."

"Mom, I'm early. I have time."

"No, you really don't." At first, I didn't have a clue about what she was doing, but then it hit me, she was trying to get me out of the house before Max showed up.

"Mom, can I at least grab a pop tart?"

"Fine," she snapped. She turned to watch me as I walked into the kitchen. "We don't have time for you to toast it," she yelled into the kitchen.

"Whatever." I would never have talked to my mom like that in the past, but I didn't care anymore.

"Don't talk to me like that."

I said nothing, just grabbed the box of strawberry pop tarts, got a pack, and walked back out to the living room.

"Are you ready now?"

"I guess." In the foyer, I grabbed my backpack and coat, then opened the door.

"Come on, let's go. Quicker." She was totally trying to get me off the mountain before Max drove up.

I got in the car and slammed the door shut as loudly as I possibly could.

She got in her side and started the car to warm it up. I was freezing in my small skirt. She turned to me, "How DARE you talk to me like that in front of your father?"

"What are you talking about?"

"After everything we've gone through, you will respect me in front of your father."

"Why do you care? He already saw you hit me."

"Right, well. It will happen again and again if you keep this up. YOU are the reason he kicked me out." She was pointing her long finger at my face. "If it weren't for you, we would have been fine. But because of you—YOU—I had to stay with your grandmother."

"How is that my fault? He saw who you really were for a brief moment." I was feeling brave.

"That's just because you are a disrespectful little bitch. He didn't know the whole story, but now he does. I filled him in. And you being brought home by the cops last night played right into my proof. So thanks for that."

"Mom, nothing happened. It was all very innocent."

"I'm sure, who would want to have sex with you?"

My mouth fell open. "What?"

"Now your father knows he has an unruly teen at home, one that he can't possibly raise by himself. Face it, you helped me get back into the house for good."

"Mom, you were there when I got home. It sure looked like that decision had already been made before I got there."

"You cemented it. I should be thanking you." She laughed again. "In fact, he's going to be traveling again. So it will just be you and me."

I looked out the window and refused to talk anymore. She drove off the mountain. When we hit the stop at the bottom, Max was there getting ready to turn toward my house. He saw me in my mother's car and frowned. I tried to give him a sheepish smile, but my mother saw and laid on the horn. He jumped at the sound. I stared at her. She rolled the window down and stuck her arm out. What was she doing? Then her hand raised in a gesture I knew well. She gave him the finger.

"Mom, what the hell are you doing?" I screamed.

She balled up her other fist and hit me in the thigh. When she took her right turn, I looked out the back window and watched his truck get smaller and smaller in the distance. I swallowed hard and bit my tongue. I was not going to give her the satisfaction of seeing me cry.

- Chapter Thirty-Three -

I walked through the double doors at the back of the school. I decided that I needed to hold my head high, not let Everly see that she had any effect on me. My leg hurt where my mother had punched me, but I ignored it. It wasn't the first time I had ignored the pain inflicted by my mother. I walked forward.

Everly was standing at my locker with her arms crossed. I could see her looking through the crowd of morning students. I paused, uncertain whether to stick with my morning routine or to avoid confrontation. *Meh.* I raised my head and decided to keep on with my course. I was not going to hide from her. What more could she do to me?

As I approached, a sly smile spread across her face, but I stared her right in the eyes.

"Hello, Everly."

"Oh. I didn't realize I was standing in front of your locker."

"Yes. Excuse me, please?"

"Of course." She moved her body slightly to the side to allow me a small space to open my locker and put my coat away.

"I saw the police driving down that old dirt road Max likes so much."

"Yeah. How about that? Strange." I looked directly into her eyes and shrugged.

"You know, he used to take me there all the time." She laughed a bit, then continued. "Yeah, that's where we always went when we wanted–you know–privacy."

"That's nice. Well. As you know, we didn't get any privacy last night."

"Well, that's a shame. Isn't it."

"Nah, I'm not too worried about it."

Her smile faded just as I felt arms wrap around me and lips graze my neck.

"Oh. Hi, Everly. I didn't notice you there," Max said. I turned into his embrace. My lips smashed into his and we kissed, right there in the hallway.

"Whatever!" Everly said.

I turned my head to see her walking away.

Max placed his hands on the sides of my hips and stepped away from me a bit.

"You didn't text me back last night. Are you okay?"

"I'm fine. My mom stole my phone and blocked my internet access."

"Oh. Yeah. My parents weren't too happy with me either. Well, my mom wasn't, anyway. She yelled, but my dad fist bumped me."

I was embarrassed by his last comment but chose to ignore it. "So, you aren't in trouble?"

"Not really."

The first bell rang. I had to get to class, but I needed to know what had happened last night–before the police got there.

"Can I ask a question?"

"Sure."

"Don't you want me?"

He took a step back. "What do you mean?"

"I mean, we were kissing, then you pushed me away and got in your truck. You left me there."

He ran his fingers through his hair. "Right, well." He shifted his weight back and forth from one foot to the other as if the question made him more than just a little bit nervous. "We don't have time to talk about it right now. Can I drive you home?"

"No, my mom will be picking me up. I'm on lockdown, apparently."

"Okay. Lunch? We can find somewhere to talk."

"Sure." Now I was nervous. He seemed upset.

"Okay. I have to get to pre-calc." He walked away, then called over his shoulder, "I'll see you at lunch."

I stood there for a while, right in the middle of the hallway. People passed me on both sides. One person knocked into me. "Get out of the hall-way, GAWD!" Harsh words shook me from my trance.

I decided to go to the office instead of class. I couldn't text Sophie, but I knew the office would let me call the hospital.

As I walked through the doors to the main office, the secretary asked, "Hi, dear, what can I do for you?" Her smile was more welcoming than usual.

"I lost my phone, I was just wondering if I could call the hospital to check on Sophie?" That was a lie, of course I had the phone Sophie's mom had given me. But she made sure I knew to just use it for emergencies. I didn't think checking up on Sophie was an emergency.

"I'm not supposed to let anyone use the phones, but yeah, of course." She got up from her desk and beckoned me over.

"Thank you so much."

I sat in her chair. "Just dial nine, then the number."

"Can I have help finding the main number to the hospital?"

"Sure, dear." She squatted down and tapped on the keyboard to pull up the hospital website. Once it came up, she smiled at me and left the room. I scrolled through the hospital's page until I found the main phone number.

I reached for the phone and dialed.

"Hi. May I have Sophie Keller's room?"

I heard the phone click, then ring through.

"Hello?" Sophie answered.

"Hey, Soph."

"Mia! What are you doing calling the hospital number? Why didn't you call my cell?"

"My mom took my phone last night, and I couldn't remember your number."

"Where are you?"

"School."

"How are you calling me?"

"Main office phone."

"They let you do that? Why didn't you use my mom's phone"

"Yeah. I mean, I was calling you, and everyone loves you. So. And, this isn't exactly an emergency."

"Anyway. Your mom? Is she back? What's going on?"

"I'll tell you, but first. How are you?"

"I'm okay. Ryan is coming home next weekend, so I'm trying to get out of here as quick as I can."

"Did you ever tell him you were in the hospital?"

"No. And you know why. So shut it."

"Fine. I will send you healing vibes."

"Thank you. Do you still have the rock I gave you?" she asked.

"Of course. It's in my backpack right now."

"Okay. Good. Now, what's going on?"

"Well, my mom is mad that the police brought me home last night–"

"WHAT?" She actually shrieked.

I told her the entire story. In my mind's eye, I could see her sitting there with her mouth wide open. The thought made me smile.

"So yeah, that's what happened."

"Wait, he just let you stand there after pushing you away, then the police showed up?"

"Um hmm."

"I mean, I guess thank goodness for small miracles. Could you imagine how embarrassing it would have been had the police driven up when you were mid-grope?"

"I hadn't looked at it that way, actually. Besides, no real groping occurred."

"Do you know why he freaked out like that?"

"Nope, no idea."

She lowered her voice a bit. "Would you have gone through with it?"

"Gone through with what?" I asked.

"Would you have had sex with him?"

I lowered my voice to a whisper. "I mean, that was the plan. But I'm not sure."

"Girl," she said.

"Girl," I said back. "Stop." I was getting embarrassed.

We both started laughing, then she coughed a little bit.

"But really. How are you feeling?" I asked.

"I'm getting better. My mom seems more positive too. Maybe they've changed their minds about the transplant." She took a breath before continuing. "My doctor explained it to me last night. It's not as scary as I thought. It's just a way to get me on the list so that when I need it, I can be at the top of the list. So, I'll be on the list, but not active. Meaning, lungs will go to the next person on the list, skipping me, but I'll save my place for when it's actually needed."

"Okay, that doesn't sound as bad as I thought."

"Nah. I'm not freaking out over it. They can put my name on the list for that. I'm fine with it."

"That way you can just make a decision later?"

"Yeah. I'll make the actual decision later. When I need to."

I sighed in relief. "Thank God." I felt like I was going to cry. I didn't want to lose Sophie, ever. And the fact that she wanted to get on the list at all, made me feel like there was some sort of hope.

"Okay, I need to get to class. I probably won't be able to see you today. My mom is pretty pissed."

"WAIT!"

"WHAT?" I said, laughing.

"What's going on with your mom? We didn't talk about that."

"I told you about how my dad was acting weird, right?"

"Yeah?"

"When I was brought home last night, my mom was there in a house robe. Nothing has changed."

"Okay. I'm talking to my mom. You're moving in."

Instantly I felt guilty. "No. She has enough to worry about. It will be fine. It's high school. There will be a million reasons to be out of my house over the next few years."

"We'll talk about it later. Okay?" Sophie said.

"Fair."

"Love you. Don't murder Everly. 'K?"

I laughed. "I'm going to kill her with kindness. Love you, too." I hung up the phone, got up, and walked to class.

- Chapter Thirty-Four -

By lunch, I was incredibly nervous. I hadn't seen Max at all the rest of the morning, and it was freaking me out. I got to my table and threw my bag under it.

Lily was seated across the table, already eating. "Have you seen Max?"

She shook her head, no. "Not yet."

"Okay."

I went to get in line. I scanned the lunchroom. Still no sign of Max. Emma came up behind me. She made some small talk about theater auditions and a movie she had seen. I wasn't really listening. I added in little comments here and there so she didn't think I was ignoring her. My scan of the lunchroom was still producing no results.

"Hey, have you seen Max? Is he with Alex?" I asked her.

"Oh no. Alex is at home sick. He has a sore throat."

"Oh. Max and I were supposed to have lunch together."

"I mean, yeah, you have every day for a week."

"No, I mean, we have stuff to talk about."

"Well, that sounds serious."

"I'm not sure," I answered.

"I'm sure whatever it is, it will be fine."

The senior girls showed up and got in line behind us.

"Hello, freshman ladies. Still stealing all our guys?" Reagan said.

Behind her, Larkin and Marco were holding hands talking quietly. He was telling her what she should eat. She seemed annoyed by it but just kept smiling. I would have hated that, some guy telling me what I should eat. But she had been sick a lot, so maybe he was just taking care of her.

"So, how are Alex and Max?" Brooke asked.

"Good, they're good," I answered.

"Where did Max go? He just walked out. I guess he left for the day?" she asked me.

"He left school?"

"Yeah, you didn't know?"

"No. We were supposed to have lunch and talk."

She whispered under her breath, "Ohhhh–"

"Why? What's going on?"

"Nothing. Nothing at all. I'm sure it's fine." Brooke smiled at me and nodded her head up and down.

I bit my nails.

Larkin chimed in. "No, really. I'm sure there's a perfectly logical reason," she said.

"You're probably right," I answered.

"Did something happen?" Larkin asked.

"Kinda." I scanned the lunch room one more time and realized Everly wasn't in the cafeteria either. "Where's Everly?"

Larkin looked around the cafeteria. "Hmmm, I don't know." She shrugged her shoulders and turned back to Marco.

The looks on the faces of the senior girls triggered suspicion. Like they were simultaneously worried and knew something I didn't.

"What's going on?" I demanded.

Reagan inhaled loudly. "Okay, remember the whole thing I warned you about? That these guys will break your heart?"

I nodded, but just barely. I was biting my thumb nail trying not to cry.

"So, yeah. They dated this summer, right?"

I just kept nodding.

"They've slept with each other on and off all school year. So while they weren't really together? They've kind of been together this whole time."

I felt like I was going to throw up.

I didn't say a word. I didn't know what to say. *Why didn't anyone tell me?* I just stood staring at Reagan.

"I mean. I thought they wouldn't be doing that anymore since he started dating you," she said.

Still staring.

Reagan tried again. "I mean, I haven't seen them together at all. I'm sure it's fine."

"Did he leave with her?" I asked Brooke.

"I… don't know," she answered.

Still biting my nails, I got my lunch and went back to my seat. I sat and ate in complete silence. I had no idea what anyone was talking about. Anytime someone came into the cafeteria, I would jerk my head to see if it was either Max or Everly. Neither appeared. I had my answer. He was still with her. That's why she was acting psycho, and also why he pushed away from me. It was all becoming so clear. He was using me to make her jealous.

- Chapter Thirty-Five -

I went through the rest of the day on autopilot. I walked from class to class, not speaking to anyone. I was in a complete daze. Finally, when the last bell of the day rang, I walked to my locker, got my stuff, and met my mother in the parking lot.

"Hello, dear." She was putting on her sweet mom act. I was sure that would change swiftly.

"Hey, Mom."

"What's wrong, you look upset?" she asked.

"I think Max is with someone else right now." I'm not sure why I started talking to her about this. I had never told her anything important in the past. But I needed to talk to someone and the words just leaked out.

"Oh, honey. Are you sure?"

I just nodded.

"Okay, I'll tell you what, let's go for coffee. Okay? You can get that mocha with whipped cream you always like. Does that sound good?"

I nodded.

We sat at Capital Joe's Coffee. She ordered my coffee and a few chocolate chip cookies for us to share.

We took our coffee and cookies to a table and sipped.

"Do you want to talk about it?"

"I'm not sure. And I don't know for sure that he is with her."

"Her who?"

"Everly."

"Oh, that girl. She's always so prissy and bitchy out there on the football field cheering. She rubs me the wrong way."

"Yeah, well. I didn't realize she had something with Max." I thought that maybe talking to my mom would help our relationship.

"Is that the boy I saw her kissing behind the bleachers after homecoming?"

I shoved a cookie in my mouth to avoid replying.

"Well, then it's a good thing you were brought home last night. Look at it as a strong red flag." She picked up her purse and started digging. She pulled out my phone and handed it to me. The kindness of this act shocked me.

"Aren't I still grounded?"

"No, I think the whole situation was scary enough. And now he's not a problem anymore, is he?"

Those words stung. "I guess not."

"Do you want me to drop you off at the hospital?"

"Really?"

"Sure."

"Yes, please?"

"That will give your father and me some personal time. We have a lot of work to do since you convinced him I was evil."

"Mom. You–"

She held her hand up. "Stop. Don't explain. I might have a bit of a temper. It's true."

I thought to myself, *a bit?* But I didn't say it. She was actually being nice to me for once.

We sat finishing our coffee and the cookies. Then got up, threw away our cups, and left. The sky was beginning to get darker.

"Are we supposed to get snow?"

"I don't think so."

"It smells like snow."

"I'm sure it will be fine. You need to spend time with Sophie!"

Once inside my mother's car, I flipped through my phone. Tons of messages from Max.

Max: Are you okay?

Max: Mia. Are you okay?

Max: Why aren't you answering?

Max: I'm so sorry that happened. I've been there a million times before and no one ever called the police.

Yes, I already knew that, didn't I?

Max: Are you mad?
Max: I'm so sorry.
Max: Mia, please answer me.
Max: Damn it, Mia.

It went on and on like that. He seemed like he was freaking out. But I really didn't understand anything. If he was that upset, why did he just stand me up at school? Why didn't he ever tell me he was still sleeping with Everly. Why did he kiss me like that this morning in front of her? Why was he doing this to me?

I looked out the window for a few blocks, wondering if I should ask him where he went. I wrote a message out several times and kept deleting it. I didn't know what to do. Finally, I typed.

Mia: What happened to lunch?
Max: You got your phone back?
Mia: Yes. What happened to lunch today?
Max: Can I come over?
Mia: I'm on my way to see Sophie.
Max: After?
Mia: idk
Max: What's wrong?
Mia: Where were you at lunch?
Max: I went home.
Mia: Why didn't you say anything to me?
Max: I didn't see you and you didn't have your phone.
Mia: Was Everly with you?
Max: We need to talk.

By saying that, he just admitted it. I put my phone down on my lap and cracked my knuckles.

"Everything okay?" my mother asked.

"No. I think it's over with Max."

"I'm sorry. He was too old for you anyway."

"Apparently."
I looked out the window until my phone buzzed again.

Max: Mia. We need to talk.
Mia: Thanks, I'm good. You have fun with Everly.

He didn't say anything else and neither did I.

- Chapter Thirty-Six -

I woke up to the light of Sophie's bedroom window hitting me in the face. I sat up slowly, trying to remember where I was. Sophie had been released from the hospital and we were having our own private slumber party. I cleared the sleep from my eyes and saw Sophie sitting by her window staring outside. She heard me and broke her stare.

"Good morning, sunshine." She smiled at me. The sun framed her face in multicolored light, almost like she was glowing rainbows. I'd never seen anything like that before.

"The light! Did you put a prism in the window?" I asked.

"What? What do you mean?"

I rubbed my eyes and the colors went away. "I don't know, there were a ton of colors surrounding you."

"Well, obviously you are just waking up. Or maybe, it's my AAAAUUUR-RRAAAAA!" She waved her hands around her face, right where the lights had been.

We both laughed, then I threw my pillow at her. "Must have been my eyes."

She threw the pillow back at me. "Well, I AM radiant, so… yeah."

"Did you do your treatment yet?"

"Yep."

"But I didn't hear you."

"Yeah, I did it in my parent's room. I didn't want to wake you."

"So, we have the whole day. What are we gonna do?"

"I don't know. It's actually going to be in the 50's today. I want to do something outside."

I couldn't get that old house out of my mind since the night I had been brought home by the police. Something about it was calling me back. "So this is going to sound strange. Can I take you to the old abandoned house Max brought me to?"

"Why in the world would you want to go there?" She looked at me like I was insane. "I mean, that's where everything went bad, right?"

"Well, yeah. But for some reason, I feel like I have to go. I mean, like it's calling to me."

"Sure, but I'm not bringing a Ouji board or anything." She was still looking at me like I was stark raving mad. "I'm not in the mood to commune with the dead just yet."

"Oh stop!" The 'just yet' shook me inside a bit. "Think of it like an adventure."

"Okay. Let's do it. We need to do something exciting." She giggled. "And hey, maybe we'll get brought back by the police."

"I mean, why not?"

We both sprang up, ran downstairs, and told Sophie's mom where we were going–just in case we actually were brought home by the police.

"Girls, seriously?" Lisa asked.

"Oh come on, we'll be safe."

"Okay. I'm going to allow this. Yes, it's trespassing, but I also remember the thrill of doing something similar."

"Oh really?"

"Sit, sit, sit. I feel a story time coming on. I'll bring the donuts in and grab coffee and hot chocolate."

Sophie and I looked at each other with wide eyes. We couldn't wait to hear the story.

She put three mugs on the table, opened three packs of powdered hot chocolate, put them in the mugs, then added coffee and heavy whipping cream. I grabbed a mug and a powdered donut.

She told us about how everyone used to talk about a haunted house on the mountain, not too far from where I lived. She said that people used to go there to party, but she and her friend were never really the partying types, so they never went. Then one day after school she and her friend, Rachel, got this idea to drive up the mountain to the house to see what the big deal was. They were always hoping to run into something supernatural. It never happened, but not for a lack of trying. When they got to the house, it was a huge wooden, Victorian-style home with white paint peeling off of it.

Lisa said they parked the car and got out, then walked right up the steps to the porch and peeked in the windows. They saw spray-painted walls and beer bottles everywhere. They weren't creeped out, because they were there in the middle of the day. But then they heard footsteps from inside the house. They could tell the footsteps were walking toward the door. They didn't stick around. Instead, they bolted off the porch and back to the car. Rachel started the car and turned it around to make their escape, trying to get away from the house as quickly as possible. Once they hit the road it sounded like something was hanging on to the car. Thump, thump, thump. There was no one behind them, but still, it was like something was there. They drove as fast as they could down the mountain back to Rachel's house and ran inside, completely freaked out. Breathing hard, they looked out the front window to see if they had brought anything back with them, but still, there was nothing there. They calmed down and pulled out their homework to start working. That's when Rachel's dad got home and came into the kitchen looking mad.

"Where did you two go today?"

"What? School," Rachel said, shrugging.

"Really? Then why is an entire tree limb attached to your back bumper?"

They looked at each other and ran outside. Sure enough, there was a large tree limb, with leaves and everything hooked on the bumper. They started laughing, but Rachel's dad didn't laugh.

He asked one more time, "Where did you go today?"

"Dad, we swear we went to school."

He sighed, threw his hands up in the air, and walked back into the house saying, "Girls. I'll never understand girls."

They had to pull hard to get the limb out from the bumper, laughing all the while.

Lisa said that they never found out about the footsteps they heard. The whole time she told the story, Lisa was smiling like it was such a good memory.

"So, yeah. I'm going to allow this. I feel like you need good memories too."

Sophie and I looked at each other and smiled.

Sophie raised her eyebrows and said, in a very creepy voice, "I wonder if we'll hear footsteps?"

"Oooh, I hope so! What's the point otherwise?" I replied.

"Let's go get dressed."

"Wait, wait, wait. Where is this house, exactly?" Sophie's mom asked.

I told her where it was, and even told her the entire story of what happened.

"Okay, well. Try not to come home in a police car. Mmmmkay?" she said, pointing her finger back and forth between the two of us. "So, it's a close walk then?"

"Oh yeah."

"Okay. Just make sure your phones are fully charged. Got it?"

"Of course."

We jumped out of our chairs and ran upstairs to get dressed.

***

We left Sophie's house, turned right, and started walking toward the river. As we passed the diner I tried not to look in, but I knew the upperclassmen would be there having breakfast. It was a tradition for them on Saturdays.

Sophie looked, then turned her head to me, saying, "Don't look. Don't look. Don't look."

Which of course made me look. I turned my head to see Max and Everly standing in front, holding hands, talking to Luke. They were HOLDING HANDS.

"I told you not to look," Sophie whispered.

I snapped my head back to looking straight forward. Then took one more look at them. Max saw me. Our eyes met, but only briefly before he looked away.

"Mia, don't get upset. You knew this would happen. Let's move on."

"I'm trying."

"Are you going to put him out of your mind? I mean, can you?"

I nodded, "Yes."

"Okay, because we are going on a mission here, and you can't be filled with negative emotion. Remember what I always say—"

"You have to be positive to have positive outcomes."

"Right."

I smiled slyly. "Okay, but what are the positive outcomes in this case? I feel like we are going to this place with the actual intent of getting freaked out." I cocked my head and looked at her. "So. How should I approach this."

"True, true. Okay. Feel positive that we will have an adventure."

I nodded. "I can do that."

We came to the old dirt road. It looked completely different in the daylight. It was incredibly overgrown. I couldn't believe Max had even been able to get his truck through there that night. We started the long journey down the road, on foot. It was a longer path than I remembered.

"Are you sure you're okay doing this?

"Mia, I'm fine. Really."

"Okay."

We walked for ten more minutes before the trees started to clear. There, in front of us was the old house. We walked forward a bit more, then Sophie stopped.

"I hate to bring this up, but right here? This very spot? Is this where he freaked out?"

I looked around. From what I could tell, it was the exact spot where he had stood, changing his mind drastically about me. One minute I had been ready to give myself to him, the next he was breaking up with me. "I think so. Why?"

"I don't know. There's some bad energy here. I feel it. It's making the hair on the back of my neck stand up." She looked around a bit. "Wait, can we back up a little?"

"Sure?"

"Do you think this spot holds the energy of that night?" I asked.

"I'm not sure. But I feel like if someone stands here long enough, they'll be affected negatively."

"I don't understand."

"I'm not sure if I can explain it right. But some places just feel happy, and some sad. This spot feels bad to me." She looked at me. "Let's just walk away. Okay? I'm not feeling well."

"Of course."

We turned and walked back for about a minute.

"Okay, now I'm starting to feel better." She shook her limbs a bit. "I just want to make sure we are protected."

She held her hands out to me. I returned the gesture and grasped her hands in mine. She started breathing deeply, so I closed my eyes and did the same. It just felt like the right thing to do.

She whispered soft words under her breath, asking for safety, for the white light of protection, and for nothing to approach us. Then she took another deep breath. We both opened our eyes.

"I thought the point was to get freaked out."

"Not that kind of freaked out. What I felt just then was really bad. I mean, freaked out, sure. But I don't want to bring anything back with us."

"I hadn't thought of that."

"I didn't either until just then."

"Are we protected now?"

"Almost. Wait, I feel like I need to find something special for us to carry." Sophie often found things in nature and gave them special meaning. She stepped off the road a short way, climbing around in the trees and low shrubbery. When she returned, she was carrying a feather and a piece of iron ore rock. "These will keep us safe." She handed me the rock. "Iron will keep ugly stuff away from you."

I took the rock in my hand. It was large and heavy, and I felt safe with it. If something tried to attack us, I could just throw it at them and do some real damage. That was not, at all, Sophie's intention, but that's how I felt.

She kept the feather. She couldn't hurt someone with it but it seemed appropriate for her. I had no doubt about the spiritual power of anything Sophie claimed as her own.

She held the feather up to the sky and asked for safety. Then she took my hand that was holding the iron ore rock and said the same prayer. As she spoke, she glowed. Emotionally, yes, but it looked to me like she was actually glowing, like light.

"How do you know how to do this stuff? I really do feel safer."

"I have no idea. It just sort of comes to me."

And that was true. She had been doing things like this since kindergarten. This part of her was something that we all accepted. Something that was getting more and more powerful as time went by.

We started back to the house. When we came to the clearing again, we stopped in the same exact spot as earlier.

"Do you still have that bad feeling?"

She smiled and shook her head. "No, not at all."

I breathed a sigh of relief.

"Is that water?" she asked.

"I hear it. I think so." I smiled.

"Let's go!" She started walking toward the river. She loved any chance to sit beside the river. "How did I never know about this place? I mean, we must have tubed past here a million times."

"In the summer it's probably all completely overgrown. I bet you can't see it from the water when the leaves are out."

"It's like a secret oasis. Oh my gosh. This all must have been so beautiful when someone was living here."

I looked back up at the house. I could see the beauty. It seemed so much less creepy when you imagined it in its glory. Sophie had entirely changed my perspective with her ritual. Somehow she had helped me to no longer think of this spot as something scary. Now, I gazed through the evergreen limbs to see the bright blue sky, then looked down at the dirt road. There I noticed small pebbles in many different colors, shining up at me, saying hello. I bent over and picked up a red one in the shape of a heart. I cupped it in my hands and instinctively held it up to my mouth and blew on it. It just felt right to do that. It had been lying exactly where Max had kissed me before he freaked out.

Sophie called my name, so I put the rocks in my pocket and looked up at her. Once again, the sun was framing her body with rainbows. She was waving her arms at me, "Come on, Mia! You have to see this."

As I got closer to her, the strobes of light framing her body thinned. She pointed out to the river. "Isn't it just beautiful?"

I stood by her side, curious. I mean sure, the Susquehanna River is beautiful in sections, but it's not like I'd never seen it before. I tried to look deeper, beyond the obvious. Maybe she was seeing something I wasn't.

"It's all just so beautiful," Sophie said, tearing up at the sight. She stood there smiling at the river, tears in her eyes. Still, I couldn't see what she saw. The other side of the river was nothing but leafless old oaks and elms with evergreens peeking out. They were the same trees we always saw whenever we were on the river. We'd been tubing down it since we were able to walk. I strained my eyes, wondering what she saw.

"What am I missing?"

"Are you serious? Just look at how green the trees are."

"The evergreens?"

"Yeah. Just beautiful. Don't you think?" Then she pointed up the river. "And look, look at the ice collecting on the island."

I started to look past her up the river but stopped. The sun was shining around her again, so brilliantly, like she was made of diamonds. She turned her head and smiled at me. I looked back toward the water and suddenly I could see the beauty she saw. It was magnificent. The evergreens were brighter. The water, though it was the same murky brown shade, sparkled somehow as the light rippled through it. The ice bunching up in front of the island was bobbing up and down as if to a rhythm, a music all its own.

"I could stand here all day and just breathe the air. Can you feel it? It feels lighter here. Sweeter almost," she said.

I could actually taste the sweetness of the air. I really could. I knew I must be feeling just a small amount of the wonder Sophie felt every day of her life. No wonder she collected so many little mementos. The rocks, sticks, and feathers were all absolutely beautiful to her. I took a deep breath in, feeling the sweetness of the air.

We heard a car engine and turned. Max's black truck was coming down the road. The spell broke. I lost the music of the water. He was ruining this moment with Sophie. I was kind of upset, but then another part of me was excited. He had actually come looking for me. Me.

"Oh, lookie. It's Max. Great." Sophie expressed her low opinion of him.

I said nothing but started toward him, my feet with minds all their own.   He jumped out of the truck. As he headed in our direction, he called out, "What are you two doing here? It's not safe."

"Why isn't it safe?" I asked. "You brought me here yourself."

We met each other in front of the old house, at the same spot where we had kissed.

"You walked here?"

"Yeah. It's not that far from Sophie's house. I don't understand what the problem is."

"A lot of strange things happen here, is all I mean," he said, standing perfectly still, hands in his pockets.

"Then why did you bring me here?"

He didn't answer.

"Where's Everly?" I asked.

He shifted his eyes to his feet. "She's at the diner."

"Does she know where you went?"

"No."

"Why are you here?"

He looked me deeply in my eyes. "What? I'm not allowed to worry about you?"

"We are fine." I turned to look at Sophie. She was throwing rocks into the river, giving us privacy. I looked back at Max.

He opened his mouth a few times as if to speak but kept closing it. Finally, he blurted, "I just … I guess I just wanted to check on you and tell you that I'm sorry."

"Can I ask you a question?" I said.

"Sure," he looked up at me again.

"Why did you start going out with me, when you were still with her?"

"I wasn't with her."

"You're with her now."

"It's a long story." He shrugged.

"You realize she's the one who called the police?"

"She was jealous."

"She is a psychopath," I said. She wasn't ever just jealous. "But if that's what you are looking for."

"As I said, there's a lot going on." His hands were still in his pockets. "I feel like I owe her a part of me."

"Why? Why do you owe her a part of yourself?"

"Do we have to talk about this now?"

Three crows circled above us. I turned my head to look at Sophie. She was happily staring at the birds.

I returned my attention to Max. "Yes, now."

He looked at me, then straightened his back and took a deep breath before speaking. "I got her pregnant last summer."

When those words came out of his mouth, I felt dizzy and tasted bile. I was sure I was going to be sick. One word was all I could manage, "What?" I grasped my ears trying to stop the dizziness.

"Yeah. It was the first time for both of us. We didn't think about protection or anything. We weren't thinking at all, in fact."

I could barely breathe. "But… but she's not pregnant. I never saw her pregnant. And I'm pretty sure she doesn't have a baby." I was confused.

"Right well, that's why I got so freaked out at the hospital. She had a miscarriage." He looked back down at his feet. "She wouldn't stop bleeding. Her parents were on vacation so I had to drive her to the hospital. She bled all over my truck"

"I… I didn't know."

"No, of course not. No one did."

"Wait. No one?"

"No. Not even her parents. I pulled money out of my savings to pay for the ER visit so that it wouldn't show up at her house in billing."

"But the ER is expensive."

"I know," he nodded. "It cleaned me out."

"They didn't call her parents?"

"No."

"So, is that why you went back to her?"

"I feel like I have to take care of her." He finally pulled his hands out of his pockets and wrung them together nervously. "I caused what happened. It's my fault."

All of this was beyond me. Completely beyond my capability of understanding. "But didn't you like me? Like, at all?"

He looked deflated. "Yes. Yes. I did. No. I do. I do like you." He looked me straight in my eyes and said, "I was falling for you."

"Is that why you pushed me away? You could have told me."

"Yeah. Well, I didn't want to ruin you the way I ruined her."

I stopped breathing. *You can't ruin a person, can you?*

"I'm sorry," he said. Then he stepped closer and wrapped his arms around me. "I'm so, so sorry." He put his chin on top of my head the way he used to do.

Sophie cleared her throat. Max let go. I looked toward her, she still had her back to us.

"Do you guys want a ride home?"

Sophie yelled to him, "No! We're happy. You aren't needed. Thanks."

I laughed a little bit. She had no intention of hiding her opinions about him at all.

"It's fine. I don't think we are done here."

"Okay. I'll see you later then, I guess." He turned and walked back to his truck.

My body was shaking as I watched him go. No, not my body, my soul. My soul was shaking. I needed to work through my thoughts, so I walked slowly back to Sophie. I wish he had told me all of that when we were dating. It all made so much more sense. I was still mad, but it made sense. I guess?

"So, what was THAT about?" Sophie asked.

"Nothing. He just wanted to apologize for being a jerk. And he was worried about us being out here for some reason."

"Just because he apologized doesn't mean that he's no longer a jerk," she answered.

"Come on, let's throw more rocks."

- Chapter Thirty-Seven -

One month later

Sophie and I walked to her house after school, the spring crocuses were starting to bloom. They were beautiful peeking through the little patches of snow that still lay on the ground. Her parents had told us to come home immediately after school. We did as they asked, but we had no idea what was in store. We had gotten into the habit of stopping by the old house on the river every day after school. It felt like it had become a part of us. It welcomed us to its land.

I had been staying with Sophie for about a week. My mother had started hitting me again once my dad went back on the road. After one particularly bad night, I had been able to text Sophie about what happened. Within a half-hour, headlights appeared driving up my dirt road. Sophie's parents had come to get me. Sophie wasn't with them though. Not knowing what they were walking into, they'd left her at home. I grabbed my bag and met them on the porch. They asked if my mom was awake. She wasn't, so Sophie's parents had called the police non-emergency number to let them know they were taking me and why. At the police station the next morning, we made a report and met with a woman who told me I would be safe. They let Sophie's parents take me home with them "until further notice," and I'd been living with their family ever since.

As soon as Sophie and I entered the dining room, we saw her dad sitting there with a woman we didn't recognize. She was wearing a suit and writing notes on a notepad. When she saw us enter she stood. "Hello, Mia! Sophie! How are you both?"

"Um, good?" Sophie answered.

It took me a second to figure out that this was a social worker. She must be there to check up on me. Sophie's mom came out of the kitchen with a plate piled high with cookies and brownies. "Oh, hello, girls. Mrs. Brown is here to go over some paperwork with us. Sit down, have some cookies."

We both sat. "What's going on??"

"We are filling out the paperwork to apply to be your permanent foster parents."

My eyes open wide. "What?"

"Honey, your father isn't able to find work that doesn't include travel, and we have no idea what's going to happen with your mother." Lisa took my hand in hers. "Your father approached us looking for help. He doesn't want to be separated from you, but you need some amount of peace. He's going to spend time with you whenever he is in town, and he'll call you."

"But why all this? Why does it have to be so formal?"

"Because you need someone to look out for your interests."

"My dad agreed?"

"Yes."

Mrs. Brown spoke, "Is this what you would like to happen?" She looked at me intently.

I looked back and forth from the social worker to Sophie and then to Lisa. "Yes. Yes, I think I do." My eyes darted back and forth between Sophie's mother and father. "Really?" I asked them.

"Yes. We love you, Mia, as if you are our own. We know this is hard. We aren't taking you from your parents. We are just making sure you are safe."

Sophie started crying. She jumped up and hugged her mom, saying, "Thank you, Mom, thank you," over and over again.

"We don't think there will be any problem getting this through," the social worker explained. "Given that Mia's mother is currently waiting for her trial. Drunk driving and reckless abandonment are serious charges."

I didn't know how to react. I didn't know if this was really the right thing to do, but I knew I didn't want to go back, couldn't go back.

Everyone signed papers. Then Mrs. Brown packed up her bag, wished us well, and left the house with one last cookie in her free hand.

I stayed sitting at the table. I was stunned. I guess it was official: I was safe.

"Mia, we are worried about your mom coming to the school. She's out on bail right now so we will go talk to the school tomorrow to let them know that we are your guardians now. That should help if she shows up."

I just nodded. I was ecstatic and sad all at the same time. I didn't know whether to cry, smile, or even laugh. I had no idea. I sat there, disconnected from space and time.

After a while, I noticed Sophie sitting next to me. "Are you okay?"

I just looked at her and nodded.

"You don't seem okay."

I shook my head back and forth. "No. I'm fine. I guess it all seems more real." I rubbed my hands over my eyes. Tears were starting to form. "You know, sometimes I thought I was making it all up. Like, I deserved what she did to me?"

"No. You never deserved it."

"I mean, I know that, but my brain tricks me sometimes. What if I'm lying? What if it's not that bad. What if she truly loves me?"

"Mia, you aren't lying. You had bruises on your body from her. Lots of bruises."

"Am I abandoning her?" I looked at Sophie, tears now streaming down my face. "What if your parents realize how horrible I am?"

"Mia. This is our dream. We are actually going to be sisters now. Don't you see?"

I smiled at the thought of becoming Sophie's sister.

Lisa sat down next to me on the other side from Sophie. "Are you okay?"

"I think so. It's a lot."

"It is. Of course it is." She took my hand in hers. "Look, you never deserved what happened to you. There was nothing you could have ever done that warranted what she did to you. Do you understand that?"

"I think so." I nodded. "Sometimes I just think it's not real."

"It's all confusing. I know. We are going to make an appointment with a family therapist to work through some of this. Also, I think we are going to get a restraining order. Are you okay with that?"

I nodded.

The week prior, Sophie's parents had made their den into a third bedroom for me. It was just a small daybed, but it was enough. I was able to put my computer on the desk, and if I folded my clothes neatly, they fit on the bookshelves with a little room to spare. Her parents wanted me to have a space of my own, but I ended up sleeping in Sophie's room most nights anyway. I just didn't want to be alone. Luckily, neither did Sophie.

- Chapter Thirty-Eight -

The doorbell rang over and over again. There was even pounding on the door. It was around 11 pm. The whole family was already in bed. Startled, we all found each other in the hallway. Sophie's dad sent us to Sophie's room and said not to go downstairs for any reason. I already knew it was my mother, had to be. Sophie and I did as her dad instructed.

In her room, Sophie said, "What do you think is going on?"

"I guarantee it's my mom."

"Really? But she hasn't contacted you so far."

"Oh, it's her."

We heard a commotion downstairs followed by a high-pitched shrill scream. My mom was putting on a scene. Fleetingly, I wondered about her makeup.

I got off of Sophie's bed and tiptoed to the door.

"Mia, no. Don't leave this room. You have a restraining order against her for a reason. Remember?"

"I just want to crack it so I can hear what she's saying."

Sophie jumped up and came behind me, putting her hands on my shoulders. "Okay, you're right. I want to hear too," she whispered.

We cracked the door open just enough to make out words.

"Why have you taken my bayyyybeeee from me?"

"Kim, we didn't. You made it unsafe for her to stay with you," Lisa answered.

"Look, you are going to have to leave." That was Sophie's dad. "You are violating the restraining order."

"How can you do this to me?" My mother was slurring her words, obviously drunk. "I might as well kill myself."

"Okay, Kim. That's enough," Lisa said. "How did you get here?"

"That's none of your business." My mother yelled then, her voice so loud we could have heard it with the door closed. "Mia! Mia! Mommy is here for you baby." Sophie and I jumped back. "I won't let them kidnap you from me like this." We closed the door quickly. Sure enough, my mother's voice still came through loud and clear. "Come down to Mommy."

"Okay. Kim. Back away from the steps," Lisa said. "You are not allowed to be with her at this point."

This went on for about ten more minutes until we saw red and blue flashing lights shining through the outside windows. The police knocked on the door. We couldn't hear them very well as our door was still closed, but it was clear they came in. We heard a bit of rustling, more crying, and a lot more shrieking. I hated hearing my mother like that. A part of me wanted to go downstairs to save her. To stop them from arresting her. An even larger part of me felt upset at myself for putting her through this pain. I put my hand on the doorknob again, but Sophie stopped me. She held me by the shoulders and turned me toward her.

"Listen to me. Do not go down there. What do you think would happen if you went down there right now?"

"Maybe I could at least stop her from being arrested."

"No, Mia. Listen to me. There's nothing you can do. She made her decisions. She made the decision to drive here drunk. She made her decision to violate the restraining order. She did that. Not you. This is not your fault."

I started sobbing. She wrapped her arms around me and we fell to the floor together. She cradled me in her arms as I wept.

Then, as suddenly as it had begun, it was over. The lower level of Sophie's house was quiet. The flashing lights went away. No one was shrieking anymore. There was no more commotion. Sophie and I heard footsteps approach the door. Someone knocked and then turned the doorknob.

"Girls?" Lisa saw us on the floor and sank down with us. She wrapped us both in her arms and rocked us. "She's gone. Are you okay?"

I nodded. "Did they arrest her?"

"Yes, they arrested her."

"Is it my fault?"

"No dear. Not at all. This is one hundred percent on her. All of it. You have done nothing wrong."

I started sobbing again, not just for my mom this time, but for me. For me because no matter how much they love me, no one understands how I'm feeling. Good intentions don't fix anything. Not really. All that's left is confusion.

"Will she be in jail long?" I asked.

"I have no idea, honey."

"Okay."

"You two need to get to bed. Come on now, let's get up. Okay?"

We all got up together. "Mia, why don't you sleep in here with Sophie tonight. Okay?"

I nodded.

Lisa pulled out the trundle bed and went to the closet to get sheets. She made the bed while Sophie used the bathroom. I just stood there in a daze.

Once the bed was made, I climbed on top and curled up in a fetal position. When Sophie returned to the bedroom, she didn't climb into her bed like she was supposed to. Instead, she lay down with me on the trundle.

"Okay, it's fine," Lisa said. "But just for tonight. Okay?" Her words were soft. Then she grabbed the Amish quilt that was on Sophie's bed and laid it over the both of us. It felt warm. Having someone hold me while another made sure I was tucked in made me feel loved in a way that I don't think I had ever experienced before.

I fell asleep quickly. Before I knew, it the alarm was going off, telling us to get up and get ready for school. Sophie was already up doing her breathing treatment.

"Good morning," I said. I watched the vapor escape the top of the mouthpiece on the nebulizer.

"Oood mmmm." Sophie couldn't talk with her mouth around the mouthpiece, but she waved. That was enough for me.

I sat and watched her, then I got up and looked out the window. A cardinal was sitting on the tree limb outside of Sophie's room. The same cardinal that always seemed to pop up whenever she was having breathing problems. At least I think it was the same one. The cardinal worried me, so I turned to Sophie and said, "Soph, are you feeling okay?"

She nodded then took her hand and waved it in a way that said, "Sort of."

I walked away from the window and the watchful bird, and sat beside Sophie. I could hear her chest bubbling. I took the nebulizer out of her hand and held it for her. Sometimes the medicine made her shaky, so it would get hard for her to hold it. I wanted to help. She smiled at me as she took deep breaths pulling the medicine into her lungs. I held the mouthpiece in place for the next ten minutes. When she was close to the end of the treatment, I took the nebulizer and shook it up a bit, hoping to free up more of the medicine. Then I put it back into her mouth. Once it was obvious she had gotten all she could out of the treatment, I took the mouthpiece and put it next to the nebulizer unit on her side table. When I looked out the window, the cardinal was closer. That beautiful bird was actually standing on the outside window sill, watching us.

Sophie laid down on her stomach for me to do percussions on her back. Percussions helped to break up the phlegm in her lungs, so I started hitting her back with a rhythmic thud. I had a fun technique, percussions to the beat of songs we liked with me singing along. Every once in a while, Sophie would laugh at my horrible singing. This, of course, would trigger a coughing fit that actually helped her to cough up the stuff that was in her lungs. After about fifteen minutes, I finished and sat back.

"Are you okay?" I asked.

"Yeah, of course. Why?"

"The cardinal was out there."

"Oh, my cardinal? Really?"

"Yeah. I always notice it when you are really sick."

"Nah. He was probably just checking in," Sophie said.

"Do you think any animals watch me the way they watch you?" I asked.

"Of course, you just don't notice them."

"You think?"

"Absolutely."

I walked to the window to see if there was an animal outside looking out for me. I didn't see anything at all. I sighed and frowned, then turned around and helped Sophie up from her spot on the bed.

***

Later that day Sophie and I were barely keeping our eyes open. Both of us were more exhausted than we ever had been. I had spent the whole morning worried my mom would show up at the school, but then I remembered she had been arrested. She was probably still in jail.

I stood at my locker, grabbing everything I needed for the next two classes. Someone tapped me on the shoulder and scared the hell out of me. It was Everly.

"Max told you?" she asked.

"Told me what?" I knew exactly what she was talking about, but it had been a few weeks since then and she had startled me. I didn't know what else to say.

"Max said he told you."

"Oh, oh, right." I furrowed my brows and nodded my head.

"If you tell anyone, I'll kill you."

With everything my mother had done to me, that's one thing she never said. My mom never said she would kill me. Confused now, I pressed back into my locker to gain more distance from Everly. "I… I… I would never tell anyone," I stammered. "It's none of my business." I looked at her straight in the eyes, so she knew I was being honest. "I mean, I've known for weeks and haven't told anyone at all."

"Just make sure you don't." She put her hand on my shoulder and pushed me into my locker. "Anyway, he's mine again."

I didn't reply. Now I was sure Everly was just as psychotic as my mother. They were the same, the two of them so I knew exactly what each was capable of. I'm glad that I had kept my mouth shut.

Her threat delivered, Everly turned then and walked away. I finished zipping up my backpack, shut my locker with a shaking hand, and walked one step in front of the other. About three feet ahead of me, Max was coming out of a classroom. He saw Everly, walked up to her, and kissed her on the top of the head, just like he used to do with me. I hadn't seen that before. I thought kissing me on top of the head was my thing—my private thing with me and him. My stomach dropped to the floor. I took a deep breath in, and before I was ready to let it out again, Emma called my name.

"Mia!" She ran up next to me. "Are you guys coming to the Prom Walk?"

"The what?" Despite all the banners and announcements, I had completely forgotten about the prom. I had way too much happening in my life to care. Besides, I was only a freshman, first-years didn't usually go to prom. Only juniors and seniors could go unless someone invited you. I had once had dreams of going this year since Max was a junior, but that didn't work out, obviously.

"I just thought you guys would want to come and cheer for me?" Emma's boyfriend, Alex, was a Junior.

"Oh, right." I realized the prom walk was important to her. "Yes. This weekend?"

"Yeah. Friday at 4:30." She jumped up and down cheering that Sophie and I would be there. "Oh, Mia, you should see my dress! It's baby blue and has tulle surrounding it. I feel like a princess in it."

"I can't wait to see it."

She was only half-listening to me, talking a mile a minute, "And my mom bought me a tiara to wear… I think I'm going to do an updo."

"That sounds pretty." I was trying to be supportive, but I couldn't be genuinely enthusiastic. After all, Max and Everly would probably be there together.

Lily popped up just in time. "Hey, can I sit with you and Sophie at the prom walk?" she said. "Since my bestie will be walking, I can't sit next to her, obviously."

"Of course. Just be at Sophie's at 4:00 on Friday."

"Thanks!" She and Emma linked arms and walked off together.

I walked into the classroom and sat next to Sophie. She smiled at me but was busy texting. "Who're you talking to?" I asked.

"Ryan, I'm trying to get him to come home this weekend. I haven't seen him in a while."

"It's been a long time. Is he avoiding you?"

"I don't think so. No," she said, looking down with her face red like she was about to cry.

Realizing my mistake I quickly said, "I doubt he has much control over that, though. You know?" I tried to let her know that it probably had nothing to do with him avoiding her.

"I guess." She nodded.

I knew their relationship was strained. He was hinting that he couldn't deal with her health problems. She kept pushing for the relationship anyway.

I wanted to get her mind off of him quickly. "So, I told Emma we would go to the prom walk and cheer for her."

"Oh yeah? Okay! That will be fun."

"I think so. Lily is going to meet us at your house and go with us."

"Okay." She gave a small smile.

"Oh, also, Everly pushed me into my locker."

"What?" Sophie looked angry. "Why?"

"I'm sure it has to do with Max," I said.

"But you broke up months ago."

That stung. "Yeah." I felt like I'd been slapped in the face.

"Sorry. That was insensitive."

"It's okay. It still stings, I guess." I paused. I needed to tell her the whole story, even though it wasn't mine to tell. "I actually have more to tell you. A lot more."

She looked at me intently.

"But it's just between you and me. Okay?"

She nodded. There was no way I could keep secrets from her. Not with how much we had been through.

"Everly had a miscarriage in the summer."

Her eyes widened. "What?"

"That's why Max was so uncomfortable at the hospital. Her parents were out of town, and he was the only one there helping her through it. I guess it was really traumatic."

"I guess so."

"So, that's why I'm not fighting for him," I explained. "But that doesn't mean it doesn't hurt."

- Chapter Thirty-Nine -

I stood looking in the mirror of the bathroom, trying to make myself look good for the Prom Walk. It was completely insane because I wasn't going to prom. Still I wanted to look good. I knew it didn't matter, but I wanted Max to see me and realize what he had lost. It was a petty thought, but I just couldn't wrap my mind around why he stayed with her. What was wrong with me? I stood there thinking. He couldn't have any idea what I was going through. I had never really talked to him about it. I hadn't told him much about how my mother hit me, not just once but all the time–so often it felt normal. Or that I had walked through a snowstorm with no coat and no phone. He probably had no clue that I was living with Sophie, or that my mother was out of jail on bail for drunk driving and breaking a restraining order. He had no idea that my father had not contacted me once since I moved in with Sophie. I realized that Max knew absolutely none of it. So much had changed, maybe I was a totally different person than the Mia he had known. Still, I wanted him to know. I wanted him to remember that he had invited me to the prom. I wanted him to see me there in the crowd, watching him walk down the sidewalk with the person who threatened my life. And I wanted to look good for it. I didn't want to go overboard, of course. I didn't want it to be obvious, but I did want to look good. I didn't want to hide in the shadows.

I walked out of the bathroom.

Sophie was brushing her hair. "What?! Are you going to prom and I didn't know?" She walked up closer to me to inspect my face. "Are you wearing false eyelashes?"

I laughed. "Yeah. I guess I just wanted to look good."

"Okay. Well, you do! Mission accomplished." She went back to brushing her hair. "What time is Lily getting here again?"

"Four."

"Okay, cool. I have to do a breathing treatment a little before then. I'll start it now."

"Okay."

"You might have to go down and keep Lily company."

"Sure."

"She's never seen me do a breathing treatment. I just… I don't want to do it in front of other people. I don't like them treating me like I'm sick."

"No problem. I completely understand. I'll hang out with her."

A few minutes later the doorbell rang. Leaving Sophie to finish her breathing treatment, I went downstairs and welcomed Lily in.

"Do you want something to drink?"

"Um sure." She seemed uncomfortable.

"Okay. Follow me, let's find you something."

I got her some iced tea and we sat at the dining room table.

"So you're really living here now?"

"I am."

"What happened?"

I was used to questions by that point, but this was the first time Lily had asked.

"My dad needed to continue traveling, and my mom has some issues she's working on, so everyone agreed that it might be best for me to live here."

She nodded. "It's nice they let you move in."

"Yeah. It really was." I nodded. "Are you excited to see Emma in her dress?"

"I guess," she said in a low voice. "I mean. I just don't see what the big deal is." She shrugged.

"Don't you like Alex?"

"He's fine. There's nothing wrong with him."

"Emma seems happy." I pointed out.

"Sure."

"You don't seem happy though."

"Nothing. It's nothing." She nervously fiddled with her necklace. "I guess it's just hard when you spend your entire life with someone." Lily paused. "And, well, then, you know, somewhere along the line, you maybe, kinda, sorta begin to love them."

I realized what was going on. I reached out and held her hand. "Lily. I had no idea."

She nodded. "It's okay. I mean, it's not like I wanted this to happen. It just did. And I don't know what to do with it."

"I understand."

"And I mean, look at her. She's so obviously boy-crazy. So I will just be her friend. She doesn't want a girlfriend. Not like that. Not like me."

"Does she know?"

"No."

"Do you think you should talk to her about it?

"No."

"You don't think she'll understand?"

"I mean, what good would it do? She loves Alex and she mildly humors me."

"I don't think she mildly humors you. You're her best friend."

"Right. Which is why I can't tell her. I don't want to make it weird. Her friendship is more important to me than, well, than anything else."

"Okay."

We heard Sophie coming down the stairs, so I let go of Lily's hand. She whispered to me, "Don't say anything."

I mouthed, "I won't."

"Hey, ladies, are you ready?"

Lily turned toward Sophie and nodded. "Yep, let's go."

We left the house and walked the short walk to the school. The cardinal flew past us on the way. I gave a knowing glance at Sophie and smiled. She laughed just as Lily said, "Wow, did you guys see that? That bird just flew at us. I've never seen that happen before."

Sophie and I just laughed and laughed. Sophie tried to explain through her laughter. "Oh no. That cardinal is my guardian angel."

"What?"

"Nothing, never mind."

"Alrighty then," Lily said. She must have thought Sophie had lost her mind.

We got to the top of the hill and saw tons of people standing outside the school, crowding along the front walkway.

"Oh. Maybe we are a bit late."

"Nah, we'll push our way to the front," Lily said forcefully. And that's exactly what we did.

The prom participants walked out the front doors of the school as their names were called. Then they stopped and posed for pictures under a balloon canopy before continuing to their cars or limos. From there they would drive to the banquet hall for prom.

One by one each couple was called until finally the announcer said the names I was waiting for, "Miss Everly Murphey being escorted by Maximilian Rossi." Everly and Max had a cheering section all their own. Everly was wearing a sleek black gown that showed off her perfect figure. Her hair was in an updo and, except for bright red lipstick, her makeup was minimal. She looked… stunning. I was instantly angry. I made my way to the front of the pack of people, hoping Max would see me standing there watching him. I pushed past a group of sophomores who were cheering for them, then I stood, staring at him, willing him to look at me. It worked. He saw me, did a little half-smile, then looked quickly away. Moments later he looked back up at me and gave me a sheepish smile, but he was not the only one to see me. Everly saw me, too. Her top lip curled up into a sneer to show her distaste. I didn't care. I smiled at her and waved. I actually yelled out, "Everly, you look so nice."

She took her middle finger and scratched the side of her perfectly coiffed up-do. Obviously, that was meant for me. Sometimes I was afraid of her, and yet others, I wanted to agitate her. I should have felt bad about that, knowing all she'd been through. But no. *Would he have to marry her because of what happened last summer? Was she expecting him to spend the rest of his life with her?* I wondered how far he would take the relationship. How powerful was the pity he had for her?

I felt two people slide up, one on either side of me: Sophie on the right and Lily on the left. Sophie grabbed my hand. "Don't cause a scene," she said quietly out of the side of her smiling mouth.

"I'm not. I just told her she looked good," I said in a sing-song voice, never breaking my smile.

Lily was standing up on her tiptoes looking in the school building for Emma. "I don't see her. Do you guys?"

"No, not yet," Sophie replied.

Finally, we heard their names. "Emma Wagner, escorted by Alexander Baker."

Sophie and I started cheering, but Lily just stood there. Emma really did look like a princess. She saw us and smiled brightly. She was so happy. But then she looked at Lily and her smile dimmed.

She mouthed, "What's wrong?" to Lily.

I elbowed Lily in her ribs to shake her out of her jealousy. Lily smiled and mouthed to Emma, "You are beautiful."

Emma beamed and walked past us.

I looked over at Lily and asked, "Are you okay?"

She nodded but then turned and pushed her way through the onlookers. I could tell she was holding back tears.

"Soph, I'll be right back, okay?"

"Okay." Sophie just kept clapping for those who were talking on the red carpet in their formal wear. She didn't notice what was happening with Lily.

I wove through the mass of people and tried to catch up with Lily, but she was already running down over the hill. I tried to chase after her, but she was a track star for a reason, and I was not. Finally, she plopped down in the back of a tree and curled up. That's the only reason I was able to get to her.

I heard her sniffling as I got closer. I walked around to the side of the tree she was sitting by and sat down next to her. I didn't say a word. I didn't think I needed to. I just sat. This was something Sophie did for me so often. She would just sit and I would feel her energy and feel better. But in that instant, I realized I had something to give Lily, something solid.

I reached into my pocket. I had two stones that I had been carrying around with me. I pulled them both out. The first was the stone Sophie gave me. The second was the red stone I had found when Sophie and I went to the old abandoned house, the one in the shape of a heart. I put Sophie's rock back in my pocket and held the heart stone in the palm of my right hand. I closed my fingers around it and greeted it with intention. I thought, "Whenever Lily touches this rock, she will be reminded to love herself, and that she is loved and special." Sophie always told me to trust my instincts and right at that very moment my instincts were telling me to blow on the rock. So I did. When I did that, my palm got warm, and a small rabbit hopped by me. It stopped and looked at me, then cocked its head, and hopped on. I felt like the rabbit was sending me a message, telling me to give Lily the stone.

Lily was holding her head with her hands, rocking, her knees pulled up to her chest. She looked up at me and asked, "Why am I this way? I don't want to be different." Tears were streaming down her face.

I didn't know quite what to say to that so I continued with my plan. "Lily," I said. "I found this rock a few weeks ago, and I think it's supposed to be with you. So, can I give it to you?"

She nodded through her tears and put her hand out for me.

With the stone balled up in my hand, I reached out and released it into her hand. I didn't pull back right away. Instead, I did what felt right. I kept my hand over hers for a moment, to let her know that love was being passed to her.

When I removed my hand, she looked at the stone. She took her pointer finger and ran it around the shape of the stone, then looked up at me.

"This seems really special. Are you sure you want to give it to me?"

"This is meant for you." I sat closer to her and put my arm around her shoulder as she stared at the stone. "Keep it in your pocket, or backpack, or whatever. It's to remind you to love yourself and that the universe loves you."

She started tearing up again. "I don't love me."

"But you should. This rock will help you. It will remind you to love yourself. Don't you see? You are worthy of that love." I stroked her hair. "That's how I know this rock was meant for you. I think the only reason I found it was to give it to you."

"How do I love myself? I don't know how."

"Hold onto it and remember that you are special. There is only one of you, and you are here for a reason." I looked out over the graveyard that sat behind the school. While living with Sophie I had started to see the beauty she saw. The earth and nature and animals and bright colorful rays of light shining. Compared to Sophie, I sensed only glimpses, but I was training my eye to see the world as a beautiful tapestry. And I knew this was a beautiful moment.

"Thank you," Lily said, wiping her face. She stood up and put the rock in her pocket. "I don't even know how to tell you how thankful I am for it."

"You don't have to. Just help me up." I held my hands out and she pulled me up. By the time I stood, she was smiling.

We walked back up the hill to where the crowd was still at the Prom Walk. Lily noticed Emma standing next to Alex's car. She ran to be with Emma before Emma drove off to the prom. I could tell Lily was feeling better, her spirits were lifted and she immediately started joking and laughing. I took a deep breath, happy that I had been able to help. Then I turned to find Sophie in the crowd.

- Chapter Forty -

The Monday after prom, I exited the school building to walk home, to my new home. Sophie hadn't been at school that day because she had appointments at Children's Hospital in Philadelphia. They had asked if I wanted to come along, but I had decided to go to school instead. They would be discussing new treatment protocols, and I didn't want to get in the way. So, they had dropped me off at school and left for Philly.

The entire day had been exactly like every other day. I went to class. I ate lunch. I fielded dirty looks from Everly. Max ignored me. The usual. At the end of the day, I walked to my locker, got my stuff out, and said goodbye to Lily and Emma. Emma was hanging onto Alex's arm. Then I headed out of the school building. I knew everyone would be home late, so I planned to take my time getting home.

I had just dawdled my way to the end of the parking lot when I saw my mother's car driving over the top of the hill from the cemetery. I stopped cold. I didn't know whether to run and hide or stand there. I ended up standing there, not because I wanted to face her, but because I couldn't move.

The car came to a screeching halt right beside me. I felt like I was going to puke. I wished I could evaporate and just stop existing. But instead, I just stood there.

My mother opened her car door, got out, and then slammed the door shut. The sound of the door slamming made me jump even though I was fully expecting it. "Who do you think you are?" she said.

I said nothing.

"You little bitch. Not only did you run away, making everyone believe I kicked you out, but you also made everyone believe you. Then I was arrested."

I still said nothing.

I felt a presence off to my side. My feet were stuck.

"You've ruined me. YOU'VE RUINED ME. I should have had that abortion or given you up for adoption. I should have dropped you off in the cold next to the firehouse."

Someone, I don't know who, suddenly grabbed my hand. Someone else came around the other side of me, walking up to my mother. This gave me a second to figure out who was holding my hand. It was Larkin. Larkin was holding my hand while Reagan charged my mother.

"Who the HELL do you think you are?" Reagan was standing right in front of my mother, with her hand against my mother's chest. "You need to go, NOW."

My mother started laughing. "Oh, little girl, you know nothing," she said to Reagan.

"Oh, I know your type," Reagan said. "GO! LEAVE!"

My mother tried to push Reagan away from her, but she didn't realize Reagan's strength.

"There is no way we are letting you get past us," Larkin yelled, right into my mother's face.

I looked at Larkin, confused. Why did they care?

Larkin looked at me and said, "Come on. Let's go get in my car."

I didn't move.

She took a deep breath, then whispered, "Mia, you don't need to be here for this. Please. Let's go to my car and I'll take you home."

I couldn't move.

Larkin wrapped her arm around my back, supporting me without making me move.

"You're no longer my daughter." My mother spat in my direction after saying that.

"Oh no! Nope! You're done," Reagan yelled, still putting pressure on my mom's chest. Reagan looked back at us, her eyes wide at Larkin. Taking her cue, Larkin then pulled out her phone and called 911.

After Larkin disconnected the call, Reagan turned to me and said firmly, "We need to get you to my car. Or inside the school building. Come on." She pulled me away from the situation. "Car or school building?"

I probably should have said school, but all I could think about was getting home. "Car," I said.

Larkin and I started walking. I could hear a small tussle, and then heard Reagan say behind us, "Oh no, you're staying here." Just then the sound of sirens made themselves known.

"Just come on," Larkin said. "Let's sit in the car. I'll turn up the volume and lock the doors."

We got to Larkin's blue Scion XB. She started the car, locked the doors, and turned up the music. Soon two squad cars parked on either side of my mother and her car. That's when I saw the principal run toward the situation. I watched as the officers talked to Reagan, who was pointing at Larkin's car. An officer walked toward us. She looked non-threatening. I unlocked the car door and got out to talk to her.

I approached the officer and explained the situation as best I could.

"Your mother doesn't have custody of you?"

"No, ma'am."

"Why did she come to the school?" she asked.

"I don't know. To yell at me? She's probably drunk."

I could hear my mother screaming. That did it. I started crying. I just couldn't hold it in any longer.

Another officer approached. He pulled the officer talking to me off to the side and said something I couldn't hear. My officer nodded and walked back to me.

"Okay, we want you girls to go home."

Reagan came over to us. Her face was red and it was obvious she was out of breath. She got to me and said, "Come on, let's go."

We both quickly got into Larkin's car. I sat in the back. Reagan sat in the front. Reagan was visibly shaken. She looked like she was trying to hold back tears. Larkin looked at her and put her hand out for Reagan. They clasped hands for a moment, just before Reagan said, "It's so much worse."

"I know it is," Larkin said, nodding.

Reagan started crying. She looked back at me.

"I'm so sorry. I am so, so sorry. I understand. I really do."

I still felt frozen. Frozen and cold. I wasn't crying, but I was shivering. Cold. I was so cold. I turned to look out the window and saw the male officer putting my mother in the back of the squad car. That's when the tears started again. No, not tears, wailing. I started wailing. Reagan got out of the car and came around to the back. She climbed in beside me and wrapped her arms around me. Together we cried the entire way to my new home.

No one was there when we got home, so Reagan and Larkin decided to stay. Reagan took Larkin's car to get pizza for us while I sat with Larkin in the living room.

"I'm so glad we saw what was happening. I don't know what would have—" Larkin stopped talking. I wasn't sure what she was going to say after that. She took a few deep breaths and began again. "Look. Reagan and I both understand the troubles everyone faces, without anyone knowing. We've both been through our fair share of hard things, and we both still struggle." She scooted over to sit right next to me. "Consider us friends, okay? You can trust us. We are here to talk. We've got you."

All I did was nod, then sob again.

Reagan showed up with the pizza. We sat and ate. I told them everything that had been going on. They sat in shock as I retold how my mother kicked me out of the house in the snowstorm without any winter clothes or my phone. They were in shock hearing about how she showed up at Sophie's house drunk. They looked relieved to hear that Sophie's parents took me as a permanent foster child. Then I listened to them as they told me all the things they had been going through. I was surprised to hear that Reagan's mother was similar to mine. Not as bad, mind you, but bad enough to make Reagan act out. Larkin told me about her head injury, which had taken her out of school for a while and had developed into an eating disorder. She also talked about her problems with her boyfriend. She loved Marco, but she felt like all he ever did was try to make sure she was okay and that she was eating. She said it made her feel like a precious porcelain doll. Like she could break any minute. She didn't want to feel like that. She wanted to feel strong. She even went to the hospital once, because of the eating disorder. She had broken up with him then, but they ended up getting back together, mostly because she liked having someone care for her. But now, now she felt like she was past that and she didn't want anyone to dote on her anymore.

Then they asked me about Sophie. I had just told them about how the doctors were looking for new treatment options for her when the front door burst open quickly and hard. Sophie's dad came in and rushed to me. "Mia!" he said. "We've been calling you. The police contacted us. We sped all the way home."

I looked at my phone. There were at least fifty calls from them that I had missed. I had forgotten to turn the sound back on after class.

"I'm sorry. I didn't think…"

Lisa followed behind him, "Oh God, we are so glad you are okay."

I stood. "I'm so sorry. I didn't… I've been kind of in shock."

She hugged me. "It's okay, it's okay. Just make sure to keep in contact with us."

Sophie came in the door and grabbed the two of us in a hug.

"Next time you are coming with us," Sophie said.

Sophie's parents thanked Reagan and Larkin for helping me. Luckily, Reagan had brought enough pizza to feed an army. So we all sat around and talked while Lisa and Robert and Sophie ate.

After we'd all eaten our fill of pizza, Reagan and Larkin decided to leave. Robert called the police station for a report of what had happened.

When Sophie was finally able to ask, "What happened?" I told her everything.

- Chapter Forty-One -

Sophie started to kick me from the bottom of the bunk. I laughed as my mattress shook up and down. I bent my head over to talk to her. "Are you ready?"

We had finally made it to Naturalist Camp and were resting before our big hike. We could not wait. Ever since the day that we had gone to the old abandoned house by the river, we'd been spending more and more time there. Sitting with the trees beside the river had become a habit. Every day after school, we would go there during our walks home, even if just for a few minutes. We had started getting super excited about the Naturalist Camp once spring buds started showing up on the trees. Camp and the big hike had been all we could think about.

Max was at camp, too. But he was a camp counselor, so we never really saw him. The most contact I had was a head nod as he was ushering a group of six-year-olds to the pool.

Our relationship was cold. After the prom, it seemed like he'd gotten more serious with Everly again. I tried not to pay attention to them, but Everly didn't make it easy. She constantly flaunted their relationship in front of me. I missed Max. I missed him a lot. I had actually hoped that I would be able to talk to him more while at camp, but he was too busy for me. Maybe that was on purpose.

I sat up and jumped down from my bunk. Sophie was still lying there laughing at how she could make me bounce. "Let's go grab breakfast." She got up out of bed and started dancing around the cabin. She didn't care at all about what the other campers thought of her. "We're doing it! We're finally doing it," she sang the words.

I decided to join her and dance. She and I had been waiting so long for this day and now it was finally happening. I didn't care if the other campers thought we were insane. A little bit of insanity can be a good thing. Sophie's doctors had never let her hike like this before; because of her lungs, they were always worried about the steep inclines. But Lisa had put her foot down and said that Sophie needed to be able to try. Finally, her parents decided that if I was there and a camp counselor stayed with us every bit of the way, Sophie would be okay. We would just have to move more slowly than the rest of the group. They even got her doctor's approval.

We got ready and then left the cabin for the cafeteria. The campers were moving slowly because it was the end of the camp week and everyone was tired.

Once we ate, we made our way to the start of the trail where everyone gathered to take roll call. Sophie was ready to be surrounded by nature, to climb the rocks, and maybe even pick up a few sticks or rocks that spoke to her. She had put a special bag in her backpack for the little items she picked up on the way.

I looked around for the counselor who was supposed to stay with us if we fell behind, but I couldn't find her. "Soph, have you seen Sonya?"

Sophie was too busy being excited to care. "Huh? No," she said, not really paying attention to me.

I looked around some more. I asked the girl standing next to us, "Did you see Sonya?"

She shook her head back and forth, "No, sorry."

"Soph, I'll be right back, okay?"

She nodded.

I walked up to the lead counselor. "Is Sonya coming on the hike?" I asked.

"No, she got a summer cold. She's staying behind."

"Okay. Will there be someone else assisting Sophie?" I was starting to get nervous.

"Oh, don't worry about it," the male counselor said. "We won't be moving that fast."

"No, Evan." I shook my head at the camp counselor who looked to be only two years older than me. "You don't understand. She can't do this on her own. We won't be able to keep up with you."

"Nah. You guys will be fine. Get back in line. We are going to start counting heads soon."

"I mean no disrespect, but Sophie has Cystic Fibrosis. We need some-one who knows the way."

"Look. I don't even know what that is. We are going to be moving very slowly. You need to get back in line, if you don't, we will leave you and your friend here at the camp."

I huffed a bit, balled up my fists, and stomped back to Sophie. "Soph, I don't think we can go on the hike. Sonya isn't working today. She was the one who was supposed to accompany us."

Sophie looked at me like she was going to tear my head off. "Mia, I have been waiting for this for so long. I have to go."

"Soph—"

"No! We are going. I need to experience this." She stomped her foot.

I just stood and nodded. "Ok. Ok. Fine. We'll do the best we can."

"Yes, we will." She gave me a stern look. "Besides, the forest always takes care of me. Don't forget that."

"Okay, I won't." But I was worried. Very worried.

We were fine at the start of the hike, it was only a small incline through the forest. We had absolutely no problems keeping up with everyone. In fact, we weren't even the slowest. To see Sophie look up at the canopy of the forest and listen to the birds was magical. She was happier than she had ever been. Her smile was radiant. I breathed a sigh of relief, thinking that this was the right move. We would be okay. The forest loves her and the counselors would never leave us behind, lost. Right?

Sophie kept pointing cardinals out to me as if to say, "See? I told you it would be fine."

I stopped worrying and started enjoying myself. Every once in a while I would bend over and pick up a small rock or stick that I found interesting, then carry it for a little while before placing it off the side of the trail.

The farther we went, the rockier the trail became. Boulders lined the path. Some campers would get up on the boulders and mess around. We didn't climb any of those. Sophie accepted her limitations, and I wasn't going to do it without her. While everyone else took time to mess around, we went searching for trinkets the Earth left out for us. Sophie found a beautiful white feather. She decided not to put it in the baggie in her backpack. She wanted to hold it in her hand the rest of the hike.

With the feather in Sophie's hand, we followed behind everyone as they took off for the first hard part of the hike. This part became more of a true hike than a leisurely stroll. It was tougher, but we were still able to keep up. I did get a little worried, especially since the counselors seemed to be in sort of a love affair and only worried about each other. They weren't making sure everyone was following. No one else seemed to care. After all, we are all older than the younger group of campers. But nobody else had to keep Sophie alive, that fell on me. I was her sister now. I had to protect her.

At certain points, it felt like we were actually rock climbing. Even though I knew that it wasn't truly rock climbing, it was probably the closest either of us would ever get to that experience. Sophie began to struggle. She had to take her inhaler a few times. I ended up climbing in back of her to make sure she didn't fall behind by herself.

At one point her face turned bright red and she started coughing. She tried walking while she coughed. She didn't want to give up. I hoped the counselors would notice, but they were too far ahead and probably wouldn't have cared anyway. Sophie's coughing became more shallow, more troubling. She had overdone it.

I found a larger flat rock that she could sit on safely. "Soph, sit here. I'm going to run ahead and let them know that we'll follow the trail back to the camp."

I knew we were in trouble when she nodded. I thought I would have to fight about it, but she didn't fight. She knew it was too much. She climbed up on the rock and worked on catching her breath while I ran ahead to the group to let the counselors know.

By the time I reached the head of the group, I was out of breath. "Hey. Sophie can't make it any further. I'm going to walk her back to camp."

"Yeah, okay," Evan said half-heartedly. He seemed put out by this entire hike and the fact there were younger teens following his every move. "As long as you stay on the path you'll be fine."

"Okay. Cool. Should someone come with us?"

"No, we can't do that. We can't be alone with kids. It's the law."

"Oh. Okay." I didn't think anything of that answer; I just accepted it. I turned and ran back to Sophie.

We sat for a bit until she was able to catch her breath, then we started backtracking. We didn't leave the trail once. After we'd been walking for what seemed like hours, we got hungry. We had water in our backpacks, so that was fine, but the lunches were with the counselors in the larger backpacks. I started to become concerned about food.

"Soph, how long were we on the trail before we stopped."

"I'm not sure. I think an hour?"

I grabbed my phone out of my back pocket. "So we left around ten?"

"No.... I think earlier than that...." She was huffing and puffing.

"Should we rest again?"

"No.... I'm fine."

I was pretty sure she was being stubborn. "Okay. Maybe we should slow down." I looked her in the face, specifically at her lips to make sure they weren't turning blue. "I'm just worried that we've been walking longer on the trail than it took to get here."

"You… think we… are… lost?"

"No. We can't be. We never left the trail." I kept looking around seeking some sort of sign that we were on the right path. "I mean, they'll probably come back this way, so if anything, we'll meet up with them again soon."

"Yeah," she said, growing more and more out of breath.

"I think we should find a place to sit."

Sophie just nodded.

As we walked, my eyes searched between the trees for a place to take a break. Finally, after about a half an hour the trees broke and a small meadow appeared. "Here, let's go there," I said, pointing.

She only nodded, again.

"I don't remember this meadow. Do you?"

She shook her head back and forth. I looked at her lips, they were tinged with purple, making me even more thankful that we could rest for a bit.

We walked off the path toward the meadow. As soon as we passed the last line of trees everything became much brighter. The meadow was completely flat, which was perfect for Sophie. The grass was the most vibrant green I had ever seen. There were bright purple violets mixed with yellow dandelions. Light flooded into the meadow in rays that seemed otherworldly. Honestly, I wouldn't have been surprised if we had seen a couple of fairies flying around. It was that kind of beauty.

We walked to the middle of the meadow and collapsed. I had been worrying about Sophie so much that I didn't realize how exhausted I was. It's not like I was an athlete at all. We both lay there staring up at the sky. A cardinal landed next to Sophie, and that was the last thing I remembered. We must have fallen asleep because I blinked and the sky had turned darker.

I stood up in a panic. "Shit, shit, shit." I bent down to wake Sophie.

"Soph. Soph, wake up." She stirred. Her eyes opened. She was in a daze. Then she opened her eyes fully and jumped up too.

"We fell asleep?" she asked.

"Apparently."

"It's almost dark. What time is it?"

"It's 9:00," I answered.

"At night?"

"Yeah."

"What happened?"

"I have no idea. I don't remember falling to sleep."

"What do we do?" She started freaking out. I reached out to her and held her hand.

"Soph, don't get upset. We'll be fine. This is a state park. How bad can it be?"

She looked at me with wide eyes.

"Should we stay here or keep walking the trail?"

She was starting to panic. "I need to take my breathing treatment."

"Then we will walk," I said, keeping my voice calm.

"Okay." She grabbed her backpack and pulled out her phone. She looked at the screen. "I don't have a signal. Do you?"

I already knew the answer, but I looked just in case a miracle occurred. "No. I don't either." In fact, I was losing battery power as well, but I kept that information to myself. I looked at her. "How's your battery power?"

"I don't have much. I was taking pictures."

I started to freak out a bit, but I tried my hardest to keep it low key. We hadn't pack flashlights because they said there would be no way we would still be out there in the dark. Everyone was probably getting ready for the bonfire by that point. I wondered if they even realized we weren't there? Probably not. *SHIT!* "Okay. We're going to be okay." I nodded. "I'm sure they sent someone to look for us. Let's just get back on the trail. They'll be looking there."

She nodded, then got her inhaler out of her bag and took a few puffs. I hoped that helped her because I had a feeling we had a ton of walking to do. I crossed my fingers that she would be able to walk quickly. She put the inhaler back in her backpack and picked the white feather off of the ground. She wrapped her fingers around the bottom of it. I think it gave her a sense of safety, but I was nervous. They kept telling us to stay on the path, and we didn't. I guess this was exactly why.

We walked as quickly as possible down the path or what we thought was the path, anyway. I wasn't sure we were even going in the right direction. I finally had to turn on my flashlight when we started tripping over roots and divots. I was used to the level of darkness from growing up on the mountain, but this…. This darkness gave me the chills. It was different.

Sophie grabbed her phone and turned on her flashlight too. I had a bad feeling about it and thought that we should use only one phone at a time to save battery power, but she felt safer in the light so we left them both on. An owl screeched. We heard coyote cries—at least I thought they sounded like coyotes. Whatever they were, they gave me shivers.

I tried to pick up the pace, but Sophie needed to rest often. I shined the light between the trees hoping to find another meadow for us to rest for the night, but there wasn't one. At least I couldn't see any.

The coyote cries started sounding closer and closer. "Are you okay?" I asked Sophie.

"Yeah," she said quietly. "Is this what it was like that time your mom kicked you out?"

"Sort of? But it was snowing then too."

"She didn't let you use your phone, so how did you see where you were going?"

"It was a full moon. I could see enough to make my way."

"It's not a full moon tonight."

"No. No, it's not."

Sophie started shivering. It wasn't cold, so I was sure she was getting scared.

"Soph, we are fine. Remember, I grew up on the side of a mountain."

"Promise?"

"Yes."

We heard an animal running beside us in the trees. Sophie grabbed my hand. The animal never bothered us, but it was scary enough just to hear it there.

The flashlight on my phone went out. We were left with only hers, and it was now the dead of night. As we walked, I listened for a search party. I never heard anything that sounded human. I tried to sniff to see if I could smell the campfire, just to see if we were close. I didn't smell smoke. I had to be honest with myself. I had no idea where we were, but with this unknown animal in the treeline, following us? I wasn't stopping to rest again. I would do anything I could to keep Sophie going, even if it meant carrying her on my back.

At some point, we would have to hit a road and be able to find a house. I just kept telling myself these things over and over again. We would be fine.

Then Sophie's phone went out. We stopped walking. We didn't know what to do. We were completely covered in darkness. We clasped our hands tighter to each other. "What do we do now?" she whispered.

The animal walking with us in the trees stopped moving, but for some reason, that no longer scared me. We tried to take a few more steps. When we did, the animal moved with us. Sophie reached out to touch my face, trying to figure out where I was.

She whispered to me, "Don't be afraid of the animal. I think it's watching over us." We stopped walking again. It stopped. She squeezed my hand and just sighed, "Yeah."

We both got the feeling of protection at the same time. That gave me a sense of peace. I know it was a crazy thought, but it felt like the same coyote who had walked with me off the mountain all those months ago.

We walked a little more, but it was impossible to see. Finally, Sophie knelt down. She was out of breath. All of this was too much for her lungs. She started coughing as I felt around her and grabbed her backpack to find her inhaler. I found it and handed it to her. She took far too many puffs of it. "I missed my treatment."

"I know. Can you keep walking? Or should we try to rest here? I can watch over you while you sleep."

"No. We need to keep moving."

I sat down next to her and saw two eyes staring at us. It was a coyote. I didn't react.

"Don't move," Sophie whispered.

Its eyes glowed up at me. It let out a whine, then started walking away from us. Then it came back, each time with a whine when it looked at us. We got up. It walked in the opposite direction from where we had been going. We didn't follow, so it turned around to us again, walked up to me, set its head on the path, and made a whining sound again.

"I think it wants us to follow him," I whispered.

I bent over to help Sophie stand up. "It's really trying to help us. Isn't it?"

"I think so. We should trust it."

A gentle wind blew in the same direction the coyote was going. As we stood, it blew harder, as if it was pushing us to follow the animal.

"What's happening?" she asked.

"You told me nature protected you. I think that's what's happening."

Then her flashlight turned on again. It made no sense.

"I thought your phone was dead," I said, my voice still a whisper.

"It was." She tapped on her phone screen, but it was dead. "My phone is dead."

"How's the flashlight working?"

"I don't know."

I shivered as I thought back to all the times that I had looked at her recently and seen a spectrum of light shining around her. Now there was light shining from her dead cell phone.

"Remember I told you that you had an animal protecting you, too?" she asked in a hushed tone.

"Yeah?"

"I think this is the animal. Was there something walking with you that night when your mom kicked you out?"

"Yes.

"I bet it's him. Come on. Let's follow him and get back to camp."

We followed the coyote, with the wind constantly pushing at our backs. Soon enough, we could see the light from the bonfire at the camp.

"Sophie, we did it."

She stopped walking and looked at me. "I wouldn't have survived without you. I love you."

"I love you, too." We squeezed our hands together. "We kept each other alive." I nodded, smiling from ear to ear. "But, come on, we gotta get back."

"Mia! Sophie!" They were calling our names.

"Mia! Sophie!"

"Can you hear us? Mia! Sophie!"

I answered back. "We're here." I could see flashlights in the distance. "Over here!" I yelled back one more time. The flashlights started moving toward us more quickly. Whoever was looking for us started to run.

The coyote seemed to nod his head, then ran a ways away. He stopped and looked at us one last time, let out a huff, and then was gone.

Sophie's flashlight began to fade as the search party's light got close enough to see us. There were three people, but I couldn't make out who they were. We stayed where we were because we couldn't see without Sophie's cell phone flashlight, and they weren't close enough yet.

I heard a voice I knew. "Mia, is that you?"

"YES!" It was Max.

Sophie started laughing; it was pure nerves.

He and two others ran up to us. Max grabbed me in his arms. "Oh my God. Oh my God. I thought you were gone forever." He started kissing the top of my head over and over again. "I couldn't bear it." He was crying and holding me so close to his body that I was having problems breathing. I allowed myself to fall into his hug, then he said the words that brought me back to reality, "What would have happened had I not found you?"

I pushed out of his grasp. "No!"

He looked confused. "What?"

"I said, NO!" I backed further away from him. "Sophie and I saved each other. We worked together and got all the way here." I started laughing. "You found us right at the moment we could see the campfire. We knew where we were going."

"But we have been searching all afternoon. All night."

"And we thank you. But we saved ourselves," I replied proudly.

The other two people were the camp director and the nurse. They both tended to Sophie. They had her sit by the side of the trail to make sure her breathing was good enough to continue without being carried.

"I'm glad you are okay," Max said.

"Thanks. We were strong through it all. We are fine."

The camp director knelt down and had Sophie climb onto his back. "Ready to get back to camp? You need that treatment, Sophie."

It didn't take long to get back to where everyone else was enjoying the campfire. The director and nurse took Sophie to the nurse's building to make sure she was okay and to start her breathing treatment.

Max grabbed my hand. "I'm never letting you go again."

"Max. No. Not now. This isn't about you. I'm shaken and really just want something to eat," I snapped. I didn't mean to, but I did. I walked away from him, leaving him stunned. I didn't want to be mean, but he'd basically ignored me for months. Now suddenly he wants to play my savior? No. Just no.

I needed a moment to myself to think about what happened and about how things lined up for us perfectly to get out of the woods safely. Sophie's flashlight, the coyote, the meadow. THAT MEADOW. Where did it come from? It was like we entered a space that was separate from the rest of the world. I wondered if I could ever find it again.

I walked to the bonfire. It looked like everyone had been having a grand time while we were lost. I didn't care. We were safe. We were protected. I sat down on a log bench and wrapped my arms around myself. Max was behind me.

My stomach let out a large growl.

"Are you hungry?" he asked.

"Yes."

He walked away to get me a hot dog and soda.

Despite the heat of the fire, I was shivering. I closed my eyes for a moment, then opened them. I looked over to the forest edge and saw a lone coyote standing in the middle of the trail, just beyond the clearing. I kept my eye on it, watching it lower its head and walk away. That's when I noticed something, a white ball of light flitting around further down the trail. It wasn't so small that it was a lightning bug. It looked like a beam of light from a flashlight. But it was moving back and forth quickly, obviously not being held by a human, it was too high for that. I rubbed my eyes, thinking that I was seeing things. When I opened my eyes again, it was still there but was growing dim. Then it just sort of vanished down the path.

- Chapter Forty-Two-

Many Years Later

I threw my backpack next to the car, then walked to the back where a little head was bobbing up and down to the music in her own soul.

"Are you ready, Peanut?"

Two arms clothed in pink reached up to me. I smiled to myself as I unbuckled her, picked her up, and set her down on the gravel road. She jumped up and down, clapping her hands.

She stopped jumping, looked at me seriously with her head cocked, and asked the most important question, "Mommy, will we see a bunny?"

"I'm sure we'll see lots and lots of bunnies."

My little girl started spinning, screaming, "Bunnies! Bunnies! Bunnies!"

I'd done small hikes with her in the past, but this was our first large one. She was definitely at home in nature, so I had no qualms about taking her on this tough hike. She was only three, but goodness did she came alive in nature. It was her element.

I bent over, grabbed the backpack, and opened it, making sure I had enough water and snacks. I checked the flashlight. It was daytime, but, well, you never knew. Then I closed the bag and slung it over my back.

"Is Daddy gonna meet us?" she asked.

"Not this time. Maybe the next time."

"Okay!"

"Let's go!" I said, enthusiastically.

She started running immediately, which was perfectly normal for her.

"Hey, Peanut, get back here!"

She turned around and ran back to me. A strand of hair was stuck across her face. She wiped it away and grabbed my outstretched hand.

"Let's go over the main rule one more time, okay? What is it?"

"We don't leave the path."

"That's right, Peanut. Let's go!"

We both ran to the clearing before the path. I looked around remembering. Ten years. It had been ten years since Sophie and I had gotten lost. I stopped and looked around, breathing in the air.

"Mommy, let's go!"

"Hang on. Give me a moment. I haven't been here in eight years." I bit my tongue to stop my tears. "I've been here twice. Once by myself, to try and find something very special. Then the time before that was with Aunt Sophie."

"THAT long ago?" she asked. "Mommy, were you looking for the fairy meadow?"

"Yeah, baby." I bit my tongue again. "I was." I smiled to myself. It all seemed so long ago, like a dream. I wasn't even sure if I could trust my memories at all. "I've been waiting until you were old enough to do this with me." I squatted down to look her in her eyes. "Do you think you're old enough now?"

"YES!" she said with a cheer. She stopped jumping. "But Mommy, tell me about the fairy meadow again?"

I sat on the grass and she plopped down into my lap, sideways so she could see me. "Well, when I was here with Aunt Sophie, we got lost. But it was because we found the fairy meadow."

"Mommy, how do you know the lights were fairies?"

"I actually don't know, for sure," I answered, stroking her hair. "But I can tell you, I felt magic that day."

"What did you see, Mommy?"

"Well, I saw lights, but it was more than that. It was a feeling. Like nature would take care of us and lead us back to camp again."

"Were you scared?

"Very. But we were okay."

"Do you think we'll find the meadow today?"

"No. I don't think so. But we'll have fun trying." I clasped my hands around her tiny face. "But what's the rule?"

"Don't leave the path," she said, nodding.

"Even if?"

"Even if we find the fairy meadow."

I took one more deep breath in and looked around. In my memory, I could smell the bonfire, and hear the other campers laughing. I shook my head to bring me back to the present. "Okay, Peanut. Are you ready?"

She jumped up, turned toward me, and held out her hands like she was going to help me get up. I grabbed her hands and stood.

As we walked, I pointed out birds and plants. Sometimes she would pick up things that interested her. She found the most spectacular stones and sticks. She gathered more and more until she couldn't carry them anymore. After that, we started putting her finds in the front pocket of my backpack. I promised her we would find a special place to put them in her bedroom. Then she found a white feather. She held it up into a stream of sunlight that broke through the trees. As she did, it seemed to glimmer.

Her eyes and mouth widened. She looked at me, and whispered, "Mommy, is it the fairies?"

"You know what? I bet it's Aunt Sophie."

"I love you, Aunt Sophie."

Just then a butterfly flitted between the feather and her face.

"MOMMY!"

"I know, Sweetie."

"It's magic," she whispered.

We started walking a little more. A cardinal landed a few feet in front of us.

"Aunt Sophie really wants to talk to you today, doesn't she?"

The little girl jumped up and down and ran to the cardinal.

"Peanut! Don't scare the bird!" I called to her.

She whispered back, "Mommy, shhhh." Slowly she bent over, delicately picked it up, and kissed it on its head, then showed it her white feather. After that, the bird flew off. She ran after it. It kept circling her like it was playing tag with her.

"Sophia, don't go too far ahead of me," I called after her.

Sophia stopped quickly and turned to the right. A bright light was shining on her face. "Mommy," she whispered, then pointed into the forest.

I got to her, picked her up, and turned to see what she was looking at. It was the meadow that Sophie and I had fallen asleep in years and years ago. It was just as beautiful as I remembered. "Sophia, isn't it beautiful?"

Sophia placed her little hands on either side of my face and turned my head toward hers. "It's just how I remember it." She turned her face back to the meadow.

"How do you remember it? You've never been here."

"It's OUR meadow. Don't you remember? I haven't seen that shade of purple violets ever since. Remember?" Then she pointed to the far corner of the meadow. "Look at that! That light. Do you see it? It's so bright."

My eyes focused on what she was talking about and there it was, a bright light, shining just at the top of the treeline. We stood staring at it for a while before it flew up in the sky and disappeared.

A single tear fell from my eye. I understood. I finally understood. Sophie had meant what she said. She would never leave me. And she never had.

And I held her tightly against me.

Forever and always.

It's never the end.

In the next book, *This Is Meant for You,*
Lily finds herself and begins to make peace with who she is.

Don't forget to check out *The Art of Drowning* by Abigail Wild.

Larkin and Reagan have always been at odds, competing for everything.

Larkin lost two years of her life to post-concussion syndrome. As she stands at the beginning of her new life, she wonders if she's even the same person she once was. Abandoned by friends when she was injured, she takes her first step toward her future: alone. Was it a mistake for her to go back to school for her senior year? Will they laugh at her panic attacks? Will they notice she isn't eating? Will she even make it through the first day?

Beautiful, tough, popular . . . cunning, Reagan puts on a good show. No one notices the pain she holds deep within and she prefers it that way. Her life is nothing, just like her mother says, but it looks perfect. When Larkin went down, Reagan stepped into her shoes. Two years later, Reagan has her senior year all planned out. One perfect year leading to the day she can finally escape her mother's grasp and leave for college. Her nightmare over. Or is it?

When Reagan and Larkin find themselves face to face on the first day of their senior year, lightning strikes.

Abigail Wild dwells inside her dreams where creativity thrives. As a child, she focused on visual arts, but after twenty years as a graphic designer, all the stories she held captured in her mind clamored to be set free. She put down her tablet and picked up the pen. She went back to school, earning an MFA in creative writing, and began her new life's work: writing the stories of her heart. Today, Abigail is a novelist, writing coach, editor, competition judge, and writing teacher. She particularly enjoys working with emergent writers, often giving them the same pep talks she received years ago. She lives in central Pennsylvania with her husband, three children, and three budgies. The budgies tend to make a racket while Abigail is trying to write, but she is not deterred!

www.ingramcontent.com/pod-product-compliance
Lightning Source LLC
Chambersburg PA
CBHW050850190726
48286CB00007B/2310